BLACK'S CREEK

'Sam Millar didn't invent the noir crime novel but, as Black's Creek indicates, he might as well have. This wondrously written and terrifically told tale is a book with a heart, however dark, that will evoke comparisons with Lorenzo Carcatera's Sleepers, John Hart's The Last Child and Dennis Lehane's seminal Mystic River. Millar is more than up to the task of following in such lofty footsteps, and Black's Creek will haunt you long after the final page is turned. Powerful. Not to be missed!'

Jon Land, **New York Times** *bestselling author of* **Strong at the Break and Betrayal**

Black's Creek is a profoundly disturbing, psychological coming-of-age thriller filled with enigmatic characters and astonishing scenes of originality. Millar brilliantly executes a combination of suspense and terror from beginning to end, with just the right balance of dark humor to calm the nerves. Terrific page-turning noir.'

'Reminiscent of Steven King's classic, Stand by Me, and Dennis Lehane's Mystic River, crime writer Sam Millar's Black's Creek is an atmospheric must-read, page-turning book.'

'Sam Millar's latest novel – Black's Creek – kicks off with suspense and mystery on page one, and doesn't let the reader off the hook until the shocking denouement on the last page. A powerful story of murder and revenge, brilliantly told.'

'Black's Creek will have you breathless from start to finish. An unput-downable crime story from a truly great writer of the genre. Loved it.'

Sheila Quigley, bestselling crime author, **Thorn In My Side**

'Black's Creek is evidence of a writer performing at his peak. Millar's finely crafted tale grips from the first taut line and never lets go. It's difficult to fault a book that has it all: economic prose, fully-realized characters, suspense, pace and every act of alchemy that makes a work great. Well done, Mr. Millar. I'd take my hat off to you if it hadn't been blown away with the rest of me somewhere around the first chapter.'

Tony Black, bestselling crime writer, **Murder Mile**

'Noir favorite Sam Millar is in terrific form with his latest book of murder and revenge. Black's Creek is an original page-turner of a book, shockingly told with brutal honesty, in Millar's usual dark and edgy voice. Yet, for all this, it remains hauntingly beautiful, and perhaps his best book to date. A genuine tour-de-force, superbly plotted by Ireland's king of crime writing.'

Noir Journal, *USA*

Also by Sam Millar

Novels:

Dark Souls

The Redemption Factory: finalist, *Grand Prix De Littérature Policière*

Darkness of Bones: finalist, *Le Prix du Meilleur Polar*

Bloodstorm: A Karl Kane Novel

The Dark Place: A Karl Kane Novel

Dead of Winter: A Karl Kane Novel

Memoir

On the Brinks

Stage:

Brothers In Arms

Radio:

Rain, performed by the BBC

Anthologies:

Requiems for the Departed, a Karl Kane story, Winner of
    Spinetingler magazine award for Best Anthology, USA

Breaking the Skin: 21st Century Irish Writing – Volume 1: Short Stories

Emerald Eye: The Best Irish Imaginative Fiction

Belfast Noir, a Karl Kane story, USA

Awards:

Aisling Award for Art and Culture

Martin Healy Short Story Award

Brian Moore Award for Short Stories

Cork Literary Review Writer's Competition

Golden *Balais d'or*, France, for Best Crime Book

Le Monde's Top Twenty Thrillers 2013 for *On The Brinks*

Website: www.millarcrime.com

Email: karlkanepi@hotmail.com

SAM MILLAR

BLACK'S CREEK

BRANDON

First published 2014 by
Brandon
An imprint of The O'Brien Press
12 Terenure Road East, Rathgar,
Dublin 6, Ireland.

Tel: +353 1 4923333; Fax: +353 1 4922777
E-mail: books@obrien.ie
Website: www.obrien.ie

ISBN: 978-1-84717-528-1

1 3 5 7 8 6 4 2
14 16 18 19 17 15

Printed and bound by CPI Group (UK) Ltd, Croydon, CR0 4YY
The paper in this book is produced using pulp from managed forests.

The O'Brien Press receives financial assistance from

DEDICATION

For Bernie. My wife. My rock. My best friend. My love.

APPRECIATION

Many thanks to all my fellow authors for their kind words on Black's Creek. A special thank-you to all the crew at The O'Brien Press, especially Eoin O'Brien for his patience and dedication to the book.

Prologue

Science, my lad, is made up of mistakes, but they are mistakes which it is useful to make, because they lead little by little to the truth.

Jules Verne, **Journey to the Centre of the Earth**

'Black's Creek Murder To Be Reopened' screams the region section in this morning's *New York Times*, the moment I sit down to breakfast. As I read further, my stomach does an involuntary little somersault; one of those pre-indigestion alerts sent out when getting mugged by the unexpected. For a second, I become dizzy. My brain burns in a bad way. Blue and red flashes cloud my vision. To make matters worse, the scar beneath my lower lip and the one above my left eyebrow begin throbbing. For a second, the darkness of my past hits me like a Muhammad Ali special, forcing me to think of the two people who caused those scars and the connection we had with the murder.

'Tom?' Concern etches my wife's beautiful face. 'You okay?'

'Huh? Oh! I'm fine. Just heartburn, Belinda.' I try to sound calm, but the words come out jagged, rehearsed. I can tell she's not convinced. She's worried that it could be the start of one of my blackouts.

The blackouts have become more frequent, less predictable. My last major one occurred about a month ago, while doing a reading from my latest crime book, *The Darkness of Night,* at a bookstore in Astoria, Queens, a few blocks from where I live. I heard about it later, of course. I had been reading the final chapter, where the protagonist shoots the murderous crime boss, right smack in the middle of the forehead. The small gathering of fans applauded, thinking it was part of the act, as I crumpled to the ground, banging my head solidly on the store's solid oak floor.

On the bright side, I sold more books that night than at any other book-signing event. My agent, Tina Winters, suggested I do the head-banging manoeuvre at all future signings, as sales had been criminally low of late. I'd been doing everything *but* making a killing from all my killings.

'You're pale, Tom,' Belinda says, bringing her face closer to mine. 'Sure you're okay?'

'Sure I'm sure.' I force a smile.

She returns the smile. Small. False. Just like mine – but at least it's a smile of sorts. She reaches out, touching my face. Her tender touch has a calming influence, but only for a few seconds.

I go back to reading about the investigation, dreading each dark word that marches along the paper's paleness.

DNA Evidence Reopens Murder Case

Prosecutors say they have obtained new DNA evidence concerning the murder of a suspected pedophile and child murderer, over twenty years ago. They have reopened the cold case, hoping to make arrests …

Despite the summer warmth in the room, dry ice brushes the stepping-stones of my spine. I immediately stop reading.

'I'll finish the coffee in the garden, sweetheart.'

I stand, folding the newspaper and tucking it under my arm. I feel sweat stains developing exactly where I've snuggled the newspaper. 'The caffeine'll give me a boost on how to finish that brain-numbing chapter I've been working on.'

'Stop being so hard on yourself.' Belinda gives me an encouraging look. I see pity in it. 'The words will come to you. They eventually do.'

'Such a fibber, but I love you anyway.' I reach over and kiss her forehead.

'I love you, too. I'll be out in a few minutes to join you.'

In the garden, the early-morning sun is melting away the slime-like mist on the grass. It's going to be a scorcher of a day; the kind of day that always manages to make you feel glad to be alive, even if the opposite has become a closer relative.

BLACK'S CREEK

Finding a comfortable place in the shade, I sit down to read the story, fearing what new evidence the police have uncovered. After all these years, the past has caught up with me. I can hear its footsteps. The only question is: how near are they?

The murdered man's name appears on the first paragraph, and a sickening déjà vu kicks me back through all those years; to a time I had hoped would remain buried, days and nights filled with madness and nightmares, when I was barely a teenager, with cold-blooded murder in mind …

CHAPTER ONE

Darkness in the Afternoon

*… the companions of our childhood always possess
a certain power over our minds which hardly any later
friend can obtain.*

Mary Shelley, **Frankenstein**

Fourth of July. Friday afternoon. Our town – Black's Creek, a small enclave in upstate New York – found itself in the middle of a brain-melting heatwave. Some inhabitants barbecued hotdogs and hamburgers in their garden, while others indulged in barbecuing themselves at the local beach, or residing in cool bars with cold beers. Not me, though. I – along with my two pals, Brent Fleming and Charlie 'Horse-shoe' Cooper – continued working on the cheaper, more exciting alternative of skinny-dipping in Jackson's Lake and drinking Coke chilled in the lake's belly.

Jackson's Lake was a stretch of filthy water surrounded by a forest, barely a mile from where I lived. Most times, the lake coiled out like a black ribbon of silence, but when it willed, it could be crafty in its nature, lassoing the unsuspecting with a ripple. Trees from the forest threw charcoal shadows across the lake's edge, helping to entrap the unsuspecting. Further up, the lake cleaved the hunting area of the forest in two, where carcasses of rusted household goods festered alongside piles of animal dung from adjacent farms.

Police danger signs were posted along the lip of the lake, warning people to stay away, that under no circumstances should they go swimming in it. Of course, this only heightened the adrenaline thrill for us naked teenagers, and we dutifully disobeyed.

The heat that particular Friday afternoon was oppressive. I'd just stepped naked out of the lake when I spotted a lone figure on top of the dusty hill, a small distance away.

'That looks like Joey Maxwell,' I said, pointing to the hill, as the hot sun dried my skin.

Brent – de facto leader of our motley crew – stopped sipping the Coke we'd got from Gino's Bar and Grill, and glanced towards the hill. He'd been reading *The Amazing Spider-Man*, having just won the important argument with Horseshoe on which artist was best at drawing the webbed hero. Horseshoe had championed Steve Ditko, but Brent loved John Romita's rendering. As for myself, I was more a DC Comics aficionado, believing them more superior and intelligent to Marvel. Secretly, I read *Gold Key* also, but limited my collection to *Magnus Robot Fighter, Doctor Solar Man of the Atom* and *Space Family Robinson*. I never told Brent or Horseshoe my terrible secret, as every other comic book outside DC or Marvel was frowned upon as sacrilege and betrayal. Perhaps even borderline sissy.

'Yeah, you're right Tommy, it is Joey,' Brent said, plucking one of his mom's pilfered cigarettes and Zippo from his jeans resting on the ground. He fired up the Zippo, its flame long and thin, and gave life to the cig. Releasing a prayer of smoke from his nostrils, he nodded to himself with satisfaction, just like the Marlboro Man in the snowy wilderness.

I didn't smoke, except for once the year before when Brent coerced me into trying weed. Realistically, I had neither inclination nor balls for smoking. Mom would have killed me if she suspected I'd even entertained the thought.

'Joey always creeps me out, the way he just stares and stares,' Horseshoe said, as he added some shading to a drawing of a superhero in his gray sketchpad. Horseshoe was good, his drawings so life-like you swore to god they were coming right at you off the page. He'd gained the nickname Horseshoe because he was so lucky. He had everything – from the talent to draw so beautifully, to plenty of money and the best of everything else. A nice family, good looks … So damn lucky in life, we kidded he was born with a horseshoe shoved up his ass.

'He creeps *everyone* out,' Brent said, spitting a splinter of tobacco from his mouth.

'Why the hell doesn't he listen, Tommy, and stop trying to hang out with us?' Horseshoe added.

'Who the hell knows?' I said, shrugging my shoulders before grabbing a sweating Coke. 'Joey doesn't listen to anyone.'

Joey was twelve – two years younger than the rest of us – so there was no way we could be seen with him. As well as becoming the laughing stock of the town, our status as tough guys would have been destroyed. Besides, the horrible incident from last year was still fresh in our minds. Even though it wasn't Joey's fault, we no longer felt comfortable when he was anywhere near us.

He had changed after the incident. Prior to it, he'd been the town clown, willing to do anything for a dare, just to make everyone laugh. Now, he just stared at people with his dead shadowed eyes, saying nothing, creeping everyone out. He had changed from a boisterous, good-humoured kid to a brooding recluse, scary to look at.

'He's getting closer,' Horseshoe said in a worried voice, as if fearful of being in range of Joey's shadow.

Joey edged closer to the other side of the lake, where disused railway track ran alongside the river. During hot days, heat rose off the tracks in crimped patterns, making them look soft and familiar in the baking distance. Occasionally, Brent and I would challenge each other to a 'track burn', resting our hands on the hot metal until one of us shouted uncle. Most times I pulled my hand away first, the blotchy redness covering my palms like a tattoo. But sometimes, on a rare occasion, it was Brent who surrendered to the excruciating pain. Sour in his defeat, he always had a begrudging answer, usually blaming Horseshoe for distracting him, or some other made-up excuse.

'Joey! What the hell're you doing!' Brent shouted, throwing an empty Coke bottle across the lake in his direction. 'We don't want you near us! Fuck off!'

Of the three of us, Brent was the only one to ever use the 'f' word. Horseshoe and I were always terrified to swear, fearful our parents would get wind of it. Mom threatened that if she ever heard I used such language, she would staple my tongue to the inside of my mouth. I remember the day she produced Dad's Swingline stapler. *Click-click,* she had said, clicking the stapler close to my petrified face. *And don't think I won't, Mister. Click-click!*

Joey didn't reply to Brent's shouting. Now, he was inching into the lake, the water up to his ankles. Perhaps he hadn't heard him – though I doubted that. Brent's voice sounded like a cannon releasing verbal volleys, and had a similar range.

'Leave him alone, Brent,' I finally said, bringing the Coke to my mouth. 'As long as he stays where he is, he's doing no harm.'

As I sipped my drink, Joey made a slight movement with his hand. I thought he was running the hand through his hair – a nervous habit he'd acquired since the incident – but Horseshoe and Brent had different takes on it.

'He's flipping the bird at us, Tommy. Can you believe his balls?' Horseshoe said, almost in shocked awe.

'Naw. He's waving. That's all,' Brent said. 'He knows better than to flip the bird at me. I'd kill the little prick.'

Joey continued walking into the lake, with zombie-like slowness.

'He's going for a dip, with his clothes on,' Brent said, grinning.

'You're right, Brent,' Horseshoe agreed, wiping Coke spillage from his mouth. 'He's trying to give us a laugh, like the old days. Go on, Joey! You can do it!'

'Joey! Joey! Joey!' Brent chanted.

The deliciously fear-charged entertainment increased every moment, as the lake's surface slid up to Joey's shoulder. It was like watching a magic eraser making his body disappear.

The three of us began counting out, daring him to break Jimmy 'Fish Face' Nugent's record of one minute and twenty-nine seconds for staying under.

'One … Two … Three …'

The top of Joey's hair disappeared beneath the skin of water. Seconds later, calmness returned to its surface, as if he had never been there at all.

We cheered louder, continuing our hypnotic drum-roll call.

'Nineteen ... Twenty! ... Twenty-one ...'

On and on we counted, our voices rising with each fading second.

'Fifty-nine ... *Sixtyyyyyyyyyy*! ... Sixty-one ... Sixty two ...'

At seventy, our voices filtered out, leaving an eerie silence. The world was caught in freeze-frame, the silence like sharp stones trapped in the pit of my stomach.

'Someone's gotta dive in there, see what the little bastard's up to,' Brent said. He looked nervous, probably believing as leader of our gang he might be held accountable for Joey's actions. 'Tommy? You gotta do it.'

'Me?' I said, edging away. 'Why me?'

'You're the best swimmer by far, that's why.' It was more a plea than a command.

'You know you are, Tommy,' Horseshoe said, nodding in agreement with Brent's words. 'You gotta do something. I swim like a rock, otherwise I'd go after him.'

I doubted Horseshoe would have braved the deeper part of the lake to jump in after Joey, but I didn't want an argument. I wished now I hadn't won all those medals for swimming, at school. I didn't want to be part of anything happening under the water, but I had little choice.

'Okay, okay! Just shut the hell up!' I said, walking towards the filthy water.

For some inexplicable reason, the water felt colder as my

bare feet touched it. I shuddered before glancing back at Brent and Horseshoe.

'Hurry!' They kept shouting in unison. 'Hurry!'

Seconds later, I was in, propelling my body downwards in the foul-tasting and murky thickness. Visibility was virtually nil. Worse than land fog. I went deeper, wishing I had the capability of shouting underwater for Joey.

Don't give up on him, a pleading voice entered my head. *He's here somewhere. Find him. Please …*

I stayed down until panic started building up inside my burning lungs. I would need to resurface for air – and soon. Then, just as I twisted my body to head upwards, an old wreck of a car came into view. Ghostly green, its smashed windows stared out like the gaping eyes of an old haunted house. I wanted to swim away from its skeletal form, but a strange magnetism drew me closer and closer.

And that's when I spotted Joey.

His body was motionless, standing as if trapped in a giant test tube. He seemed to be holding the car door, as if wanting to get inside.

I went torpedoing forward.

A moment later, I was at his side. I took hold of his arm, pulling on it. He looked around at me, his face expressionless in the godless gloom. Only his eyes seemed to have life. I would never forget how they looked; how they blinked at me in surprise.

Grabbing the back of his shirt, I yanked hard on it.

Nothing. His body resisted. A ton-weight of unmoving mass.

I pulled again on the shirt, but my lungs were on fire. Feeling dizzy, I swam empty-handed to the surface, grateful to be gulping down the beautiful hot summer air.

From the embankment, Brent kept shouting, 'Where is he, Tommy? Where the fuck's Joey?'

'Get … help … hurry …' I stuttered, plunging back down into the nightmare.

Under the water, I searched again for the old wreck, but the water had now become black as oil spill. I could find nothing, other than a forest of thick weeds. I tried to swim through them, but they were becoming entwined on my legs. It felt like someone trying to wrestle me down. I pictured Joey grabbing at my ankles.

Panicking, I kicked out at the weeds, but their grip became iron. Water rushed into my mouth, filling my nostrils. I was becoming disorientated. A gathering hurt assembled in my lungs. I held the pain there as long as I could, trying not to breathe, trying to think about anything other than the pain.

No! Not like this! I screamed in my head. *Don't die like this.*

I remember Horseshoe dragging me back to land, and that was all. Later, Horseshoe laughed, saying he wasn't willing to give me the kiss-of-life; that it was lucky for me I didn't need it.

'He's ... he's down there, Horseshoe,' I spluttered, coughing up filthy water. 'Joey's not moving ...'

'Brent's getting help. Don't worry. It'll be okay ...'

But I could tell from the way his hands shook, he understood it wasn't okay.

By the time an ambulance arrived in tandem with a police car, I knew it was too late. Joey was gone. I also knew I was in trouble, as I watched the sheriff emerging from his car. Thin as a line but commandingly tall, he came rushing towards me, rhino-like in his speed.

'Are you okay, Tommy?' he said, bending down beside me.

I nodded. 'I'm fine, but Joey's down there, Dad.'

'Don't worry. We'll find him. In the meantime, don't move from here. One of the ambulance crew'll take you to hospital. Clear?'

I nodded again, not caring about the ambulance crew or about anything else at that moment. I suspected Dad would have more to say to me later on. I was very aware that it was he who had placed most of the danger signs at the lake. I also suspected he'd have something to say about Brent. Dad didn't approve of my friendship with Brent, who he regarded as a future felon, just like Brent's father, doing big time in a south Florida prison for possession of drugs.

'Sit tight,' Dad said, running off in the direction of the lake.

It took police divers forty minutes to locate Joey, but another two hours to bring his lifeless body to the surface.

He had handcuffed himself to the door of the old wreck; the same handcuffs his father used as a prison guard in the penitentiary.

Later that evening at home, Dad both praised and cautioned me.

'That was brave what you did, Tommy, trying to save Joey Maxwell; but also foolish. I noticed that Fleming kid there when I arrived. Did he put you up to it? I want the truth.'

'It had nothing to do with Brent. I was the best swimmer there. Aren't you just glad I tried to save Joey?'

'Of course I am, but it meant putting yourself in danger. We could've been dealing with two deaths this evening, instead of one. There's an old saying: fools rush in where angels fear to tread. Perhaps you can remember that in future. Clear?'

I nodded. 'Yes ...'

Mom hovered in the background like a vulture, waiting for Dad to finish so she could get pecking at me. Mom never praised. It just wasn't in her nature. But she was a specialist at warnings; that was her second skin.

'What did I warn you about being with that Fleming boy? Did you have cotton stuffed in your ears when I warned you I didn't want you with him?'

'Brent's okay, Mom. It wasn't his fault.'

'You arguing with me, *Mister*?'

Mister? Only Mom had the ability to send shivers up your spine with one word. Mom was smaller than Dad by a good foot-and-a-half, but she always seemed to look bigger when she was angry. The room seemed to get smaller, to close in around you. Dad always said not to be fooled by Mom's size; that dynamite comes in small packages.

'No … I'm not arguing.'

'If stupidity ever becomes a currency, you'll end up a millionaire. Don't *ever* let me find out you're hanging about with that Brent Fleming again. Understood, Mister?'

'Yeah …' *I'll make sure you don't find out.*

'What?' Mom's mouth dropped open. She looked as if I had just sworn at her. 'What did you just say?'

'Yes. I meant yes.'

'Don't let me *ever* hear you talking like that again. I didn't raise some corner boy with his "yeah" gutter language. Got that?'

I sighed. 'Yes. Can I be excused now? I'm going over to Horseshoe's to watch *Planet of the Apes*.'

'*Planet of the Apes*? Ha! After all your monkeying about at the lake, the only planet you'll be seeing for the foreseeable future is the globe in your room. You're grounded until further notice.'

'What? But …' I looked over at Lawyer Dad, hoping he would raise an objection. But he knew better than to argue with Judge-Jury-Executioner Mom when it came to the law in her territory. So did I.

We both watched Mom leave the room, to go out onto the porch. I swore I saw smoke coming from her ears, even though she didn't smoke.

'Why's Mom always like that to me, Dad?'

'Like what?'

'Mean.'

'Mean?' Dad looked evenly at me for a moment or two. 'Oh, I see. "Mean", as in petrified about you almost losing your life today? Perhaps you meant "mean" as in the terror in her voice when I called to tell her what had happened, and why you ended up in the hospital?'

'I didn't think she cared,' I replied in a near-whisper.

'Let me tell you something, Tommy, and I hope you listen carefully to it. When you become an adult, and if you're blessed with a child, and God forbid that child does something so foolish he or she is almost killed, then all I hope is that you're as mean as your mother when it comes to showing what true love and protection really is.'

'What's that suppose to mean?'

'Figure it out for yourself.' He ruffled my hair, then smiled. 'Now, if you don't mind, I've a beautiful girl I need to be seeing.'

He left the room, to join Mom on the porch. I watched through the window as he sat, his arm resting on her shoulder, and she leaned into him. The sun was going down, and its dying rays etched the shape of my parents onto the glass, a silhouette surrounded by faded hues of gold and blue. A soft, warm breeze sneaked in through the partly open door, and rested on my face, and for the first time that day, it felt good to be alive, as the solid mass of my parents seemed to lift the cares from my shoulders.

Little did I know, but all that was about to change.

CHAPTER TWO

A Gathering of Conspirators

Shedding the blood of their brothers ...
Emiliano Zapata

Joey's horrific death was the main headline for days in the local newspapers. The reports suggested his suicide had been triggered by the attack in Black's Wood, last year, where he had been sexually molested. They also noted, ominously, that his attacker had never been apprehended. Police had a suspect, but they couldn't arrest him through lack of evidence.

Over the next few days, journalists and TV reporters came by to interview me about Joey. I was portrayed as a hero, trying to save a pal – much to Brent's annoyance.

'Shit, I called the ambulance,' Brent said, four nights later, as we sat around a makeshift campfire at the lake, drinking Coke. 'They didn't even mention me.'

'Me neither,' Horseshoe added, as he tossed a piece of wood

on the fire, causing devil sparks to dance in the darkness. 'I pulled you out of the water, Tommy. I should've got my name in the paper as well. I was a hero too.'

I nodded in agreement. 'I know. You both were heroes. I told them about the two of you, but they didn't put your names in the story.' I didn't mention the recurring nightmare I was suffering each night, watching ugly little green fish peel the skin off Joey's face with their tiny razor-like teeth. Then Joey would grab me, handcuffing both of us to the old wreck. His eyes are everywhere in my room, accusing me. Perhaps if we hadn't encouraged him to go deeper into the water, he would still be alive?

'Everyone's saying it's because Joey was molested,' Horseshoe said, before slugging down a bottle of Coke in one long gulp, a feat that never failed to amaze me.

'That pervert Not Normal's the scum bastard who did this, by molesting Joey,' Brent agreed, spitting into the fire. 'Made poor Joey go and kill himself.'

'*Shhhhhhhhh!*' I hissed, glancing nervously over my shoulder. 'Only a few people know Not Normal's a suspect. If my dad ever finds out we know, he'll figure I've been listening to his private conversations in the hub. Then I'll be in for it.'

'Don't worry, Tommy,' Horseshoe said. 'Your dad'll not hear a thing from us. Right, Brent?'

'Well, it doesn't change a fucking thing,' Brent said, ignoring Horseshoe's assurance. '*We* know it was Not Normal.'

Not Normal – Norman Armstrong – worked as a part-time janitor at the Strand movie theatre. Completely hairless, he suffered from alopecia universalis, the rapid-hair-loss ailment. The creepy loner acquired his unfortunate moniker due to his name being pronounced wrong by every kid in town.

Normal, can you tell us if there's a cartoon before the big movie today? Will there be ice cream for sale today, Normal? Will I be allowed to watch that horror movie, Normal, even though I won't be thirteen 'till next month? Normal, can you tell me if –

This went on for months, until one night, he had had enough. *I'm Norman!* he screamed, in utter frustration, before making himself a legend with the following classic statement: *You bunch of little rubber-mouth bastards! I'm not fucking Normal!*

'His ugly face is like a *piñata*: should be whacked hard and often,' Horseshoe now suggested.

'Never mind hitting him. They should shoot the bastard,' Brent said.

His fixation on the subject had become so relentless it was starting to scare me.

'Yeah,' Horseshoe said, making an imaginary gun with finger and thumb. 'Shooting him would be much better.'

Brent nodded. 'Right in the nuts. That would stop him, the perverted bastard.'

'Yeah. Pervert. In the nuts. *Bang!*' Horseshoe nodded, before loudly belching out Coke gas. 'He's nuttier than a squirrel's turd. Gives me the creeps. Have you ever seen that evil smile he has, with those rotten teeth of his?'

'We should make a pact, like they do in the movies,' Brent said. He loved nothing better than a good murder movie, full of mystery and intrigue.

'Yeah, like in the movies.'

'Are you game, Tommy?' Brent was looking hard into my eyes.

I watched the flames flickering over Brent's face, distorting his features. It made me think of Dr Jekyll morphing into Hyde. I shivered.

'Game for what?' I finally said, knowing full well what he was hinting at.

'Justice for Joey. Pay that pervert Not Normal back for what he did. We take an oath, right here, right fucking now.' He held out one hand, and with the other produced a penknife from his pocket. 'A blood oath.'

'Blood ...?' Horseshoe said, his voice thinning.

I thought Horseshoe was going to faint. Everyone knew he loathed the sight of blood – especially his own.

'Yes, *blood*,' Brent said, never taking his eyes off mine, ignoring Horseshoe. 'If the oath is betrayed, the traitor will go straight to Hell and be fucked in the ass by the devil's flaming cock, forever and ever. Agreed?'

Even though I knew this whole blood-oath thing was just bluster and talk, the hairs on the back of my neck began nipping my skin. Night sounds whispered secretly behind me. I felt darkness on my mouth. 'Okay ...' I finally said.

Brent smiled and held out his thumb, curving the knife inwards. His skin tore. An inkblot of blood appeared. Even in the dull light, I would never forget its colour: deep crimson, like the bloodshot eye of a trapped animal.

'Here,' Brent said, handing me the knife and holding his bloody thumb outwards.

I held my breath, and then cut along my thumb, brave-facing the instant jolt of pain. A bubble of blood appeared.

'Now you, Horseshoe,' Brent commanded, handing the bloodstained knife to Horseshoe.

Horseshoe swallowed hard. His Adam's apple bobbed up and down in the dim light. It looked like a robin's egg.

'Can't I ... just swear something, instead?' Horseshoe asked.

'No, you can't! It's like the three musketeers. All for one, and one for all.' Brent's face was becoming harsh. 'Stop being such a sissy. Just fucking cut.'

Reluctantly, Horseshoe took the knife, his hand shaking terribly. Breathing deeply, he pierced the skin on his thumb. He swooned slightly. '*Ohhhhhhhhhhhhhh.*'

'Now, thumbs together,' Brent urged.

We complied.

'Let the oath of blood-brothers and secrecy live with us forever,' Brent continued, forcing the three thumbs tightly against each other, allowing our blood to mingle like spilt ink on a page. 'Let any traitor burn in hell, forever and ever.'

For the longest ten seconds of my life, I waited to take my thumb away. It felt on fire.

'See?' Brent said to Horseshoe, finally breaking the bloody link. 'Wasn't so bad, was it?'

Horseshoe didn't answer. His pale face looked damp, glistening in the dancing firelight.

For the longest time, no one uttered a single word. The night seemed to grow denser, and the intense silence began closing in on me. It felt claustrophobic, like a funeral shroud.

'Are we finished?' I finally asked, feeling bone weary. 'I've got to head home. I'm still under night curfew.'

'Finished, and just beginning, blood-brother.' Brent grinned. His face looked strange. 'Call over to my house, tomorrow. I'll come up with a plan.'

I left my two friends there, with the dying embers for company, and the soft slapping sound of Jackson's Lake spilling over the embankment behind them. There would be no plan, of course. It was just Brent, living out his fantasy, playing the leading man in one of his mind-movies.

As I made my way home in the darkness, I felt eyes on my back. I hoped it was Brent or Horseshoe, but something made me think of Joey Maxwell's accusing gaze. I swore I heard his voice calling out.

Why didn't you save me, Tommy?

I ran as fast as I could, never stopping until I reached home.

CHAPTER THREE

Sweet Lemonade and Thoughts of Murder

I know that's a secret, for it's whispered everywhere.
William Congreve, **Love for Love**

Early the next day, I went around to the back of Horse-shoe's house, and threw a couple of tiny stones up at his bedroom window.

The stones reached their target and the window opened in a flash, followed by Horseshoe's annoyed-looking face.

'Tommy, what the hell's wrong with you? You almost smashed the glass. You gonna pay for it, if it gets broken?'

'Stop moaning and get your butt out the window,' I said, grinning.

His head quickly popped back inside, and a couple of minutes later Horseshoe started climbing out the window, legs first. Balancing himself carefully, he reached out for the extended tree branch, directly across from his window. Not for Horseshoe the conventional way of the front door. Everything had to be dramatic. Crawling precariously along the branch to his treehouse door, he disappeared inside.

'C'mon, Horseshoe!' I shouted. 'Hurry the hell up!'

'Okay, okay! Give me a second.'

The rope ladder came flying out of the treehouse, followed by Horseshoe.

Horseshoe was the only kid in the neighborhood with a treehouse. I would've given anything to have one, just to get away from Mom and Dad every now and again. Even the scrawny tree at the back of our yard would have sufficed, giving me somewhere to sneak out to at night. But Mom was wise to all of that. She made sure my room was at the front, where she could 'keep a good eye on me' at all times.

'What do you think of these?' Horseshoe asked, as soon as his feet touched the ground.

He was wearing a pair of plastic X-ray glasses, ones I had seen advertised in the back of a comic. Horseshoe was gullible that way, always buying crap. His family had plenty of money, compared to Brent's and mine, so I guess his parents didn't mind. It never bothered me, the money he had. He was generous with it, and always bought the Cokes we drank.

'If you want me to be honest, they look silly, Horseshoe. Really silly. Almost as silly as when you painted your face green for Saint Paddy's day.' Horseshoe had painted his face green the year before last, for the annual Saint Patrick's Day festivities. He looked ridiculous. Both Brent and I teased him mercilessly, saying he must have been trying to look like the Hulk, but had ended up looking like puke.

'I don't care if they look silly. They work. That's all that counts.'

'They're garbage, like all the crap you buy, Horseshoe. Remember the Sea Monkeys you bought? *So eager to please they can even be trained?* Turned out to be just a bunch of dead, shriveled-up shrimps.'

'Come on, we all make mistakes every now and –'

'Or the Polaris Nuclear Sub, that was supposed to fire real rockets and torpedoes? You wasted seven bucks on that, only to discover it was cardboard, and a fart would've sunk it. You could've made a better one from an empty cereal box.'

'But these are different, Tommy. I'm telling you. Here, take a look,' he said, taking off the glasses and handing them to me. 'Put your hand up in front of them. What do you see?'

I reluctantly put the glasses on, checking first that no one would see me, and then held my hand up directly against one of the lenses.

'Wow!' I was amazed. I *could* see my hand. Chillingly, it was all bones, no flesh, like something out of *The War of the Worlds*. 'Shit, I can't believe it, Horseshoe. They actually *do* work. You've finally bought a winner.'

'Best buck-and-a-quarter I ever spent. Think of the things we can get up to with them.'

'Things? What kind of things?'

'All sorts of things. Like looking through Ann Cartwright's clothing, for starters. We'll be able to see her panties.'

Ann Cartwright was a gorgeous, big-breasted girl at our school. Everyone was in love with her. Especially Horseshoe. Even though he knew realistically he hadn't a hope in hell with her, he never gave up the dream.

'If Big Boobs Cartwright catches you gawking through her dress, you'll be in big trouble with her three brothers,' I said, handing back the glasses. 'They'll beat the shit out of you, just for the fun of it.'

'It'll be worth taking a beating just to see her panties. Bet they're pink and lacey. I can't wait until school reopens.'

I didn't know if it was just the glasses, but Horseshoe's eyes looked kind of strange when he spoke about Ann's panties.

We quickly headed over to Brent's house, in deep discussion all the way about the pros and cons of X-ray glasses. I had to admit, Horseshoe had me convinced. In fact, I had decided secretly that I'd send for my own pair, when I got back home from Brent's.

I always enjoyed going to Brent's house, because his parents were much more relaxed than mine could ever be. Mom called them 'liberal', which I took to mean something approaching Satanism.

Once, when Mrs Gleason – Mom's old school friend and card partner – was over visiting, I overheard her use the word 'swingers', in reference to the Flemings. My teenage mind summoned up a picture of Mrs Fleming swinging on their tree-swing, being pushed by Mr Fleming. Could that really have been what Mrs Gleason meant?

The Flemings also smoked marijuana, according to Mrs Gleason. Lots of it. That was before Mr Fleming went to prison, after being caught with 'a ton of it' down in Florida. I knew what marijuana was, of course. Brent smoked it occasionally. I had even tried it once, but threw up and never touched it again. Ever. Dad said if he even suspected I had touched anything like that, he'd personally lock me up, and throw away the key. I was almost certain he wasn't joking. Mom said she would kill me. She *definitely* wasn't joking.

Brent was resting beside a tree at the bottom of his garden, drinking homemade lemonade, when we approached. In his hands he had a copy of *True Crime* magazine, borrowed from me, which of course meant borrowed/stolen from Dad's collection. Brent and I had something of a lending library in miniature going on. In return for a regular supply of my dad's crime magazines, Brent would let me look at *his* father's massive collection of *Playboy* magazines. I was in love with Little Annie Fanny, despite the fact that she was just a cartoon.

Brent was totally fascinated by the crime magazines, and their grisly black-and-white photos. Their monochrome depictions of blood did more for the imagination than any Technicolor rendering ever could.

'Okay, blood-brothers?' was the first thing he said, spotting us walking towards him.

I nodded, but didn't say a word.

Horseshoe was more enthusiastic. 'Feeling great, blood-brother. Strange, I always wanted a brother, and now I've got two.'

'What the fuck've you got on your face, Horseshoe? Looks like some sort of bug,' Brent said, spotting the glasses.

'X-ray glasses. Want to try them?'

Brent looked at me, and then back to Horseshoe. 'Are you fucking nuts? There's no such thing as X-ray glasses. When the hell are you gonna grow up and stop acting like a kid?'

'Try them on and see for yourself,' Horseshoe said, offering the glasses to Brent.

'Bullshit. No such thing.' Brent refused to touch them. 'Put them away – now.'

'Try them first, and then tell me they're not real,' Horseshoe said, defiantly.

Brent looked at me. I just shrugged my shoulders.

'Okay,' he said, snapping the glasses from Horseshoe's hand. 'But if I catch you laughing …'

Brent put the glasses on. He looked so ridiculous that I almost laughed, in spite of the warning.

'Put your hand up to them,' Horseshoe instructed.

Reluctantly, Brent's hand went to his face.

'What do you see, Brent?'

'Shit …' Brent's mouth opened like a trapdoor. 'You're right, Horseshoe. They work!'

'Told you.' Horseshoe grinned with pride. Finally, after a very long list of disappointments, he had actually managed to buy something that did what it said on the can. This was major. Respect would have to be given to him, after this.

'Hold on a sec …' Brent said. 'I put my other hand up, and it looks the same.'

'Of course it looks the same. It's a hand, ain't it?'

'I know it's a hand, smart ass, but why isn't it moving when I make a fist?'

'Huh?'

'A fist,' Brent said, making one, and holding it up to the glasses. 'It's still showing a hand, not a fist!'

'Let me see,' said Horseshoe, nervously taking the glasses from Brent and placing them back on his own face. He made a fist. Then a hand. Then a fist. 'I … I don't understand.'

'Don't you?' Brent said, smirking. 'You've been suckered again.'

'What?'

Like lightning, Brent grabbed the glasses off Horseshoe's defeated face, and began crushing them in his hands.

'Hey!' Horseshoe shouted, making a grab for them. 'Don't do that!'

But it was too late. The damage had been done. Brent tore the glasses apart, and then held something in his hand.

'Feathers,' he said, grinning. 'These were stuck in between the lenses, to make it look like you were seeing an X-ray. Either that, or the feathers came from your sorry ass, Horseshoe.'

Mortified, Horseshoe could only look at his latest investment blunder withering in front of his eyes, and witnessed by the entire world. Two feathers, cardboard frames painted black and, just to add insult to injury, cheap plastic lenses. The entire kit and caboodle was the equivalent of one cent worth of crappy leftovers, sold for a buck-and-a-quarter to the biggest sucker in town.

'There ought to be a law against these sort of things,' said Horseshoe, staring glumly at the wreckage of plastic.

'Do something useful, Horseshoe. Go get you and Tommy a glass of lemonade from the fridge,' Brent said, indicating towards the house. 'Grab some more ice for me, while you're at it.'

'Why's it always me has to go?' Horseshoe said.

'Because I say so, that's why, Mister fucking X-ray Eyes.'

'Maybe I'm not thirsty.'

'Maybe you don't want to be a blood-brother?' Brent made a movement to stand, as if to confront Horseshoe.

'That's not fair. It's always me who has to –'

'Stop arguing like two girls!' I said, walking towards the house. 'I'll get the damn lemonade.'

A few seconds later, I was rapping politely on the door, even though Mrs Fleming always encouraged me to 'walk right on in, don't bother with that knocking crap'.

'Hello? Mrs Fleming?' My voice carried itself into the house. No response.

'Mrs Fleming?' I called again from the doorway, before entering.

Walking fast, I headed straight through to the kitchen, and there – to my shock but juvenile delight – was Mrs Fleming, in a pair of *very* tiny white panties, and nothing else. She stood at the open fridge, cooling her very cool body, a bottle of beer in one hand and a reefer in the other. Flaming red hair fanned onto the balcony of her shoulders. Her eyes were green and luminous as moonlight on the lake. Silver earrings were tooled tightly into the lobes of her ears. A sickly sweet aroma drifted across the room from the reefer.

I couldn't help but look directly at her crotch, where tiny sunbursts of hair pushed out from her panties.

'Oh, hey, Tommy. What's up?' she asked casually, as if being practically naked was the norm.

'I ... I'm looking for ...' My eyes went straight from her crotch to her gorgeous face, then to her beautiful bare boobs. Embarrassment bled up my neck and into my face, like a rising tide of hot oil. I tried blinking away her nakedness, but the blinking only made it worse. The more I blinked, the more naked she became, shaping into Little Annie Fanny. 'I ... lem ... lemons ...'

'Lemons?' she said, smiling sweetly. 'You want *lemons*?'

My cock began pulsing. *Oh no!* I pushed my hand down, hoping to block the bulge from Mrs Fleming's view, terrified it looked like a miniature dowsing rod.

'Lemon … ade … I mean …' My brain told me to get out of there quickly, but my crafty cock-a-doodle-doo cock paralysed my legs.

'Oh, lemonade …' She smiled, before sucking seductively on the reefer. She placed her beer down on top of the fridge. 'I'll get you some.'

Bending elegantly into the fridge, her long legs tightened. I could clearly see one of her butt cheeks as her tiny panties rode up, tight into the crack in her beautiful ass. My heart did a little double movement. I swallowed hard. Couldn't breathe. Fainting was becoming a strong possibility.

'Here you go.' From the fridge, she handed me an ice-cold pitcher, filled to the brim with golden lemonade.

Her cool fingers touched mine. I almost dropped the pitcher.

'Thank … thank you, Mrs Fleming.'

'Grab a glass from the cupboard,' she said, indicating with her head.

'Okay …' I reached and quickly grabbed two. My hands were shaking so much, the glasses began rattling horribly.

'That was a very brave thing you did, Tommy, trying to save that poor boy, Joey Maxwell.'

'I … it wasn't just me. Horseshoe and Brent helped, too.'

'But it was *you* who jumped into the water to save Joey. Not Horseshoe, and definitely not Brent. That's what distinguishes a hero. Doing what others fear to do, even if you're terrified when it's happening.'

'I … I don't think I'm a hero, Mrs Fleming.' My face was turning an even deeper shade of crimson.

'And modest with it.' She smiled. 'Bet your father's so proud of you.'

'I guess,' I replied, shrugging my shoulders, trying to maintain a cool facade. I wanted desperately to kiss her.

'No guessing about it. He's proud of you. I wish Brent would do something to make me proud. I only hope he doesn't end up like *his* useless father.'

This was just as embarrassing, the conversation's sudden turn of direction. She kept talking to me as if I were an adult. I suspected she was lonely for adult company. I doubted Mrs Fleming had many visitors. No one in the neighborhood wanted to be associated with the family, because of the drug dealing down in Florida.

'Hot outside, isn't it?' She waved away the smoke curling about her face.

'Yes,' I nodded. And then nodded some more. Like a freakish, broken toy, stuck in nodding mode.

'They say this is going to be the hottest summer on record. I just can't seem to stop sweating.' Tiny beads of sweat were trickling languidly down her stomach, congregating in her bellybutton, like a glorious garden pool. I wanted to dive right in there, and swim to the bottom, tickle her stomach.

Vast rivers of sweat were meanwhile trickling down my spine, pooling in the crack of my ass. If the sweating didn't stop soon, I'd have the cleanest ass in Black's Creek.

'Staying for lunch, Tommy?' she said, retrieving her beer from on top of the fridge.

'I don't really know, Mrs Fleming.'

'Sally. You don't need to keep on calling me Mrs Fleming. It makes me feel old. You don't think I'm old, do you?' She smiled, waiting my response.

'No! No way. You're not old, Mrs ... Sally ...' It felt distinctly weird to call her by her first name.

She smiled further, but added something to the smile, something mysteriously seductive and arresting. There should have been a law against that paralysing smile. It was criminal.

'It's only cold cuts and bread, but you're more than welcome to stay. I like seeing you about the house, Tommy. You're always a good influence on Brent, helping to keep him out of trouble. I feel much better, knowing he's with you. You're a terrific young man, growing up fast.'

Tilting her head back gracefully, she took a sip of beer. Her neck was beautiful, like a swan's. A beautiful swan. I imagined what it would be like to kiss that swan-like neck, tasting its honey sweetness.

Just as I was getting lost in the moment, a dark vision of Mom entered my head. She was holding a carving knife and the Swingline stapler, preparing to dismember my member for all my impure thoughts of swans and honey.

After I cut it off, you'll be able to staple it back on. Click-click!

'Perhaps I should give you a handsome reward?' Mrs Fleming said, thankfully breaking my thoughts.

'Huh?'

'A reward for being such a good influence on Brent. Keeping him out of trouble.'

'Oh … no, that's okay.' Handsome rewards always had a way of turning ugly for me.

'You sure?' She gave a secret smile, and moved closer to me; so close I could smell her exhilarating womanly smells and perfume.

'Tha … thank you anyway for the offer, Mrs Fleming,' I finally manage to stutter, edging slowly backwards from the kitchen.

'Sally.' She gave me a little wave. Smiled some more and then sucked very slowly on the reefer. I swore she winked.

I staggered out goofily, waiting to trip on something, but miraculously reached the front door and freedom without a hitch. I turned and fled back down the garden, towards Brent and Horseshoe.

Brent glanced up from the magazine, as I approached.

'What the hell kept you?'

Your mom, half-naked. Her beautiful lemonade boobs! I saw her sunburst of bush! And her little Annie Fanny!

'Noth ... nothing ...' I mumbled, holding up the pitcher. 'I was just fill ... filling her up.'

'Huh? Filling her up?'

'I ... I mean the pitcher ... It was empty.'

For a second, Brent looked puzzled. 'Where's the ice?'

'Ice? Oh! The *ice* ...' I scrambled for an answer. 'I ... I couldn't find any.'

'Couldn't find any?' He looked even more puzzled. 'Shit, there's tons of the stuff in the fridge. How the fuck could you *not* find ice?'

'I just couldn't find it!' My voice sounded like a choirboy with his nuts being squeezed in a vice. 'Must've been looking in the wrong place.'

Horseshoe giggled like Shirley Temple being tickled. I thought seriously about crowning him with the pitcher. I poured out a glass of lemonade instead, and drank. Just the way Mrs Fleming did, only not sexy. I imagined her long fingers in the lemonade, stirring it, before she places one in my mouth, demanding that I suck the juice clean off.

Shaking myself back to reality, I handed Horseshoe the pitcher and the other glass. He could fend for himself.

'I've been getting good ideas from this, Tommy,' Brent said, holding up the crime mag.

'Oh?' I tried looking interested, but my mind kept wandering back to the kitchen scene.

'Yeah. Lots of good ideas.'

I thought of Mrs Fleming again. Her crotch. So much red hair down there, as if it were on fire. Frightening, yet mesmerising. Who the hell needed X-ray glasses, with Mrs Fleming running about butt-naked? I quickly sat down, lest Horseshoe and Brent spotted the bulge of my cock stirring again.

'*Tommy*? What the *hell's* wrong with you!' Brent shouted, practically into my face.

'Huh?'

'I said, I've been getting good ideas out of these crime mags. Been doing a lot of thinking about our big surprise for Mister Pervert.'

'Oh, right ...'

'What kind of ideas, Brent?' asked Horseshoe, his enthusiasm renewed.

'Hurry up and finish the lemonade. I've got a little something I want to show both of you.'

'Your cock?' Horseshoe said, grinning.

'What?' Brent's face turned menacing. 'What the fuck did you just say?'

'What do you want to show us, Brent?' I said quickly, jumping in to defuse the situation.

Brent glared at Horseshoe for a few seconds before answering. 'C'mon. Let's head over to Black's Cemetery.'

Horseshoe and I quickly jumped up and followed behind. I thought I saw a smiling Mrs Fleming peeping behind a curtain, watching me leave. Perhaps it was just wishful thinking on my part. Perhaps not.

Black's Cemetery was situated in the large forest area surrounding Jackson's Lake. It always gave me the shits, even in daylight. I hated Halloween nights, because we always chose to hang out here among the dead, just to prove how tough we were. We'd be armed to the teeth, with BB guns and slingshots, hunting for squirrels or hares, pretending we were castaways, and that our very lives depended on capturing little furry creatures for food. In all honesty, we never managed to hit one squirrel or hare, despite the fact that the forest was teeming with them.

'This'll do,' Brent said, forty minutes later, stopping beside an old uprooted tree badly gone to rot in the cemetery. The fleet of unattended tombstones – the ones still standing – were covered in moss, and fractured like decaying pirates' teeth.

Horseshoe and I watched as Brent dropped to his knees, digging at the soil cushioning the tree. From another tree directly to our right, a nosey squirrel, its tail curving into a hairy question mark, vigorously scratched its furry undercarriage and watched the three of us.

'Disgusting,' Horseshoe said. 'If they're not eating nuts, they're scratching them.'

'If you gotta scratch, you gotta scratch,' I said, grinning.

A few seconds later, Brent stood back up, a dirt-covered package in his filthy hands.

'What's that?' Horseshoe asked.

Brent gave us a meaningful look, and began denuding the package. He was grinning, like a magician performing a trick. A few seconds later, he revealed a gun, wrapped protectively in polythene. It stared out at us like a mummified fetus.

Horseshoe looked ready to faint with excitement.

'*Whoa*! Is ... is it *real*, Brent?' Horseshoe finally managed to say, once his mouth had started working again.

'It's real,' Brent said, casually releasing the gun from the polythene enclosure. 'A German Luger.'

I was less impressed, having seen plenty of guns in my life, mostly courtesy of Dad's work. By the time I was seven, I had handled my first gun, but it would be three long years after that before he permitted me to fire one – albeit an old .22 handgun. As the years progressed, so did the standard of gun Dad allowed me to fire. Yet there was something different about this gun displayed proudly in Brent's hands, sending the dual shivers of fear and weariness up my spine.

'Where'd you get it?' I said.

'My grandfather's, from the war. Took it from a dead Nazi's filthy hand, after he shot him dead. It was hid in my ma's room, but I came across it a few weeks ago, when I was searching for some weed.'

This was a new Brent; a Brent with secrets. As friends, we weren't supposed to have secrets – at least not of this magnitude.

'Have you ever fired it?' Horseshoe said, his voice now a whisper of awe. He was in a trance, hypnotised by the lethal beauty of the gun.

'Old Mullan's barn, last week. Cracked a hole the size of a melon in the side. Almost shot one of his bulls.' Brent was still grinning proudly.

'No way!' Horseshoe said, returning to reality. 'That really is bullshit.'

Without warning, Brent cocked the Luger. The sound made me think of someone's knuckles cracking. Slowly, he brought the pistol up to Horseshoe's face.

'Think I'm bullshitting? Think I didn't hear that homo remark of yours, back in the garden?'

Both Horseshoe and I went rigid. Fear spread through me, and my body started tingling in a very bad way. Brent's finger began tightening on the trigger, his knuckles whitening under pressure.

'Brent ...' I finally managed to croak, my mouth dry as cotton. 'Don't mess about with –'

He pulled the trigger.

Kraaaaaaaaaaaaaaaacckk!

The sound hit me in the face. I blinked. Black splotches began spreading across my vision.

'You should've seen the look on your face, Horseshoe!' Brent was smirking like a greasy frog. 'The gun wasn't even loaded.'

Horseshoe bent over, retching violently.

Instinctively, I grabbed the gun from Brent's grip, pushing him away hard. He landed firmly and unceremoniously on his butt.

'Are you crazy?' I screamed into his face. 'What the hell's wrong with you?'

'It ... it wasn't loaded,' he mumbled, staring up at me.

Removing the magazine from the Luger's heel, I could see a bullet nestled on top, like a metal wasp. I removed the bullet gingerly, and held it out.

'Wasn't loaded? What the hell's *that*?'

It was Brent's turn to look frightened. Was it the sight of the bullet, or the fact that I'd had the audacity to tackle him so forcefully? I don't know. What I *do* know is that something changed between us at that very moment; something irreversible.

'I swear to you, Tommy, I was sure it wasn't loaded.'

'Don't rely on your gun's safety. Treat every gun as if it *is* loaded and ready to fire,' I said, reciting Dad's number one rule of his ten commandments for gun safety. I threw the gun and single bullet at Brent's feet, before turning to Horseshoe. 'You okay?'

Horseshoe nodded, but looked far from okay. He was as pale as one of Dad's starched shirts.

'I … I didn't mean anything, Horseshoe,' Brent said, slowly standing. 'Honest, I didn't.'

To me, Brent's contrite words didn't fit with the anger boiling in his mean eyes.

'It's okay, Brent. Not a big deal,' Horseshoe replied, regaining his habitual cool.

'See?' Brent said, looking right into me. 'Not a big deal.'

'It *is* a big deal,' I said, my eyes leveling with Brent's. 'You've got to be careful with guns.'

'Okay, okay! You're fucking right. I shouldn't point it unless I'm willing to use it.' Brent's commanding tone was back. 'Well, I'll be pointing it at Not Normal's nuts, once I get a plan set up in a few days. Are you with me, or are you gonna let that perv get away with killing Joey?'

Horseshoe nodded. 'Yeah … let's get the perv.'

Brent hadn't even looked at Horseshoe when asking the question. Just me.

'Well, Tommy?' Brent said.

A loud ticking was sounding in my head, like an annoying alarm clock that had yet to go off. Or a bomb.

'Okay,' I eventually managed to say. 'I'm in.'

CHAPTER FOUR

Secrets of Biblical Proportion

… and the crocodile caught him by his little nose …
Kipling, **Just So Stories**

'I wish you'd stop bringing your work home with you,' Mom would often say to Dad, attempting the impossible task of tidying the small bedroom-cum-office in our house. Dad would simply smile, knowing that within the hour, Mom would calm right down again. She understood the importance of keeping an after-hours office – 'the hub', as he referred to it – in his eternal quest to bring bad guys to justice.

I suspected he mostly just liked to get away from the stress of work by going there, browsing through his crime mags, honeycombed into wooden brackets against the wall alongside a gold rush of *National Geographic* spines. An unopened bottle of Jim Beam sat sideways atop the magazines. I don't know if the famous bourbon was a gift from someone to Dad, but I could never remember him drinking from it. In fact, I knew it was still sealed, because I had taken the bottle down one day in an attempt to sniff the flavour of its contents.

In the far corner of the room, the usual suspects of crime novels lined themselves up haphazardly against the wall, jostling for attention. In the lead were Ed McBain's *87th Precinct* books, followed closely by Mickey Spillane's hardboiled detective Mike Hammer.

Dad had recently purchased a book called *In Cold Blood*, from Mister Brun's secondhand bookstore over in Lexington Avenue. Dad said it was one of the most frightening books he had ever read, despite having read it twice in one week, and was already re-reading it a third time. The thought of any book frightening Dad perplexed me. When I asked him was it a horror story filled with monsters, he simply looked at me, and very solemnly said: 'Yes. The worst kind.'

I avoided that book for years. If it frightened Dad, the bravest man on the planet, what the hell would it do to me? Only after I eventually plucked up the courage, many years later, did I fully understand the meaning of Dad's words. The book is indeed full of monsters.

Secretly, Dad wanted to be a crime writer, a passion he kept simmering below the surface. I learned this after accidentally discovering a wooden box tucked away beneath his desk. The box was filled with rejection slips and returned manuscripts of crime stories he had penned. Some of the rejection slips were quite harsh in their criticism, and it always filled me with anger reading the to-the-bone words, more or less telling him not to give up the day job – ever.

Dad never mentioned these stories to anyone – at least not within my hearing distance – and certainly never to Mom. In all probability, he was mortified by the rejections, yet he gallantly ploughed on, waiting for that big break that would never come. Little did I know then, but I would follow in his footsteps – not as a sheriff but as a writer, collecting equal amounts of rejections slips before eventually getting my big break. Dad's rejection slips spurred me on each time I thought of giving up.

I only ever witnessed Dad crying once. That was the day he held my first crime novel in his hands, and read the dedication inside, thanking him for being my inspiration as a writer. Mom was mentioned too, of course, for being the best Mom in the world. I think she liked that, even though she just patted me on the head as if I were eight instead of twenty-two, and having a novel published was no big deal.

Dad also liked to sit the hub, listening to jazz on his old, battered radio. He would fill the room with the scratchy sounds of songs from the fifties, along with the pungent aroma of scorched tobacco from his pipe. Mom didn't approve of his smoking – or anyone else's – but it was one of the few vices he refused to compromise on. After all, Mom had her bridge club over for entertainment once a week, and Dad never complained about *that*, even though he had to endure Mrs Gleason's endless gossip and the *advice* she loved to administer, briefing Dad on how to keep the town's morals from going bankrupt and down the shitter. Though in fairness to her, I have to admit that she never once used the work shitter.

Besides my bedroom, the hub was my favourite place in the house. There was an air of mystery about it; I just never knew what I'd come across when Dad was at work and Mom out visiting her friends. The hub was next to my bedroom and, if I stayed absolutely silent, most times I could clearly hear Dad's conversations with Deputy Hillman, and anyone else invited there. I was warned by Mom to stay out of the hub, not to go poking my nosey nose where it didn't belong. Had I been told I could go in any time I wanted, I probably would have ignored the hub, its secrets no longer alluring to my adolescent imagination. A bit like Adam and Eve with the apple, I suppose.

There was always an exciting feeling about the hub; the feeling that something great was about to be discovered – provided you knew where to look, and provided you could decipher Dad's atrocious handwriting, like epileptic spiders, the words all mashed in to each other.

The very day after our gathering at the cemetery, Deputy Hillman called in to see Dad at the hub. I was in my room, relaxing, enjoying that spacious sensation a Saturday afternoon brings. I could hear their secretive voices, urgent and low, but not low enough for my keen ears.

Tiptoeing to the wall, I began to eavesdrop on the conversation. They were discussing Joey's death at the lake.

'What're we going to do about Norman Armstrong, Sheriff? There's a lot of bad feeling in town at young Maxwell's death.'

'Not much we can do, Peter. We still don't have enough evidence to arrest Armstrong – for now.'

'It's shameful. It's not as if there's a phonebook of suspects. And you're saying we can't do a damn thing about it, even though we know it was Armstrong.'

'We *suspect* Armstrong's involvement,' Dad corrected. 'There's an ocean of a gap between knowing and suspecting when you're trying to convince prosecutor Flynn. Don't get too downhearted, though. Good police work will eventually bring Armstrong to justice, Pete. That's how these things finish, nine times out of ten.'

'I don't know, Sheriff. The more I think about Armstrong, the more I think he'll get away with this, along with the other attacks we know – *suspect* – he was involved in.'

'Those other incidents took place over in Webster. We have no jurisdiction there, so let's not waste time mulling over them. Stay focused on what happened here. That's how we'll nail him.'

'It's gonna be tough. He knows how to cover his tracks. He's slippery; there's more grease on him than Amos Harper.'

Dad laughed. 'I wouldn't let old Amos hear you say that. He'll start over-charging us for servicing the squad cars.'

I could hear Deputy Hillman let out a long sigh. 'Just beats me up inside, watching Armstrong walk about town, and that sickening smirk on his face.'

'Well, it's up to us to wipe that smirk away. Good police work, Pete. That's the answer. Good police work.'

I could hear Dad moving about in the hub for a few seconds, before talking again.

'Come on. Let's go. I've got to see Judge Pickford, before noon. Need a search warrant for Cartwright's farm.'

'Don't you think we'd be better off chasing after Armstrong, rather than a small-time moonshine maker like Luke Cartwright?'

'I agree. But until we can land the big fish, little ones will have to suffice. The good tax-paying folk of the town want to see something being netted, even if it's only a minnow.'

After Dad and Deputy Hillman left, I sneaked into the hub to see what I could find. Mom had gone earlier to buy some groceries in Wegman's, and I estimated I would have a good hour before she returned.

I quickly began my search, hoping to find something damning on Armstrong. Glancing about the many shelves lining the hub, I spotted the Bible's spine protruding from an army of law books. Dad wasn't into gospel, so naturally my curiosity was piqued. Carefully dislodging the book and opening it, I discovered that its stomach was hollowed out. Inside, a small black book nestled. I eased it out from its enclosure. Jackpot!

A diary. How had I never found this before? I flipped through the pages as quickly as possible, stopping the moment Armstrong's name leaped out at me. I began to read.

Almost certain of Norman Armstrong's involvement in the assaults of children over the last three years. A gut feeling, perhaps, alongside police instinct. Nothing more at this moment in time. But that feeling has never let me down, as God is my witness. Armstrong's as sly as a fox. Interrogated him again yesterday at his place of work, the movie house. Unofficially, of course, as I had little evidence to warrant bringing him in. He just laughed in our faces (Deputy Hillman was present). Armstrong said, 'Next time, Sheriff, see my lawyer.' Still, I must remain upbeat. The secret to a good interrogation is asking the same question differently, until you get the right answer. One day I'll get that right answer, so help me God.

There is little doubt that Armstrong has done fiendish things – things I can't begin to comprehend, even after a lifetime of examining all the darkness and evil that men produce. I'm almost certain of his involvement in the sexual assault on young Joey Maxwell. If ever a devil deserves the wrath of justice, it's him. Catching a fox like Armstrong will be difficult, but not impossible. One day he'll be brought into a courtroom and made to pay for the evil he has perpetrated on the young. I think of Tommy, and I shudder at the thought of this monster lurking in the darkness.

Reading that last sentence felt like someone had taken a hammer to my chest. I knew how much Dad detested Armstrong, but this was something entirely different, seeing his raw feelings written so clearly in black and white. Perhaps it was simply therapeutic for him to write these words? If so, I could relate to that. Sometimes when I was angry, I would write terrible things down on a page, describing what I was going to do to avenge some wrong. But usually, after cooling down, I'd rip the page to shreds, embarrassed at writing such juvenile crap, even though I was still a juvenile filled with crap.

Just as I finished reading, I heard a car pulling up outside. Shit! I had lost all track of time, had become totally submerged in Dad's words. I quickly eased the diary back into its home in the false Bible – but not before committing the information to memory – and quickly hightailed it out of the hub, just in time to avoid Mom coming through the front door, carrying bags of groceries.

'Get out and bring the rest of those bags in, Tommy. Next time, I'm taking you with me, no matter how much you moan about going shopping.'

'I hate going to Wegman's. It's always filled with slow-moving people,' I said, shuffling towards the front door.

'Yes, but you don't say that when you're shoveling the food down your ungrateful throat, do you?' Mom said, her voice stinging like a whip.

I quickly headed out to the car, hoping to avoid a further lashing. It took me a few minutes to unload the groceries and bring them into the house. I found Mom staring up at the hub, before she redirected her eyes to me.

'You been behaving?' She was looking at me as if I'd been doing something suspicious.

'Of course!' I tried sounding indignant, but the glare she returned told me it was a pathetic attempt. I quickly packed away the last of the groceries, but by the time I got finished, Mom had made her way upstairs, and was standing outside the hub.

I walked up towards my room, trying to look cool and relaxed. I could feel Mom's eyes burning into my head.

'What's for dinner?' I asked, trying to sound casual despite the knotting in my stomach.

'Chicken and potatoes. You're sure you weren't in your father's office?' Mom's interrogative eyes drilled right into my head. She should have been a cop. She was worse than Dad, once she suspected wrongdoing.

'Are you roasting the potatoes?' I said, quickly heading into my room.

'Some roasting *will* be getting done …' she said, not specifying whether she meant the potatoes, the chicken or me.

Inside my room, I leaned against the door, letting my breath out gently, suspecting Mom listening at the door, suspecting me.

CHAPTER FIVE

Meeting Mean Man Maxwell

... there was about him a suggestion of lurking ferocity, as though the Wild still lingered in him and the wolf in him merely slept.

Jack London, **White Fang**

Almost four days had gone by since our campfire meeting, and there was still no word from Brent. I knew it, he was full of shit, just like his beefed-up vocabulary stolen from Dad's crime mags.

I was resting on my bed, reading a copy of *Green Lantern*. Through the open window, a warm, early evening breeze ventured in, carrying a tribe of everyday fragrances on its tail: melted tar cooling; stirred paint just out of the can; and the quintessential summertime smell of newly mown grass. The sky was everywhere outside the window, blue and perfect as only dusk on a late August day knows how to be.

I took it all in, closing my eyelids and feeling drowsy with intoxication. It was a wonderful, legal high, provided by nature and life. Who the hell needed marijuana when they could have this for free? Just as I thought of drugs, the sound of Dad arriving home from work broke my trance.

I heard the front door opening, then closing, and a few seconds later the doorbell rang.

Ascending footsteps sounded on the stairs, moving in my direction. The doorbell rang again.

'Tommy?' Dad said, poking his head into my room. 'I'm going for a shower. See who's at the door.'

'But the Green Lantern is just about to use his power ring ...'

'*Clear?*'

'Yes ...' I said, reluctantly pushing myself off the bed and heading downstairs. When Dad used the word 'clear', it was a command, but when he emphasised it, it became law.

Opening the front door, I was startled to see Theodore Maxwell, Joey's father, filling the frame of the door with his own massive frame.

Theodore Maxwell was a six-foot-three brick-building of a man. His entire body was constructed from blocks of muscle, with little wastage in between to interfere with what those blocks were specifically built for: intimidating the dangerous prisoners he guarded in the notorious Sing Sing Correctional Facility, the maximum-security prison five miles from where we lived. Sing Sing was arguably the most infamous prison in the world, where prisoners were baptised in the fire of broken bones, and strap-your-balls-on gladiatorial fights for survival.

Dad had once said that someone was making a sick joke when they named it Sing Sing, as there was little to sing about in that god-awful place. On 19 June 1953, Julius and Ethel Rosenberg were electrocuted at the prison for espionage. Despite the passing of time, their deaths continued to be discussed in bars and diners as if it were yesterday. Over the years, I had learned that our small town would grab any slice of pie to munch over, regardless of its morbid contents.

'I'm looking to speak to the Sheriff. Is he home?' Theodore Maxwell said, inching closer to me.

Theodore Maxwell's cropped, Marine-short hair was shaped like a smoothing iron, accentuating an unforgiving face as welcoming as a kicked-in door. A five o'clock shadow was crawling over that mean face, coating his ghastly pockmark-pitted skin. The pockmarks had not been caused by some childhood affliction, but by a shotgun blast, many years ago, dealt by an escaping convict named Jeff Fields. Despite being badly wounded, Theodore Maxwell had managed to disarm Fields and hold him until other guards came to help. Shortly after his recapture, Fields spent three weeks in the prison hospital, after 'falling down steps', according to the official report. Less than a week after his release from the prison hospital, Fields was mysteriously and very violently killed in his cell.

Horseshoe said he once overheard his father say of Theodore Maxwell: 'There are wannabe tough guys, and then there's Theodore Maxwell – the genuine essence of tough guy personified. Better to mess with the devil than with Theodore Maxwell. He neither forgives nor forgets.'

'Well, boy? Is the Sheriff home or not?' he said, looking at me rather sternly.

I quickly nodded. 'Yes … yes, sir. He's … he's home.'

Theodore Maxwell's mean eyes sparked with revelation. 'You're Tommy, aren't you?'

My tongue was a plank of wood. I couldn't speak. The question sounded like an accusation. A trap. He was in uniform, and a pair of menacing handcuffs dangled from his belt. The handcuffs made me think immediately of Joey. For one heart-stopping second, I thought Theodore Maxwell was here to take me to Sing Sing. My stomach began percolating with nervous acid. I instantly tightened my butt cheeks, in case I would shit my pants.

'Yes, sir …' I said, feeling like one of his convicts. 'I'm … I'm Tommy.'

'I never did get the chance to thank you for trying to save Joey. It was very brave of you, Tommy.'

I almost fainted with relief. 'I … I just jumped in … it was nothing. Really …' I mumbled, leaving out the fact that I had been one of the cowards encouraging Joey to go deeper into the water, to his doom. I wondered what Theodore Maxwell would do to me if he ever discovered that terrible truth? I shuddered inside.

'I was hoping to find you at home. I want to give you this, as a thank-you.' From the inside pocket of his dark jacket, he removed an envelope, then held it out towards me.

'What ... what is it?' I asked, not reaching for it, as if it were a miniature bear-trap.

'There's a hundred dollars in twenties inside.'

'A hundred dollars ...?' A hundred dollars was a fortune. I'd never seen that amount of money in my life, but there was something not right in accepting it. 'I ... I can't take it, sir, but thank you all the same.'

'Can't take it?' Theodore Maxwell looked puzzled. 'Don't be foolish. I want you to have it.'

He thrust the envelope towards me, but I edged away, afraid to be contaminated by the touch of blood money and a dead boy. The envelope looked like a piece of Joey's pale skin.

'Tommy?' Mom's concerned voice came from directly behind me. 'Who is it?'

'Joey's dad,' I said, relieved at her emergence.

'Oh, hello, Mr Maxwell. I was so sorry to hear of your son's tragic accident. Terrible.'

Mister Maxwell simply nodded. 'I wanted to give your son some money, as a way of thanking him for trying to save Joey, but he refuses to take it.'

Mom looked evenly at me for a few seconds. She could clearly see how troubled I looked.

'Well, that's his prerogative, Mister Maxwell,' she finally said, taking her eyes off me. 'But he thanks you all the same for the offer. Isn't that right, Tommy?'

I nodded, but didn't say a word. A migraine began drilling into the area just above my left eyebrow.

'Okay,' Mister Maxwell said, returning the envelope to his inside pocket. 'I can respect that. You have a great young man there, Mrs Henderson. A pity the town hasn't more like him.'

I felt my face redden.

'How can I help you, Mister Maxwell?' Mom said nonchalantly, not sounding too convinced about me being a great young man.

'I'm really sorry for disturbing you so late in the evening, Mrs Henderson, but it wasn't just your son I came to see. If possible, could I speak to your husband? I've just finished my shift at the prison, and when I called into his office in town, they said I'd just missed him.'

It wasn't unusual for people to come to our home, to speak to Dad. It was a small town, and informality was the norm. To the good people of our town, it didn't matter if you were the mayor or sheriff, people believed they had a right of access to you twenty-four-seven, to voice their concerns, or query you about something they didn't like – even if you were taking a shit when they were talking to you. Mom would do her best to let Dad get some peace when he had just finished work, and was pretty skilled at separating the wheat from the chaff at our front door.

'Well ... he's just got in, but you can wait upstairs in his office. Tommy'll show you the way. Can I get you some coffee?'

'If it's no bother? Thank you. Black. No sugar.'

Dark and sour. Just like him, I thought.

Showing Mister Maxwell into the hub, I was about to make a hasty retreat, when he asked, 'How well did you know my son Joey?'

The burly guard's question caught me off-guard. I didn't want to be here, with this imposing adult asking me tricky questions. I wanted to run.

'Know? Well ...' For a moment, my brain seemed to have shut completely down. 'I ... Joey was ... funny. He ... always wanted to make people laugh. Everyone liked him. Everyone ...'

Theodore Maxwell showed no emotion at my words. I wondered, had I let him down with this characterisation of his dead son? Should I have added something else, something more telling and wonderful? Thankfully, Mom arrived with the coffee, and I sneaked away unnoticed back to the Green Lantern, as he battled the evil Doctor Polaris.

But my curiosity wouldn't let me be for more than a couple of minutes, as I heard the muffled voices coming from the hub. Slipping silently off the bed, I leaned against the wall, my right ear tight against it, and listened. The conversation between Dad and Theodore Maxwell was becoming heated.

'I've read in the papers that law enforcement have a suspect, Sheriff, but for some strange reason you refuse to arrest and charge him.'

'I wouldn't believe everything you read, Mr Maxwell. Newspapers say a lot of things simply to boost circulation. I'm working every minute I can spare on this case. Believe me, if I had the evidence, someone would be answering to it.'

'But you've got *more* than evidence. Haven't you?'

I pictured Theodore Maxwell's alligator stare, drilling into Dad's equally hard stare.

'What do you mean by *more*, Mr Maxwell?'

'You've got something more than evidence – something not learned from a book; something that takes a long time to develop. It's called good police intuition, Sheriff. That's what I mean. Gut feeling. That knotting of the gut when you know something just isn't right.'

I could hear Dad hesitate before answering.

'I never go by gut feelings when it could mean a person going to prison for a very long time, or when –'

'You've had the perpetrator in the interrogation room. You've looked into the abyss of his eyes when you asked him certain questions. You *know* he's the perpetrator; you can feel it in the fibres of your body. The instinct you've fine-tuned over the years as sheriff. The same feeling that's never let you down when push comes to shove. Aren't I right?'

Once again, Dad hesitated before replying. 'I never build a case on feelings, Mr Maxwell. The district attorney would laugh me straight out of his office.'

'Flynn? He's a joke, but I ain't laughing. He's a disgrace.'

'The town elected him. He's what we have, like it or not.'

'We both work for the same purpose, you and I. Wouldn't your agree?'

'What purpose would that be?'

'The purpose of justice, Sheriff. You catch the bad guys, and I lock them up, keep them from harming good people – especially young people. It's simple, black-and-white.'

There was a two-second pause before Dad answered. 'I think you know it's not that simple, Mister Maxwell. There's an awful lot of gray in between the black-and-white called justice. An awful lot. Of all the colours that occupy my time in the pursuit of justice, gray leads the pack.'

'Sometimes justice isn't served, Sheriff. You've seen the fancy-mouthed lawyers getting criminals off, even though you know they're guilty as sin. Isn't that so?'

'I agree the system isn't infallible. Like all systems, it has its flaws. But again, it's what we have – until something else comes along to replace it.'

Theodore Maxwell's voice went harsh. 'The system didn't serve my son. Joey was sexually molested, and so far the perpetrator's not been brought to justice. Joey committed suicide because of the animal that raped him, and took away his innocence. Now you can only stand there and tell me it's all we have? There's nothing can be done?'

'I understand how you must be –'

'You understand *nothing*.' Theodore Maxwell's voice sizzled with suppressed anger. 'Until something of this terrible magnitude happens to your child, you'll *never* understand.'

Theodore Maxwell's words chilled me. I felt for Dad – he had to stand there and just take it. He couldn't defend himself, because he probably agreed with everything Theodore Maxwell was saying.

'I can't disclose anything that could jeopardise or compromise any future leads, Mr Maxwell, as this is an ongoing investigation. It's top of my agenda to arrest the person responsible for the attack on your son. I can assure you that I'll –'

'You can't assure me of *anything*, Sheriff – that's the only thing I feel assured of since this conversation began. I only hope for your sake that when this monster strikes again – *and he will* – that you won't look the parents of that child in the eyes and sell them the same brand of bullshit you've just tried to sell me.'

'It's not bullshit. I can only work within the –'

'When you see your son, Tommy, sleeping soundly in bed tonight, you think of my Joey, and pray this endless nightmare is never visited upon you or your family – or any other family. Good evening, Sheriff.'

I heard the door to the hub slam, then a minute later Mom's concerned voice.

'Frank? You okay?'

Dad sighed. 'Okay? I'm not the one who just lost a son, Helen, so I suppose I'm fine.'

'I wish people would stop using you as a punchbag, Frank. You're doing the best you can. Everyone in town knows that.'

'Do they? I just spoke to one good citizen of this town who'd strongly disagree with you. He lost his wife three years ago to a drunk driver, and now his only son is gone. Can you imagine the hell and torment in Theodore Maxwell's head?'

Everything went quiet. I could picture Mom reaching over, trying to reassure Dad with a touch. A minute later, I heard her softly exit the room, leaving Dad to his own brand of tormented thoughts. I re-ran the words from Dad's diary in my head, of poor Joey and his father. Theodore Maxwell had paraphrased the diary's contents, chillingly, almost verbatim, as if he had read the telltale book.

There was little doubt in my head that Dad was thinking exactly the same thing.

CHAPTER SIX

The Bloody Plan

*All concerns of men go wrong when
they wish to cure evil with evil.*
Sophocles, **The Sons of Aleus**

It took Brent over a week, but he eventually came up with a plan, hatched no doubt from one of the murder stories in Dad's crime mags. That Wednesday evening, the three of us sat on a small rocky outcrop deep inside Black's Wood. Our faces looked deadly serious, no longer young.

'Every Thursday, after the Strand shuts for the night, Not Normal always takes porn movies home to watch in that rundown trailer of his,' Brent said in a low voice, his face animated by the flames from our campfire.

'How d'you know that?' Horseshoe asked.

'*Everyone* knows that,' Brent said, glaring back accusingly.

From the look on Horseshoe's face, he obviously wasn't everyone. I guess I wasn't everyone either, because I imagine I had the same look on my face.

'You'll play a key role in this, Horseshoe. Very important,' Brent continued. 'You're gonna be the bait.'

'*Bait?*' Horseshoe said, frowning. 'What's that supposed to mean?'

'Something to lure the perv to where we can catch him off-guard.'

'Why me?'

'Why ...?' Brent said, hesitating.

I knew the answer, even if naïve Horseshoe didn't. With his blond hair and handsome face, Horseshoe was almost angelic in appearance. If anything could lure Armstrong to his doom, it would be this deadly combination.

'Would you rather pull the trigger instead?' Brent challenged, an Elvis snarl curling his lip. 'I'll gladly swap places with you.'

'No! No ... I don't want to pull any triggers ... Okay, I'll be the bait.'

'Good. That's settled. Tommy? You'll need to come up with some gasoline, so we can destroy all the evidence afterwards. You can siphon some from one of your dad's squad cars. You'll keep a look out behind the trailer as well. If you see anything suspicious, you'll give a squirrel whistle. Okay?'

I nodded, refusing to commit myself with words. I wanted to go home, watch some TV. 'Hawaii Five-O' would be starting shortly. It was one of my favourite shows, and I never tired of Detective Steve McGarrett's catchphrase, telling his right-hand man Danny Williams, 'Book em, Danno!'

'What about the cops, afterwards?' Horseshoe said, looking even more nervous. 'What if Tommy's dad starts questioning us?'

'Why would he question *us*?' Brent replied, looking directly at me. 'Isn't that right, Tommy?'

'Well … I …'

'Of course he won't,' Brent responded, as I stumbled to find an answer. 'We're just three kids. Who'd suspect us? Plus, don't forget all the enemies Not Normal has. Remember, someone tried to set fire to his trailer a few weeks back. That will help keep the questions away from us. Right, Tommy?'

I hesitated before answering. 'I suppose ...'

From his pocket, Brent magically produced two pairs of latex kitchen gloves.

'Once we're finished, I'll burn these. It's important we leave no prints behind. I saw an episode of 'Columbo' where the murderer was caught when Columbo discovered prints *inside* the fucking gloves. We don't want any fuck-ups like that, do we?'

Horseshoe and I nodded, and at that moment – too late – I realised I'd underestimated Brent's conviction to his hare-brained plan.

'Remember: we're blood-brothers. This secret dies with us in the grave,' continued Brent, handing me a pair of gloves. 'If any one of us becomes a rat, may he burn in Hell for all eternity. Say it.'

'May he burn in Hell,' Horseshoe echoed, his voice a nervous quiver.

'Tommy? You gotta say it too.'

I licked dry lips before answering. 'May ... he burn in Hell ...'

'We'll meet back here tomorrow night, early,' Brent said. 'Best we aren't seen together before then. And remember, blood-brothers: this is for Joey.'

As I made my way back home, a murder of crows spread out in a long black stream across the pale blue night sky. They cawed to each other in little sporadic bursts. It sounded like a warning.

CHAPTER SEVEN

Into the Fiend's Lair

He was a ferocious man. He had been ill-made in the making. He had not been born right, and he had not been helped any by the moulding he had received at the hands of society. The hands of society are harsh, and this man was a striking sample of its handiwork.

Jack London, **White Fang**

In the strange geometry of night, Armstrong's trailer had the intimidating structure of a large jail cell, an image reinforced by its barred windows and daunting metal doors. It was parked illegally on contested ground just outside town. In the iron darkness, a faint pencil-thin light filtered from the trailer's back window.

For the last hour, the three of us had been doing a stakeout from a derelict hardware store, just across from the trailer. We were like burglars, casing the place to appropriate all necessary information, waiting for the opportune moment to strike.

As Brent had predicted, Armstrong was home. We had watched him arrive less than thirty minutes ago. Deep down inside, I was hoping he wouldn't appear, praying for a miracle that he'd be hit by a speeding car, or killed by a robber watching him leave the Strand. Anything but this.

'Who the hell did an SBD?' Brent said, waving away the acrid smell of a nasty fart. 'Someone shit their pants, by the smell of that.'

It was mine, but I pinched my nose and quickly pointed an accusing finger at Horseshoe, a notorious dropper of Silent But Deadly farts.

'Wasn't me!' Horseshoe protested his innocence. Even in the dull light, I could see his face getting redder by the second. 'I swear to Jack Kirby and the Fantastic Four, it wasn't me!'

'Enough!' Brent said, glaring at Horseshoe. 'Okay, are you ready?'

'Yes ...'

'Know what to do?'

Horseshoe nodded. 'Tap on the door and ask for directions. Tell Armstrong I'm lost and thirsty.'

'It's important you don't forget to say you're thirsty. Understand?'

I didn't understand the importance of Horseshoe having to say he was thirsty. Not at that moment. I figured it was just a stalling tactic. By the time I learned the truth, it would be too late – for us all.

'Yes, I understand that part,' Horseshoe said. 'But ... but what if Armstrong recognises me?'

'Why the hell would he recognise you? He doesn't even know you.'

'He might remember me from the Strand. I go to a lot of movies.'

'Stop making excuses. Besides, it's too dark. And anyway, even if he does, it won't matter.' Brent grinned, and produced the gun. 'Dead men tell no tales.'

'Dead men? But ... you said we were gonna shoot him in the nuts. You never said anything about killing him.'

Brent brought his face close to Horseshoe's. 'You want him to come looking for us? Is that what you want? Looking over your shoulder for the rest of your sorry life, for him to dick you like he did poor Joey?'

It was a line, verbatim, I had read in one of the crime mags. No doubt Brent had practised it, maybe in front of a mirror, before using it. I was still wondering when Brent was going to call it all off. I was sure his game plan was to rely on Horseshoe or me backing out first. That way, he would save face and still be king of his imaginary kingdom. This was why he was upping the stakes to killing, rather than the plain old bullet in the nuts. He knew one of us would call a halt to this madness at any moment. None of us was a murderer, after all. We were kids, for God's sake.

'Well?' Brent said. 'Anyone got any objections?'

I was still calling his bluff, remaining silent. I knew it was only a matter of time. He'd go on to the very last moment before calling everything off. Then *he* would be the one to lose face. Not me.

'I need to piss,' Horseshoe said, moving to the back of the old building.

'*Now* you need to piss? Hurry the fuck up.'

'I don't need you to tell me when to take a piss.' Horseshoe disappeared into the shadows.

'Just don't forget and take a shit, while you're at it,' Brent smirked.

'Can't you just shut up for one minute?' Horseshoe's annoyed voice came out of the darkness.

'He's shitting himself, isn't he?' Brent said, staring at me.

It was almost five minutes before Horseshoe reappeared.

'You okay now?' Brent was grinning. 'You look a lot thinner than when you went in.'

'Very funny.' Horseshoe's petrified face was bone-pale.

'Ready to rock?'

'Yes.'

'Tommy? Got the gloves on?'

'Yes,' I said, holding up my hands.

'Good. Let's move out – *quietly*.'

I grabbed the half-can of gasoline, easily siphoned from Dad's police vehicle earlier that night, and followed behind Horseshoe and Brent into the darkness, all three of us first crouching, then crawling on our bellies and elbows. Our shadows hurrying alongside us looked deformed, misshapen.

Without a word, Brent stood and sprinted towards a family of trees ten yards from the trailer. Once there, he waved us over. We quickly followed suit.

'Leave the can here,' he whispered, as soon as I reached the trees. 'We'll come back for it.'

I set the can down, awaiting further instructions.

'We're gonna have to crawl from here, so that he doesn't spot us.' Brent immediately went back on belly and elbows. 'Come on. Follow me.'

We crawled behind Brent like characters from The Great Escape. A few seconds later, we reached the back of the trailer, and stood. Dull sounds were coming from within. We could feel the presence of the animal, lurking inside his metal box.

Brent edged his face upwards, glancing furtively in through the back window. 'The perv's watching one of his porno movies. Check it out, Tommy.' His voice was an exaggerated stage whisper, his eyes dancing with excitement.

I didn't want to check it out. My heart hadn't stopped thumping in my head for the last twenty minutes, and now it seemed to have moved up a notch. Bats were flying around inside my stomach. I wanted to throw up.

Pressing my face partially against the window, I focused my eyes. It was semi-dark inside, but the luminous light from the television helped. Armstrong's skin had the pinkish tone of a healing wound. A trellis of wrinkles covered it in thick lines, guarding eyes as dark as the undersides of decayed leaves.

His eyes are black as coffee, I thought to myself. *They've no pupils.*

Armstrong was wearing a pair of ragged jeans and a filthy vest. He was sitting on a battered armchair, bottle of beer in hand, grinning lips slippery and snail-like. His eyes kept flickering with excitement. He seemed engrossed in whatever was on the television screen. I couldn't tell if it *was* a porno, but I took Brent's word for it.

'Did you see him, Tommy?' Brent said. 'The disgusting bastard.'

'Yeah, I saw him.'

It was Horseshoe's turn to crane his neck up and steal a glance through the window.

'Okay, Horseshoe. Make a move for the door. Don't forget your story of being lost and thirsty.'

'I ... I don't know if I can do it, Brent. Not Normal looks even creepier sitting in there. What if he has a knife or something?'

'Stop being such a sissy. Anyway, it's too late to chicken out now. We'll be right behind you. Don't worry.'

But Horseshoe did look worried. He didn't move.

'You ... you won't let him kill me, will you, Brent?'

'Don't be stupid. He's the one who's gonna get killed.' Pulling it out with a flourish from the waistband of his jeans,

Brent brandished the Luger, and placed it against Horseshoe's face. '*Now, move!*'

Horseshoe edged his body painfully slowly along the front of the trailer. Even in the dull moonlight, I could see the terror on his face. I wanted to scream at him to run, to run like hell, but I was a coward, and kept my mouth shut.

What seemed like an eternity went by before Horseshoe began rapping timidly on the door.

I quickly glanced in at Armstrong. He was sipping his beer.

Horseshoe rapped on the door again.

Armstrong's face tightened. He seemed to be straining to listen. He reached over and lowered the volume on the television, before slowly walking to the door, beer in hand.

The door opened, washing Horseshoe in bleaching white.

'Yeah? What ya want?' snarled Armstrong.

Horseshoe looked like a tiny lamb, being sized up at the slaughter house.

'I'm ...'

For the longest seconds, Horseshoe said nothing. I could feel the tension radiating from Brent. I glanced at him, and he was mouthing something inexplicable, as if trying to send secret commands to Horseshoe's brain.

'What's that you say?' said Armstrong. 'Speak up, boy. What the hell is it you want?'

'I'm ... I'm lost, Mister. Could ... could you give me some directions on how to get home ... please?'

'Home? Where the hell's home, boy?'

'Fair ... Fairbanks. I live in Fairbanks.'

'Fairbanks? You're a long way out. What're you doing in this neck of the woods?'

I could detect suspicion in Armstrong's voice.

'I ... I was with a couple of friends, camping in Black's Wood, but we split up after a stupid argument,' Horseshoe said. 'Now I'm lost, and I can't find my way home. Will you help me? Please?'

'Camping's illegal in the woods. Don't you know that?'

'You ... you're not going to call the cops, are you? Please don't. My parents would skin me alive.'

'Even if I had a mind to get the cops involved, I don't have a phone, so you can relax.'

'Thanks ...'

'Well, you better come in. I'll give you directions. You hungry, boy?'

'No, sir, but I'm very thirsty.'

The trailer door slammed, cutting off the light. The night was dark as ink.

'What do we do now?' I said in a panic.

'We wait until Armstrong comes to the back of the trailer. That's where he keeps his cola.'

Brent eased his face along the window, eyeballing the scene. I took the other corner of the window. I could see Horseshoe standing at the doorway, looking petrified. Armstrong was smiling like a hungry diner reading a menu, with Horseshoe the day's special.

Without warning, Armstrong turned, and looked directly at us.

Shit!

Brent and I ducked down immediately. My whole body seized up, like a propeller on a boat coming to an abrupt, shuddering halt.

Above me, I could hear movement approaching in the trailer, then the sound of a cupboard opening.

Brent stretched his head back up, and peered into the trailer. I reluctantly followed. Armstrong was removing a bottle of cheap cola from an overhead cupboard. Easing the cap from the bottle, he began pouring the cola into a tall glass. Only now did I realise that he was using the open cupboard door as a shield. I almost missed his sleight-of-hand, as he added a little touch of clear liquid from a small bottle into the cola.

What the hell is Armstrong doing? I swivelled my head around to Brent. He was gripping the Luger so tightly, his knuckles looked like they were ready to pop from their enclosure. I watched in horror as Brent brought the muzzle of the gun up to the window, hands trembling violently.

He's going to do it, I thought, sweating prayers as he took his shaky aim. *He's really going to pull the trigger and shoot Armstrong in the head!*

All of a sudden, Armstrong swung his face around towards our window. He was so close I could see age spots running down the side of his face, like tear tattoos on a convict.

My nerves were tightening like guitar strings. I hadn't breathed in a long time. I was certain he'd seen us. He continued gazing intently at the window. A stabbing pain shot through my stomach, like my intestines were unravelling. I stifled a surge of nausea, waiting for the pervert to scream at us. He didn't. It wasn't until much later that I realised he wasn't looking at us at all, but at Horseshoe's mirrored image reflecting on the window.

Turning, Armstrong headed back down the trailer towards Horseshoe.

'Shit!' I said, releasing all the trapped air from my lungs. 'Brent? We can't let Armstrong do this to Horseshoe. That was probably poison he was pouring into the glass. He'll *kill* Horseshoe. Brent ...?'

But Brent didn't respond. He simply stood there, zombie-like, pointing the gun at the window, his face as white and stark as the moon now washing over us. It was then I noticed the enormous dark patch in Brent's washed-out jeans. He'd pissed himself.

'Brent!' I shouted, not caring any more whether Armstrong could hear us. 'Snap the hell out of it! We've gotta do something – *now*!'

'I ... I ... I ...' His lips were barely moving.

'C'mon!' I ran around to the front of the trailer. Not stopping to think, I kicked in the door and leaped inside.

Horseshoe's look of relief was matched by Armstrong's look of shock, as he spilled the cola all over his filthy vest and the floor.

'Run! Run like hell!' I shouted.

Horseshoe didn't need to be told twice. He was past me and out of there like his ass was on fire. I was right behind, picturing Armstrong breathing down my neck, ready to grab and strangle me.

We ran quickly to the end of the trailer to get Brent, but he was already running in the opposite direction, towards Black's Wood.

A hand roughly grabbed my arm, squeezing down on it.

You little bastard! Armstrong hissed. 'I'll kill you for this.'

'Keep off me!' I tried pushing away from his filthy body, but his grip was like a bear trap.

'Scream all you want. Ain't no ears hearing.' Armstrong tightened his grip. 'I'm gonna teach you a lesson you'll not forget in a hurry.'

Just as I thought I was finished, I heard a voice in the darkness, shouting, 'Leave him alone, you filthy pervert!'

It should have been big tough guy Brent doing all the shouting, but it wasn't. In a blur, I remember watching Horseshoe run towards Armstrong, a great piece of branch wood in his hands. He swung the branch in a wide arc, whacking

Armstrong across the front of the head. I'll never forget how Armstrong's head recoiled back, as if attached to an invisible elastic band.

Armstrong screamed, releasing his grip on me. He staggered back, like a drunk in the night.

'Run!' Horseshoe shouted.

We ran and ran, not knowing if we were running in the right direction, not caring.

'Run all you want, little girlies. I'm a-coming for you!' Armstrong's voice screamed, somewhere in the darkness.

Somehow, in all the confusing madness, Horseshoe and I eventually found our way home. Outside my house, we both hid in the shadows of overgrown bushes, avoiding the lights.

'That took balls, Horseshoe, what you did back there, rescuing me from Armstrong,' I whispered.

'What else could I do? You got me out of his trailer, and *that* took balls. Now we're balls even,' Horseshoe said, grinning with pride. 'What happened to Brent? Where'd he vanish to?'

I thought of all the cheap bravado pouring from Brent's mouth; how he had almost gotten Horseshoe poisoned – or worse. I thought of the accusing piss stain on his jeans. That stain would never erase from memory, and he would never forgive me for seeing it.

'I don't know and don't care what happened to him, Horseshoe. Just make sure you don't say a word about this to anyone, ever, otherwise we'll all be in the shit.'

Horseshoe looked nervous. 'Do you … do you think Armstrong recognised us?'

'Naw. Not a hope,' I said, believing the opposite. 'It was too dark. Besides, it was all over in a minute. He hadn't time to recognise any of us.'

'Then he won't be coming to kill us while we're in bed, in the darkness?'

'Don't talk silly. Get home and get some sleep. I'll see you tomorrow.'

Horseshoe walked away, glancing nervily in all directions like a fox. I watched him for a few seconds, before taking a few deep breaths and going inside, praying to be undetected by Mom.

Sneaking upstairs, I practically fell into bed. I didn't sleep a wink all night, waiting for Armstrong to come and kill me in the darkness.

CHAPTER EIGHT

The Enchantress

Great perils have this beauty, that they bring to light the fraternity of strangers.

Victor Hugo, **Les Misérables**

Next morning, my stomach churned as I heard Dad returning home from night duty. I prayed fervently that there had been no witnesses to the incident at Armstrong's trailer. I sat in the kitchen, pretending to read *The Brave and the Bold*, as Dad breezed through the kitchen door.

'Not out enjoying the sun?' he asked, taking a pitcher of lemonade from the fridge.

'I want to finish this comic first.'

'Lemonade?' He held up the pitcher.

A naked Mrs Fleming entered my head. I quickly erased her, before nodding to Dad.

He poured.

So far so good. No mention of Armstrong. But then, what could Armstrong realistically say without bringing unwanted attention to his filthy habits? Still, my head was a jumble and my nerves were frayed, fear and exhaustion overpowering rational thinking. I had stayed awake all night, waiting for Armstrong to climb in through my bedroom window, knife between his rotten teeth.

Dad handed me a glass of lemonade, and placed the pitcher back in the fridge.

'You still running about with that Fleming kid?'

My stomach did a little kick. Dad gave me one of his ten-second stares. He was very good at trapping people with that stare – just ask any of the criminals he had interrogated over the years, before imprisoning them.

'I ... well ...'

'I don't want you to lie, Tommy, so don't answer. Old man McGregor reported seeing a scuffle outside Norman Armstrong's trailer last night. He said three kids were involved. One of the descriptions fitted Brent Fleming. I went up to the trailer this morning, and questioned Armstrong about it.'

I could feel the blood drain from my face.

'Armstrong said nothing happened, so I can't investigate further,' Dad said, pausing to read my mind some more. 'Norman Armstrong is a dangerous individual, Tommy. *Extremely* dangerous. Some people would even call him evil. He is to be avoided, like the plague. Clear?'

'Yes ...'

'Now, as far as the Fleming kid is concerned, I know you

like him. He's your pal, but for your sake, I hope you've stopped hanging about with him. Some people get their ends before their starts; sometimes that's just the way it is. That boy's going to be one of them. He's cut from the same cloth as his father. Now, finish your lemonade and get out into the sun. You look pale. I don't want you cooped up in here the rest of the summer.'

Dad left the kitchen, and I downed the lemonade in one grateful gulp. I decided to take his advice and get out of the house.

Before leaving, I made a sandwich and stuck it in my back-pack, alongside a tawdry-covered pulp fiction paperback, the kind I hoped one day would have my name sprawled across the top and be sold in bookstores all across the country.

I took my usual short cut through Black's Wood, regretting it the moment the sun disappeared behind the trees' crowns of leaves. Creatures called out warning sounds – whether to each other, or to me, was difficult to determine. I walked faster. Creepy Armstrong was still fresh in my mind. He was out there somewhere, lurking.

'Why the hell did you have to come this way?' I admonished myself loudly, gaining a slight comfort from the sound of my voice. 'You could've gone over to Horseshoe's house and –'

A muted squeal-like sound abruptly put an end to my soliloquy. I glanced to my left. Between the spines of trees, a shadowy figure seemed to be observing me. Tight, against scruffy jeans, the figure held an evil-looking knife, its serrated teeth grinning wickedly. Blood was reflecting on it, wet and terrifying. Something was very far from being right, and I was right smack in the middle of that something.

I wanted to run, but my feet had become clay. Then something landed heavily beside me. My head jerked down to look at the ground. Hares. Four or five, bundled together. Dead. Paws tied with old cord. Blood stained their furry necks like little crimson ribbons.

'Shit!' This time I did run. I ran so fast I dropped the backpack. '*Helpppppppppppppppppppppppp!*' I was screaming loudly, like a big girl, and didn't give a flying fart about any macho pride. I just hoped someone would hear my screams, and come to save me.

I ran and ran, until I reached the lake. The sun was baking down on the water, reflecting off it like a giant mirror. Sure that I had escaped the forest stalker, I doubled over, trying desperately to catch my breath and ease the stitch in my side. It took almost five minutes before I was able to breathe comfortably again.

I debated with myself about getting the hell out of there, heading home the long way across Goodman's Bridge, but the water looked seriously inviting. After my near-death experience, I needed to cool down.

Despite repeated warnings from Dad after what happened

to Joey, I couldn't resist swimming in the lake. It still had that dark, magnetic pull on me, and was an oasis in a town of nothingness. More than that, to overcome the guilt I felt over Joey's death, and to stop the recurring nightmares of Joey's accusing face and pointing finger, I knew I would eventually have to conquer the water. It was the only way.

Stripping quickly, I piled my clothes against some rocks. Then I spotted someone, staring at me from the trees' shadows, deep beyond the lake's fringe.

'Brent …? That you?'

Nothing.

'Who's there? Horseshoe? Stop messing about.'

I thought of Joey Maxwell's ghost. Then Armstrong, hiding, watching me. Worse, the killer of skinny hares had come to skin the hairs on my skinny ass.

'To hell with you!' I shouted bravely, running quickly into the water, then diving into its murky underworld. It was instantly exhilarating, and I went deeper, testing lungs, resolve and nerve. If Joey's ghost was here, then let it take me, I decided. I wouldn't be held prisoner any more, not by something dead.

Joey? If you're listening, I'm sorry for mocking you. I should have stopped you going into the lake, when I had the chance. I was a coward. I'm sorry, but I can't turn back time. If you want to, you can kill me now, but please stop torturing me. Please …

I seemed to have been swimming for hours when my

head finally broke through the water's ceiling. I let a yell of joy escape from my mouth. 'I'm alive! I'm alive!' I felt new, reborn. Joey had forgiven me for not saving him.

But the euphoria quickly dissipated when I heard someone or something enter the water directly behind me.

Despite hair being cut like a boy's, to my astonishment it was a girl. Like me, she was totally naked. Unlike me, she was beautiful. She reminded me of Samantha from 'Bewitched'. I had never seen such a beautiful girl in all my life. Even Mrs Fleming and Little Annie Fanny paled in comparison. Tiny, faded freckles congregated under her eyes, giving them an unreal, dreamy look. Her upper lip slanted strangely, in a seductively sensual snarl. But it was the sight of her nipples, poking out above the waterline, that totally mesmerised me. It was terrifyingly thrilling.

'See enough?' she said.

My mouth became wood. I couldn't speak.

'Cat got your tongue, boy?' she mocked. 'Like what you see?'

'I ... I was just looking ...' My face was burning with embarrassment. 'No! What I really meant to say was, I wasn't really looking ...'

'Well, I sure *was* looking.' A small smile appeared on her face. 'What's your name?'

'Tom ... Tommy,' I finally managed to mumble, trying desperately to look away from her breasts, but failing absolutely.

'I've seen you a couple of times, Tom Tommy, swimming here with your friends.'

'You watched us, swimming butt-naked?'

'Out of sheer boredom, so don't get the wrong idea.' The smile widened, making her even more beautiful. The light in her eyes did something funny to my heart, flipping it over and slowing it right down. 'You're the one who jumped into the water, and tried to save that crazy kid? I saw your picture in the paper.'

'Joey ... his name was Joey. Joey Maxwell. He wasn't crazy. He was just ... tired of ... things ...'

'Tired of living, you mean. Tied himself to a car, according to the news. Deliberately went and killed himself. He must've been stone crazy.'

'You shouldn't believe everything your hear. It was on the news yesterday that some old lady down south saw Jesus depositing money in her local bank. You believe that?'

'Could be true – everyone knows Jesus saves! Hallelujah!' She grinned. 'They say you got a medal or something for trying to save that crazy boy.'

'More lies. I didn't get a medal. Really, I didn't want anything. Didn't deserve anything ...'

'I wish someone would do that for me, save me if I was in danger.'

'*I* would. I'd save you if you were in danger.' The words came out automatically, but they were sincerely meant.

'You would?' She looked surprised.

'Yes, I would. In a heart-beat.'

She laughed loudly, but I detected sadness in the sound. She kept looking at me strangely, as if I was some weird and wonderful creature she had captured in a net.

In a blink of an eye, she disappeared under the water, only to reappear beside me. Before I knew what was happening, she was kissing me full on the mouth. I could taste her breath, feel the eagerness of her tongue, the pressure of her breasts spreading against my chest. It was the first time I had ever been truly kissed, and I could have died with happiness, right there in the filthy lake.

'I've always wanted to kiss a hero,' she whispered between kissing.

I gasped, feeling her hands fondling my balls under the water, as if weighing them. I couldn't breathe. Her fingers moved across the shaft of my cock. I jerked back, as if I had been prodded by electricity.

'What's wrong?' she said, looking puzzled.

'Noth ... nothing ...

'Haven't you been with a girl before?' She smiled again. This time, though, there was a slight wickedness to it.

'Of course,' I lied, feeling my face peel with embarrassment. 'I've ... I've been with lots of girls.'

'I bet you have.' She laughed, and then turned her back to me. 'I've got to go.'

'But ... now?'

'Now.'

'But ...'

She swam away, towards where our clothes lay in a heap. She reached the bank and I watched her easing up out of the water, small buttocks see-sawing mischievously. A tease.

'Aren't you coming, *Tommmmmeeeee?*'

I couldn't. Too terrified she would see my cock, all stiff and angry despite the cold water. Physically, I hadn't much to boast about to the world.

'I ... no, I'm going to swim for a while.'

'Never mind swimming. Come on out. I've got something for you.' She stood there, naked, hands on hips, legs wide apart, like a fleshy pair of scissors.

'What? What is it?' Could it be what I hoped it was?

'C'mere and see, *Tommmmmeeeee.*'

Reluctantly, I stepped from the water, covering what little I had worth covering. When I reached her, she was holding something in her hands.

'Your backpack.'

'My backpack ...?'

'The one you dropped when you ran away from me in the forest.'

'That was you ...?' *Shit!* I had run screaming like a big girl from a big girl. I would never live this down, if Brent or Horseshoe ever found out.

'Don't worry. I won't tell your friends how you screamed and ran away,' she said, smiling.

'I wasn't screaming,' I said defensively, watching her putting on her clothes, preparing to leave. 'What were you doing with a great big knife in the forest, and those dead ... things?'

She bent down, and pulled the bundled-up hares from behind a rock.

'These? My ma makes pies with them. *Hmmm.*' She pretended to lick her lips. 'I'll get Ma to make you one. As for the knife? I use it to cut their throats.'

I felt my balls shrink even smaller.

'*You* cut their throats?'

'No, of course not. They do it themselves,' she said, walking briskly away.

'Your name? What's your name?'

'Devlin!' she shouted, without looking back.

'Will you be here, tomorrow, Devlin?'

She was gone without a reply.

That night in bed, I enjoyed my first good sleep since Joey's death. Instead of nightmares of him, I dreamed of a mysterious and beautiful girl called Devlin, wondering when – *if* – I would see her again. I couldn't wait until morning.

CHAPTER NINE

Under Her Spell

The course of true love never did run smooth.
William Shakespeare, **A Midsummer Night's Dream**

Next day, I was up before Mom, an unusual occurrence. All night, I couldn't get Devlin out of my head, and now I couldn't wait to see her. I left the house with hardly a bite of breakfast in my jumpy stomach, and ran as fast as I could towards Jackson's Lake.

Arriving back at the exact spot we had been the day before, I could still make out the indent of where her clothes had rested on mine. I touched the flattened grass tenderly, as if it were sacred ground. For almost two hours, I sat there waiting, but my initial burst of euphoria quickly turned to despondency. She wasn't coming. Not now. Not ever. I had been a fool to think someone so beautiful would have any interest in someone as plain and boring as me.

Eventually I returned home, defeated.

'What had you up so early this morning?' asked Mom, placing a plate of food down in front of me.

'Nothing,' I mumbled. 'Just wanted to get out of this damn boring house.'

Mom slammed the palm of her hand down hard on the table, making me jump.

'You *ever* use language like that again in this house, *Mister*, I'll staple your mouth before hurling you through to next week. Got it, Mister?' she said, giving me one of her withering looks.

'Yes ...' I mumbled. 'I got it.'

'I hope you're not up to anything with that Brent Fleming? You've been warned to keep away from him and his family.'

'I've already told Dad I've stopped running about with Brent.' Despite the hunger growling in my stomach, I pushed the plate away and headed for my room.

For three long days, I brooded about the house, until Dad finally threatened me.

'If you don't get out and enjoy the summer, I'll be forced to bring you over to the county jail. They can always do with volunteers to clean the cells. You'll even get a free haircut, just like the inmates. Clear?'

Taking the hint, I quickly got out of the house, walking in the direction of Jackson's Lake. Lost in my thoughts, I hardly heard Horseshoe behind me.

'Going for a swim, Tommy?'

'No. Just walking and killing time. What's happening?'

'Nothing much.' Horseshoe looked embarrassed, as if he'd been avoiding me. It seemed the three of us were now involved in a conspiracy of avoidance, after the botched raid on Armstrong's trailer.

'Seen Brent about?' I asked, not really caring.

'Yesterday, for a few minutes. We didn't speak much. He ...' Horseshoe peered warily over his shoulder, as if expecting Brent to be standing there. '... mentioned Not Normal.'

'Yeah?'

'Said one day he'd make him pay for what he did to Joey; said he's gonna kill the pervert.'

'Brent says all kinds of things, Horseshoe. He had his chance at the trailer, but he chickened out.' I shook my head. 'Anyway, at the moment he's not thinking straight. Best keep well away from him for a while.'

'Yeah, I reckon you're right on the nose.' Horseshoe nodded. 'I'm just glad we got away that night.'

'For all our sakes, don't mention what happened at Not Normal's to anyone. Understand? Otherwise, the devil will dick you in the ass.'

We both laughed nervously.

'Sure you don't want to go for a swim, Tommy?'

I thought about it, but knew the answer even before I spoke. 'Nah. Not today. I've things to do.'

'Well, call me when you want. Okay?'

'Sure,' I said, continuing zombie-like on my journey.

At Jackson's Lake, I could do nothing but stare at the water.

'You weren't here yesterday,' came an accusing voice directly behind me.

I turned quickly to see Devlin, holding a large leather satchel, the type Horseshoe kept some of his better drawings in. She was smiling at me, and suddenly my world was okay again. She looked more beautiful than ever.

'I'd things to do. I was here a couple of days ago,' I mumbled. 'I couldn't find you.'

'Can't find what doesn't want to be found,' she replied, cryptically, setting down the satchel. 'Anyway, we're both here now. Going for a swim, or are you just going to stand there, looking dumb?'

Before I could answer, she was stripping, her beautiful naked body emerging triumphantly from its cocoon of clothing.

'Stop gawking and strip!' she commanded. 'C'mon! I haven't all day.'

Away she went, running for the water, leaving me fumbling with my clothes and playing catch-up.

In the water, we splashed about and she dunked me twice, laughing, throwing her head back with joy. She seemed like a kid now, far from the sophisticated woman I had imagined when we first met.

'Isn't this fun, Tommy?' Her mouth and eyes were smiling.

'Yes!' I shouted at the top of my voice. '*Yessssssssssss!*'

She giggled.

I wanted this moment to last forever. I no longer cared about family or friends, life or school or work, or any of those silly things. This was what I wanted. Forever. Unfortunately for me, in Devlin's world, forever had a very short time-span.

'C'mon. Let's go,' she said, her demeanour suddenly shifting.

'What? You're going? So soon? We only got here. You can't go, not yet.'

'Don't *ever* try to tell me when I should go. I go when it suits me.' She began swimming towards land. 'C'mon! Hurry up!'

I reluctantly followed, anger and disappointment boiling in me.

On dry land she scooped up her clothes, but didn't put them on.

'This way. Hurry,' she laughed, running away from me, her clothes gathered in her arms. 'Bring my satchel.'

Snatching my clothes and the satchel, I quickly followed her into the wild and camouflaging grass, noticing for the first time the constellation of miniature horseshoe-shaped bruises on her buttocks. The marks were frightening to look at, but I couldn't take my eyes from them. I'd seen similar marks not too long ago. I shivered at the memory.

'What's wrong?' she said, stopping abruptly. I knew she'd caught me staring at her butt.

'Nothing ...'

'Good,' she said, removing objects from the satchel. 'Ever been sketched?'

'No. I mean ... I don't think so.' Actually, Horseshoe had sketched me, but I'd come out looking like Ben Grimm from The Fantastic Four.

'You don't think so? What kind of stupid answer is that? You have or you haven't – which is it?'

'Haven't, I suppose. Why?'

From the satchel, she had removed a couple of small sketch-pads and some pencils, which she placed on the ground. I grabbed one of the pads and flicked through it – page after page of rough sketches of trees and wildlife. I couldn't help but notice a family of hares, posing happily for the artist as they nibbled on grass. The morbid certainty formed in my mind that the hares she had killed the other day were one and the same crew. Once again, Devlin read my mind.

'Sketched them before I killed them. I told them I was gonna keep them alive, for ever and ever.' She gave me a wicked smile. 'Now I'm gonna sketch you, so don't even think of blinking. You move and you're dead – just like them hares.'

'I need to put some clothes on,' I said, realising just *how* naked I had become. I quickly grabbed my jeans to cover my boyhood.

'You even think of covering up, and I'm leaving. I'm naked, and I ain't complaining. I mean it, Tommy. You put those clothes on, and you'll not see me again.'

'Can't I just cover some … parts?'

'Where would the fun be in that? Those are the parts that are fun!' She laughed. 'Anyway, it's not the size of the gun, but the bullets it fires, that really counts.'

Slowly, I allowed my jeans to crumple to the ground. I was her slave, and she knew it.

'Stop fidgeting,' she ordered, selecting her weapons of choice for my death on canvas. 'Just relax.'

'Easy for you to say,' I mumbled.

I sat there naked, listening to the sandy scratch of pencil on rough paper. While she studied me, I studied her: her finger movements, her frown, as she wrestled to capture my likeness on the page.

'Do you sketch everything before you kill it?' I whispered through clenched teeth, like a ventriloquist's dummy.

'Keep talking and find out.'

A long half-hour later, it was over.

'Done,' she said, packing everything up in the satchel.

'When do I get to see my picture?'

'*Your* picture? Who said you owned it? If you're lucky you

might see it soon; you might see it later. Perhaps you mightn't see it ever.'

Without warning, Devlin pulled me down onto the grass, quickly rolling on top of my willing body. Fallen apples carpeted the grass. Their fermenting aroma was everywhere, but it was Devlin's smells that intoxicated me, filling me with a strange power I never knew I possessed. I could hear things that were impossible to hear: the mist settling on the lake; stones breathing in the baking heat. I could taste the sun in my mouth as we kissed, big wet kisses that seemed to last an eternity, bruising our mouths with eagerness.

'Squeeze,' she whispered, placing my hand on her breast.

I squeezed. Her breast was warm and small, soft as uncooked bread dough. I could feel her heart beat, pulsating through the skin. My cock was stirring. I tried desperately to will it away, fearful of what she would think of me.

'You love me, don't you, Tommy?' It was a statement, rather than a question.

'Y ... yes.'

'Say you love me.' The timbre of her breath was soft and resonant, making my ears tingle sweetly.

'I ... I love you,' I managed to say, throat sandpapery-dry with anticipation.

She began kissing my mouth again, only this time harder, her tongue stabbing in and out frantically like a tiny bird fearful of capture. Her saliva tasted heavenly. There was a soft purr in her throat, a low-frequency gurgle, elevating the mundane experience of kissing to the level of something sexually dark.

Rolling off me, she lay on her back, fully exposed. My eyes sneaked a look at her most private of areas. The skin there was coated with fine, fair hair, so fine it looked as though a breeze could steal it away.

'When you've earned it, I'll let you go further than just touching my breasts.'

'Further?' My voice was a croak.

'Much further,' she smiled, and then winked. 'I'll show you things that'll make even your mama blush.'

I wish she hadn't mention Mom. There was something uncomfortable about sex and Mom in the same conversation.

'Why do you have to talk like that, Devlin?'

'*Shhhhhhhh!*' she whispered urgently, placing a finger firmly to my lips, bridging them. The sharp attention in her eyes derailed for a second, focusing on something else. '*Someone's here, watching.*'

The sweaty phantom of fear touched me for a second, making the hairs on the back of my neck tighten. My cock instantly deflated and went into hiding. I stopped breathing, listening intently. I thought of Horseshoe watching. Had he followed me, just to see what I was up to? Could it be Armstrong? But all I could hear was the lake touching the rocks with soft groans, like the hiss of a nail in a tyre.

For the longest time, we remained motionless.

Suddenly, there was a heavy movement behind me. I wanted to get up and run like hell, but Devlin pulled down on my arm. A hare came charging through the long blades of grass, jumping over our naked bodies and scaring the shit clean out of me.

Rolling onto her back, Devlin began laughing.

'Oh, Tommy! Your face! You'd think you'd just seen a ghost!'

'You were scared too.'

'Wasn't!'

'You were!'

She stood up and started dressing.

Disappointed, I reluctantly stood too.

'Why're you going, Devlin? Angry at me poking fun at you?'

'Don't be silly.' She kissed me on the lips. 'I've got to go. My ma needs looking after. She has … problems. I can only get out for a couple of hours, every other day.'

'Oh … I'm sorry.' I was filled with remorse, embarrassed by my own craven selfishness.

'It's okay.' She shrugged her shoulders. 'I've been looking after her for years.'

'Don't you have a dad?' I asked, regretting it the moment my big mouth opened. 'Sorry … that's none of my business …'

'He's a distant rumour. Walked out on us when I was a baby. I never knew him.'

'I'm sorry.'

'*Don't* keep saying sorry. It's not a word I like. It's weak.'

Keep quiet and leave, the voice of reason kept telling me. But I was never good at reasoning with anyone, least of all myself.

'Can I ask you something, Devlin?'

She looked at me suspiciously. The skin between her eyebrows creased into a small, angry V.

'What?'

'Promise you won't get mad.'

'I don't believe in promises. They're always broken. What?'

I wished now I had let things be.

'Those ... those marks, on your ... butt ...' I felt my face getting hot.

'What about them?' Her face was nonchalant, but her voice turned cold. The pupils of her eyes looked like gunshot wounds.

'What ... what are they? They look like burn marks.'

'If that's what they look like, then let them be just that. Best they be what you think, and best you keep your nose on your face, rather than in my business.'

Had I been an adult, perhaps the corollary of her words would have had meaning, and the summer's sweetness might not have tasted so wickedly good. But it would be a long time before I knew the true meaning of those sinister marks. Too long, and too late.

'Are you finished questioning me?' she said, pulling on her jeans, zipping them so loudly they sounded like a serrated knife cutting into my bones.

'Yes.'

'Good.' She made a movement to go.

'Can I walk you home?'

'No. I can make my own way. I don't need you or anyone to walk me home. Been doing it since legs sprouted from my body.'

She was visibly annoyed now, all thanks to my stupid questioning. I felt my throat tightening, as if an invisible hand was slowly squeezing. The thought of her leaving was killing me.

'When will I see you again, Devlin?'

'When I decide. Okay?'

No, it wasn't okay. 'Okay.'

Just as I thought she was going, she turned and stared at me. Her beautiful face had lines of anger. I tried reading her thoughts, wondering what that stare meant. Was it over, our relationship? Was she deciding never to see me again?

'Follow me. Don't talk. If you talk, I'll hurt you so much you won't even feel the pain, it'll be that painful,' she said, walking briskly ahead, never looking back at me.

I followed quickly behind, like an obedient and happy puppy, uttering not a word, lest my mistress became angry.

We walked for what seemed like hours, going beyond the lake's influence, and entering into Dust Hill territory. Dust Hill was a stretch of struggling land where the poorer people of Black's Creek lived, beyond the outskirts of town, mostly in rusted trailers or homemade shacks. The unfortunates who lived here were nicknamed 'dusties', or 'hillies'. Mom had warned me plenty of times never to go near Dust Hill, as if a fate worse than death awaited anyone foolish enough to venture near it. 'They never work, but always seem to have money for liquor,' was one of her kinder descriptions of the inhabitants. Dad, outside of Mom's earshot, would say the folks of Dust Hill were just like people everywhere, good and bad.

Just as I began to wonder how much further we had to walk, an isolated farmhouse came into view. The place looked disjointed, like a mirror fractured. A massive barn clung, crab-like, to the side of the house. I could make out rusted machinery, poking from the barn's dilapidated siding. Everything seemed chaotic and unused, as if no human hand had touched it for decades. A battered, rust-covered truck stood silently like a great beached fish, its heavy shadow streaking the heads of wild and rotted wheat.

'This is where I live,' Devlin said. 'Come on, but be very quiet. I don't want Ma hearing or seeing us.'

'Okay,' I said, practically tiptoeing onwards. No sooner had we started than Devlin stopped in her tracks.

'*Get down!*' she commanded, pulling me quickly down between the skinny necks of wheat.

'What's wrong?'

'*Shhhhhhh! Over there*,' she said, pointing. '*Listen.*'

I listened, but could hear nothing other than the sound of tree branches rubbing together like stridulating crickets. The only visible movement came from a pageant of crows swooping in for landing in the haggard-looking field, where a ternary of scarecrows took centre stage. Ignoring the ragged sentinels, the crows rummaged at will, drilling with hardened beaks against the unyielding ground. The scene was like something from an old black-and-white horror movie, and it transfixed me. It was then that I noticed one of the scarecrows moving.

'*That scarecrow just moved,*' I said, pointing.

'*That's Bob McCoy. A rattlesnake. He does mostly odd jobs in some of the farms. People pay him in food. Sometimes, he sells stuff for Ma.*'

'*I'm certain he's looking over at us.*'

'*Just keep still.*'

We both did just that, for a tortuously long period of time. Finally, Devlin gave the okay by gently touching my arm.

'He's moved on. Let's go,' she said. 'Just be careful.'

Finally reaching the front of the barn, I waited for Devlin to open the doors. Up close and personal, there was something eerily quiet and intimidating about the place.

'You must never, *ever* come here alone,' Devlin said, ushering me quickly inside. 'Do you understand? It wouldn't be safe.'

'Why? What's the big deal?'

'Because Ma uses McCoy as her eyes and ears. He reports *everything* to her.'

'I'm not afraid of McCoy,' I said, filled with false bravado.

Her face became very serious. 'Just do as I say. McCoy isn't the only one you should fear.'

'What's that supposed to mean?'

She ignored my question, and flicked on a switch.

The dull light melted, magically revealing an artist's work-shop. Paintings rested on a few homemade easels, some shrouded in dustcovers. Paintbrushes lay scattered on a large, paint-stained table, alongside numerous jars of thick paint.

'Wow! Is this your art studio?' I walked over to the paint-ings and was immediately mesmerised by how skilfully they were created. 'You did all these?'

'Yes,' she said, removing dustcovers from some of the hidden paintings. Despite the gruffness in her voice, I detected pride. A small half-smile appeared on her face, and it delighted me that I should have this wondrous power.

An enormous canvas, titled 'An Effigy of Calvary', took centre stage. It depicted crucified scarecrows, barking at the moon. Barbed wire squeezed out purple blood from each ragged face, which spilled down to form a puddle, shaped uncannily like the town. The second painting was titled 'Still Life', and was similarly unnerving: it portrayed a dead baby, painted in painstaking detail, decapitated by a piano string. The child's face was fully developed, its eyes terrifyingly real.

But it was the next painting, beautiful, yet repulsive, which seemed to cast a spell over me. The painting's theme was animals – pigs, to be exact – mating, watched by a goddess, herself comprised of animal and insect parts. It was a mosaic tapestry of the exotic, titled 'Guilt of Man', despite the fact that the painting's central character was clearly a woman. The nude's butterfly-wing ears protruded from black, cascading hair, partly covering a field-mouse nose that twitched with delight. The shadowy mound of hair resting between the nude's legs resembled a tarantula wrapped menacingly around a bloody, severed-phallus-shaped mushroom. The spider seemed to stalk the canvas, as if it were ready to leap. The pigs mated in groups in the painting's background, aroused by the nude. Their faces bore grotesque, almost human similitude. A filthy-looking boar, eyes shadowed, stood over a sow, ready for mounting, its large, lance-like penis erect and angry.

I tried to look away, but failed. My heart rattled like a dried pea in a tin can. The pigs seemed to be calling me, whispering my name. *Tommy. Tommy. Tommy.* It sounded like Gregorian chant echoing through my head. They wanted me to join them. *Come and join the fun*, said the ugly boar, winking at me. Eerily, the boar reminded me of someone, but I just couldn't put a name to the horrible face.

'*Oink oink!*' hissed Devlin into my ear, making me jump, but thankfully breaking the dark, hypnotic spell the painting had put me under.

'Shit! Don't do that.'

'My paintings freaking you out? Shocking, aren't they?'

'Shocking? Ha! Very little shocks me.' I *was* shocked. I wondered what kind of mind could create such nightmarish scenes? More importantly, perhaps, why?

'I watched your face. My paintings scared you.'

'They're nothing to what I've seen in real life. I've seen photos of dead people. Some of them murdered.'

'Such a liar!' She started laughing. It annoyed me.

'I'm not a liar. My dad's the sheriff. Lots of times he brings his work home. Sometimes he has to examine photos of car crashes, stabbings … even shootings.'

She looked at me for a few seconds, her expression now one of curiosity. 'You've actually seen photos of dead people?'

'Yes, I've seen them. All in gruesome colour. If you don't believe me, I can show you one or two, the next time Dad brings them home.'

'Perhaps I could paint them, bring them back to life …?'

'Paint them? I don't think that would be a nice thing to do, Devlin. Not the dead.'

'Why wouldn't it? They're dead, aren't they? The way I see it, they aren't gonna be complaining too much.'

'I was always told to respect the dead, not make fun of them.'

'I'm tired listening to you, sounding like some old preacher from the mountains,' she said, pushing by me. 'Time for you to go.'

'Go? But … I only got here.'

She walked to the barn door. Opened it.

'You can find your own way back.' The mischievous smile was back with a vengeance. 'Unless of course you're scared of meeting someone dead on your way home?'

'Will I ... will I be able to see you tomorrow?' I said, walking reluctantly towards the opening. 'Will you be at the lake?'

'No, not tomorrow. In a few days. Perhaps a week.'

'A week? But why do I have to wait a week to –'

'*Just go!*' she shouted, practically pushing me out. 'I'm sick listening to your whining voice.'

'Okay, okay, I'm going! No need to push!'

'Remember what I told you: never come here uninvited. Ma's got ... mood swings, when she doesn't take her medicine. She would gobble up a little boy like you, turn you into something you wouldn't like.'

'She a witch?' I smirked.

'Oh, she's far worse than a witch,' said Devlin. 'She's a monster.' The barn door was slammed in my face, leaving me staring at the decaying wood.

CHAPTER TEN

The Kiss of Death

A monster horrendous, hideous and vast depraved of sight.

Virgil, ***Aeneid***

'Where've you been?' Mom challenged, as I approached the porch on my return from Devlin's barn. Mom was sitting with a copy of *Life* magazine, opened near the middle spread. Dad was reading one of the many comic strips in the newspaper, and smoking his pipe.

'Just walking about.' I wasn't in the mood for one of Mom's interrogations. Devlin and her gruesome paintings were still seared into my mind. 'Now that I'm only allowed to run about with Horseshoe, I don't have too many choices.'

'Stop with the martyr complex, Tommy. No one said you could only have one friend. That's a decision you've made. What about David Klein, across the road? He seems a nice enough boy. You could become friends with him. I always see him playing basketball with his little sister.'

'It's *because* he has no friends that he plays with his little sister,' I said, a snide smirk forming on my face. 'We asked him once, last year, to play football with us. The sissy almost fainted.'

'*Don't* talk like that in this house, calling any person a sissy.'

'I'm not in the house. I'm outside it.'

I instantly regretted trying to be smart with Mom. It was not very smart.

Mom's war face came on. She let the magazine slip down the side of her legs, as if she were going for a gun or stiletto blade. 'For your information, smart mouth, David Klein's father died in Vietnam. You should be grateful you *have* a father to teach you football.'

So far, Dad had remained neutral, not getting himself involved in the argument. Now he said, quite calmly and to no one in particular, '*Peanuts.*'

Both Mom and I looked at him quizzically.

'What? What about *Peanuts*?' I said.

'You enjoy reading *Peanuts*, don't you?'

I shrugged my shoulders. 'It's okay.' I loved *Peanuts*, the whole motley crew. But I wasn't going to admit that to Dad or anyone else.

'The Klein kid across the road. A bit like Charlie Brown. Meek, nervous, lacks self-confidence. Probably can't fly a kite and never won a baseball game in his life, never mind trying to kick a football. Doesn't make him a bad guy, does it?'

I shrugged my shoulders again. 'I guess not …'

'Who knows, then? Maybe some time you'll get the chance to show him how to kick a football or throw a mean curve ball, the way I've seen you throw?'

'Maybe …'

'Good. That's that sorted. After dinner, we're going to see *Diamonds Are Forever*. That okay with you?'

'*Diamonds Are Forever*! You bet it's okay!'

Dad smiled, popped the pipe back in his mouth and went back to reading his newspaper. He wore a pleased little smile, having successfully prevented war with his worldly words of wisdom. Mom went back to reading *Life* magazine, looking equally pleased at having just won the battle. I smiled too, went inside and up to my room, whistling the theme to James Bond.

This was what summer was all about.

'We're gonna be late!' I kept shouting up the stairs to Mom and Dad. There was panic in my voice. 'We'll not get good seats.'

'Stop shouting!' Mom shouted. 'There's plenty of time.'

She was right, but I was impatient to see James Bond do his thing, and to check out all the fantastic, futuristic gadgetry he got to play with. Plus, there was always a beautiful girl to be rescued, like Ursula Andress. Or, as Horseshoe liked to call her, Ursula Undress.

We arrived with plenty of time to spare, but like a sardine can, the place was packed to the gills. Thankfully, being sheriff brought a few perks for Dad, and we were allocated prime seating, right at the front of the balcony.

'Boy, am I gonna enjoy this,' I said.

Not if Mom had anything to do with it. 'Going to. Not *gonna*,' she said.

I stood up.

'What're you doing now?' asked Mom irritably.

'I need to *go*.'

'Go?'

'To the john.'

Even in the dull light, I could see Mom cringe at the word *john*. 'I warned you not to be drinking so much Coke. You were asked if you needed to go to the *bathroom* before we left the house.'

'I didn't need to go back at the house,' I said, easing myself out of the row of seats. My bladder was ready to explode. If I continued to have a pissing contest with Mom, I would end up pissing myself.

'Make sure you wash your hands,' Mom said, getting the last word in as usual.

The Strand's restroom was tiny, outdated and dank, but it did the job – which wasn't saying much, considering what the job was. A naked light bulb dangled from the ceiling like a hangman's noose, giving off a chalky greyness. The bulb looked to be on its last legs, crackling and spitting.

Unzipping my jeans, I leaned into the urinal and did what came naturally. My bladder slowly deflated like a pierced balloon.

'Ahhhhhhhhhhhhhh. Lovely,' I sighed with relief.

Just as I came to the end of my task, the door creaked, and then closed very quietly. Almost immediately, the ambience of the confined space changed dramatically. The damn bulb died and the room was thrown into absolute pitch blackness.

'Shit!'

I quickly re-zipped. No hand washing. I needed to get the hell out of there. I fumbled desperately in the dark for the door handle, but failed to find it.

'*Thought you liked fucking about in the dark?*' whispered a voice close to my ear, scaring the shit clean out of me. The voice had its own pungent smell. '*Not so brave without your two pals, are you, boy?*

My eyes began acclimatising. I could just about make out the shadowy figure, now standing in the far corner. Tall. Skinny. Hairless. Armstrong.

'You … you don't scare me. I know … I know who you are.'

'More importantly, I know who *you* are, boy. Took me a bit of time to figure out where I'd seen you before, when you attacked my trailer that night.' He sniggered the answer. 'In the newspapers. Pictures of you. Trying to save your little pal, Joey Woey.'

'Any second now, my Dad's gonna come through that door, and blow your stinking hairless head off, you filthy bastard!'

'Your daddy? Your daddy's sitting down there with your mama, all nice and snug. He's eating popcorn, and she's eating his tiny fat dick.'

Blood rushed to my head. I took a run at him, arms swinging wildly. 'Don't talk about my mom like that, you filthy –!'

He stuck out his leg and I went crashing against the door, banging my head. I was dazed. The blackness in the room changed to blue and red.

'You got balls, I'll say that for you, boy. Bigger than your daddy's – though that ain't saying much.' He leaned down into my face. I could smell chewing tobacco and whiskey on his breath. 'That was mighty nice of you, to come and visit me in my trailer. Well, I'm gonna return the favour. I'm gonna come visiting you, when you're tucked up in bed, give you something really nice, and it sure as hell ain't small and fat.'

'You … you better keep away from me. I … I'm warning you. My Dad'll kill you if you –'

'Bye-bye, sweetie pie, see you in a little while.' He groped my balls, before kissing me full on the mouth.

I heard the door close. Then silence. Only the sound of my heart banging against my chest. It went on forever. Then stopped. I tilted my head to the side, and vomited all over the floor.

CHAPTER ELEVEN

Painted Confusion

This painted child of dirt that stinks and stings.

Pope, *An Epistle to Dr Arbuthnot*

'You feeling better, Tommy?' asked Dad, next morning over breakfast. 'That's one hell of a bump you got. That head of yours must've made some hole in the door.'

'It doesn't hurt. I'm fine.' The throbbing black-and-blue bump on my forehead was the size of a baby's fist. It hurt like hell.

Despite brushing my teeth fifty million times and showering twice, I could still taste Armstrong's filthy presence in my mouth and on my skin. My stomach heaved again at the thought of his touch and filthy lips. I couldn't tell Dad about the encounter with Armstrong, after denying I had been to his trailer. It would open up a very nasty can of worms. I'd have to tell him about Brent, about the gun and the plan. Horseshoe would be dragged into it also. There'd be hell to pay.

'I warned you not to be stuffing your face before we went to the movies,' Mom said, full of her usual sympathy. 'Would you listen? No, of course not. Vomiting all over the place. It was embarrassing, having to haul you home last night, with all those people holding their noses. And to add insult to injury, the movie had only just begun.'

I was about to say something stupid to Mom, but Dad came to my rescue in the nick of time.

'The movie's no big deal. I can get more tickets, Helen. And as for some of those people holding their noses? I could name two or three of those nose-holders who I've had to put in the slammer overnight, for urinating and vomiting in the street. Don't get me started about those pure, upstanding citizens.'

We went back to finishing our breakfast. I was hoping that was the end of the discussion about last night. Of course, Mom had other ideas.

'You're not *up* to something, are you?' she said, looking at me suspiciously.

'What's that supposed to mean? Why would I be up to something?'

'I don't know. I can't quite put my finger on it, but you've been behaving differently of late.'

Mom was right. I *had* been behaving differently, ever since meeting Devlin.

Dad smiled. 'Men can't win, Tommy. Even when we're *not*

up to something, we're up to something. You'll discover that as you get older.'

'Just make sure you're *not* up to something,' said Mom, tightening her eyes as she watched me leave the table and head out the door.

A few hours later, I was sitting on my old rusted swing in the front garden, reading *The Flash*. Dad had just left for work. Mom was in the kitchen, making some kind of stew. Mom's stew never looked good, but always managed to taste delicious.

'Not think you're a bit old to be on a baby swing?' said a voice behind me.

It took a few seconds for me to take in the fact that Devlin was standing right there, smiling, dressed in her usual denims.

'Devlin … I … you said you couldn't see me for a week.' I tried to conceal *The Flash*, while slowly slipping down off the swing. I didn't know which was the most embarrassing: getting caught on my old swing or being seen reading the comic book.

'Not glad to see me, Tommy?' she said in a teasing tone.

'Of course I am, but … how did you find out where I lived?'

'The sheriff's house. You told me your pa was the sheriff. Remember? Everyone in town knows where the sheriff lives. Why? Is there a problem, me being here?'

'A problem? Why … why would there be a problem?' I said, thinking about the problem making stew inside at this moment.

'I brought you something to see.'

It was then that I noticed the large satchel resting at her feet. She bent down, and retrieved something from it. A small canvas.

'Well? What do you think?' she asked.

It was a drawing of someone, buck-naked, and that someone was me. Had to be, despite its strangeness and distorted lumpiness.

'You hate it,' Devlin accused, looking disappointed.

'It's me, isn't it?'

Devlin nodded. 'Yes. Perhaps not the way you see yourself, but the way I see you.'

The more I looked at it, the more the body parts, the facial expression, came together in my head. It really was me, or some part of me, hidden until now.

'It's … it's brilliant, Devlin. Brilliant …'

She smiled. It was a smile filled with pride and something else. I wanted to think it was love. It was the first time I detected a hint of vulnerability behind her tough exterior.

'Don't get too carried away,' she said. 'I made you a lot bigger than you actually are.'

'Bigger?'

She laughed at the expression on my face. Then she pointed at my larger-than-life penis on canvas.

'Very funny,' I said.

'You can keep it, if you like.'

'Keep it? You really mean that?'

'I don't usually give away my drawings, but ... well, you can have this one.'

'It's the best gift I've ever been given. I wish I could give you something in return, some sort of payment for it.'

'You can let me on your swing, for starters,' she said, quickly making herself comfortable on the swing's uncomfortable wooden seat. 'Well? Aren't you gonna push me?'

I carefully put the drawing down, rushed behind her, and began pushing.

'Harder! Higher!' she shouted, each time my palms pushed against the small of her back. '*Harderrrrrrrrrrrrrrrrrrrrrrrrrrrrrr rrrrrr!*'

She was laughing uncontrollably. I was grinning like a clown. Then I saw Mom, watching through the window. She wasn't grinning at my clowning around. I prayed to God she wouldn't come out and embarrass me in front of Devlin.

After about fifteen minutes, Devlin slowed the swinging down and jumped off.

'Tommy ... look, I really like you – a lot. You know that, don't you?'

I nodded. This was music to my ears. She had never professed any feelings towards me before. It had all been one-way street, until this declaration.

'I've already told you, Devlin, how I feel about you. It's more than like. A lot more. I ... I love you. I really do'

'That's what makes this so hard.'

'Makes what so hard?'

'I won't be able to see you for some time.'

'Some time? How long is some time?

'Long.'

'What?' An invisible fist punched me in the gut. Hard. 'Why, what's wrong?'

'It's Ma. She's become very ... unwell. A lot sicker than usual ...'

Her voice trailed off. There was a mysterious edge to it, a lot she didn't want to tell me. She looked away, embarrassed.

But her embarrassment meant little to me. I didn't care about a sick mother. What about me? If I didn't get to see Devlin, I'd be the one ending up sick. To hell with her mother.

'How long, Devlin, before I see you again?' I tried to calm my voice, but I couldn't. Panic was evident. 'I could help you with your mom, if you like, and –'

'No!' she screamed, so loud I jumped. 'No ... this ... this is something I have to deal with alone. Don't get all mushy with me. I don't like it.'

'Is that why you gave me the drawing? As a pay-off?'

For a split second, I thought she was going to slap my face. Instead, she turned to go.

I quickly grabbed her arm. 'I'm sorry. I didn't mean that.'

'I warned you about saying sorry to me.' She pushed me angrily away.

'Please don't go.' I sounded desperate. I *was* desperate. 'I'll do whatever you ask, Devlin, just don't leave me wondering when I can see you again. I can't bear it.'

She looked at me as if I were a scraggy mutt that had once been a cute puppy, but had now overstayed its welcome, shitting everywhere in the house.

'I've got to go,' was all she said, as she quickly walked off.

I just stood, watching her getting smaller and smaller in the distance, like an exclamation mark slowly becoming a period. Then the period vanished …

That same evening at dinner, Mom kept glancing at me strangely. Dad looked uncomfortable. I didn't know what the hell was going on, but knowing Mom, I could guarantee it wouldn't be long before she let me know.

'I think your father has something he wants to ask you,' Mom said, looking at me from across the table. Her face was more serious that usual, which was saying something.

Dad looked even more uncomfortable now, as if he'd just been ambushed by the best ambusher in the business.

'Yes … well … look, Son … your mother … what I mean is … is there something you need to discuss with us? Something you need to tell us?'

My mind was racing, struggling to think what the hell I had done, but before I could come up with something, Mom cut in.

'We – your father and I – are not narrow-minded, even though at times you might think so. No, far from it ...' She looked to Dad again for support.

'Far from it,' he said, nodding vigorously in agreement.

'Do you want to tell us about it?' Mom said, looking me straight in the eyes.

'About *what*? I don't know what you're talking about. Honest I don't.'

'I see. So, that's the way you want to play it?'

'Play what? What is it you *think* I've done?' I was becoming exasperated.

Mom left the table, and went into the living room. I looked across at Dad. He pretended to be eating his meal.

'What's this all about, Dad?'

But before he could answer, Mom's footsteps came towards us.

'I discovered *this* about an hour ago while cleaning your room,' said Mom, face as red as Rudolph's nose. She placed something on the table. 'Well? What do you have to say about it?'

Shit! It was Devlin's drawing.

'I ...' My throat went dry. I could feel the blood draining from my face.

'A naked man?' Mom shook her head. 'I can't believe you're doing this to us.'

'I'm not doing anything! It's only a drawing.'

'Look, your father and I know young people your age go through different stages, until you mature. Young people like to … well, they like to … experiment.' Mom looked at Dad. 'Isn't that right, Frank?'

Dad sighed. 'What your mother is trying to say, is that we know your hormones are driving you nuts at the minute, and experimenting probably helps to control them. Sex can be confusing at your age.'

I was cringing inside, my face rapidly going from white to deep scarlet. 'Dad, this is embarrassing. I know all about the birds and bees, and all that crap.'

'Watch your mouth, *Mister*,' Mom said, speaking with the confidence of someone who never had to repeat herself. 'And don't interrupt your father when he's talking. This is for your own good.'

'What's for my own good?'

Dad was starting to look flustered. 'Tommy, what we're saying is that sometimes growing up can be confusing and complex, and sex is all part of growing up. That's all we're saying.' He looked over at Mom. It was her turn to carry the ball.

'Before you try to lie your way out of this,' Mom said, glaring at me. 'I saw the way you were … behaving with that boy, this afternoon.'

'Boy? What boy?'

'What boy, he says!' Mom rolled her eyes heavenwards. 'The one you were pushing on the swing. *That* boy. What was that all about, giggling and laughing for all the neighbours to hear and see? I saw him hand you that drawing. I want the truth, and I want it now. What's going on between the two of you?'

'The truth, Tommy. We want the truth,' Dad said, voice soft and controlled. 'A lie is like a boomerang. It always comes back to you, hits you on the back of the neck. Your mother and I are not here to judge, just to help.'

'First of all, I don't need help about anything. Devlin's *not* a boy. She's a girl; a beautiful girl,' I said angrily. My face was as red as Mom's. 'That's how she likes to dress, in jeans. So what? Is that a crime?'

'A girl …?' Mom looked unconvinced. 'Didn't look like a girl to me. So stop trying to be smart, when you know you're anything but.'

'I'm not trying to be smart. I'm telling you the truth! Can't you see?'

'Whatever you're selling, Mister, it sure ain't the truth, and I ain't buying. And that drawing? This Devlin, why on earth would she give you something so … something so vulgar?'

'It's not vulgar! It's …' I almost said 'me', but thankfully managed to grab my tongue in time.

'It's what?' Mom said, folding her arms.

'Well … she's … she's an artist … that's her latest drawing.'

'An artist? Ha! If that's true, then what were you doing with it, hid under your bed?'

'I … well …' *I didn't want you to have a heart attack, seeing your son's cock-a-doodle-doo, that's what.* 'She let me borrow it. I … I was going to let Horseshoe see the drawing, compare it to the stuff he does.'

'I don't believe a single word you've just said.'

'That's nothing new. You never believe me, do you?'

'Watch it with the mouth, Mister! One way or another, I'm going to find out what this is all about.'

'Devlin?' said Dad. 'What's the rest of her name?'

'I don't know.'

'Ha! What'd I tell you?' Mom said triumphantly. 'He's lying through his teeth – as usual.'

'Surely you know her second name, Son?' asked Dad. It sounded like an accusation. 'If we know her full name, it'll make it easier and quicker to contact her parents.'

'She only has her mom. They live over beside Stockman's Field. A big farmhouse sort of place. I don't know the actual address.'

'He's making it up as he goes along.' Mom closed her eyes and sighed. 'Get out of my sight. *Now*. Go to your room. Stay there and don't come out. You're grounded. And leave that disgusting drawing there. I'm going to burn it.'

That was when I saw blood.

'You're *not* burning it! It belongs to me. I won't let you burn it.' I stood and grabbed the drawing.

'Put that thing down, *now*, while you're still breathing, *Mister*.'

'Dad?' I looked directly at him.

He sighted. 'We can't burn someone else's property, Helen. We could end up being sued. It'll have to be given back to the young girl. I'll put it in the trunk of my car. It'll stay there until I find out exactly where she lives. Tommy? The drawing.' He held out his hand.

Reluctantly, I handed it to him.

Mom glared at me with eyes that could have stripped paint from a wall. 'You must have a twin, *Mister*, because I already told the other one to get to his room, four-and-a-half seconds ago. Now move it!'

Like a chastised dog, I quickly disappeared upstairs to my room, wondering why the hell bad things always happened to me.

CHAPTER TWELVE

Hare-Raising Experience

Prying curiosity means death.

HP Lovecraft, **The Rats in the Walls**

So far, Mom had refused to relent on the life sentence of solitary confinement she had imposed on me. A full week had gone by – seven days, 168 hours, 604,800 seconds – and counting. In all that time, I barely slept, as insomnia took over. The purplish bags under my eyes began turning into something sinister, like Vincent Price in a horror movie. I couldn't get Devlin out of my head. What if she'd gone back to the lake, just to see me? What would she think, with me not being there?

On the eighth day of my imprisonment, at breakfast, Mom offered some kindly advice.

'You better start behaving, quit all this nonsense of pretending not to sleep. You're not a three-year-old kid – just acting like one. But, hey, you want me to treat you like one? No problem. I can start by reducing this week's pocket money to what a three-year-old would get, and putting you to bed good and early.'

'I think Tommy's seen the error of his ways, Helen,' Dad said, looking at me from across the table. 'Right, Tommy?'

'Yes,' I replied.

'You better have, because next time there won't be a next time,' Mom said.

'A beautiful day like this, seems a waste to be stuck inside,' Dad offered, glancing out the window at the cloudless sky. 'I'm sure if you said you're sorry to Mom for shouting at her, she would be generous and let you out.'

I hesitated for a few seconds before gritting my teeth. 'I'm … I'm sorry, Mom,' I mumbled, hating myself for giving in to her, even though I was in the right.

'Get out of my sight, and keep away from trouble,' she said, not even bothering to look at me.

Once outside, it took me less than an hour to do what Devlin had told me never to do.

The second I stepped out into the forest clearing, the isolated farmhouse came into view. I studied the eerie-looking place for a few minutes, debating with myself. I wasn't yet fully committed to the mad plan in my head.

'To hell with it. Stop being such a sissy,' I finally told myself, agreeing to the madness.

I made my way cautiously in the direction of the barn, avoiding the carved path leading to it. The ground beneath my feet felt slightly sodden and spongy, from a thunderstorm the night before. It smelled of wet mushrooms and turned-up soil. Overhead, the afternoon sky was fading to the colour of dry clay, with tongues of darker grey clouds. Another storm seemed imminent, despite Dad's earlier prediction.

Reaching the farm, I eased the barn door open and slithered in, like the snaky, obsessive bastard I had become. Pitch blackness greeted me. I waited a few seconds for my eyes to become accustomed to the gloom. All I could think about was how the hell I was going to find Devlin.

Suddenly, I heard something behind me. Unfortunately, I hadn't heard it suddenly enough. The barn door snapped open and, before I could move, the place became filled with the day's dull, oppressive light.

'Private ground, boy. Trespassing gets you killed,' said a voice directly behind me. Turning, I managed to say the word 'shit', before my mouth froze with fear.

A woman, her face shadowed from the dull light, stood in the doorway, sucking on a hand-rolled cigarette. Its hot nipple glowed like a ghostly SOS message. A warning too late, it would seem, as I stared at what her arms harboured: a lean and mean pump-action shotgun, housed in the crank of her elbow. She cradled the gun affectionately, as if it were a sleeping child. An ugly-looking weapon, it was speckled with tiny

freckles of rust that teased out the metal into an uneven surface. More worryingly than the gun, I could detect the stench
of booze coming from the woman's mouth.

Behind her stood a bear of a man, his massive face covered by
a forest of unruly beard, his eyes flat as flint. What skin could
be seen was jaundiced-yellow, and the colour was matched
by his sporadic teeth. He smiled craftily – an unreal-looking
smile, like something he'd just bought from a pawnbroker. He
was wearing history clothes – someone else's history – and a
wine bottle protruded from his pants like a pickpocket's fist.

'That's him, Miss Jessica,' the man said, pointing gleefully at
me. 'Saw him snooping about the place. He thought I didn't
see him. Got to get up earlier if he wants to try and fool me.'

'You can return to your work now, Mister McCoy,' Miss
Jessica said, her eyes never leaving mine.

McCoy nodded to Miss Jessica, before giving me a smug
smirk. He looked like a fox with a chicken clamped firmly in
its jaws as he exited the barn.

'What's your business snooping about my property, boy?'
Miss Jessica said, her face tightening into a spider's web of
suspicion.

Despite her slenderness, Miss Jessica's arms looked muscu-
larly chiselled, just right for giving headlocks. I would certainly
have hated it to be *my* head in any wrestling match with her.

A million lies went racing through my head, competing for
attention. I quickly selected the best one. 'I was … searching

for a friend of mine. I thought I saw him head this way, but I must've been mistaken, ma'am. I'm sorry if I –'

In an instant, she brought the shotgun to my face, barrel in line with my nose. I went cross-eyed. She cocked the weapon. I could feel my face screwing inward like a bathtub draining. I was no longer conscious of my own breathing. Distressingly, I smelled shit. My own. I'd just crapped my pants.

Miss Jessica's nostrils flared. If the smell bothered her, she didn't say. What she did eventually say bothered me.

'*Ma'am*, is it? Very polite – for a thief and trespasser. What were you planning on stealing, boy? The answer better be good, or else it'll be bad – for you.'

My balls, at that particular stage in my development, were about the size of small plums, but within seconds of having the evil-looking gun glued to my face, they had shrunk to pea-size. My stomach churned, making a disgusting farting noise. I knew I was about to shit myself again, any second now. I prayed I wouldn't faint, lest any sudden movement would cause her to pull the trigger.

I forced my lips to move. 'I ... I wasn't gonna steal anything. Honest, ma'am. I wasn't.'

'Your eyes do a strange twitch when you're lying, even in bad light. Look like a captured rat's. Did you know that, boy?'

'No, ma'am.'

'Soiled your pants, too.'

'I ... I'm sorry ...' I wanted to cry with embarrassment.

'You're really something, ain't you?' she said, in such a way as to let me know I was anything but.

'Yes, ma'am – I mean, no, ma'am.'

'*Move*,' she hissed, indicating with the shotgun. 'Don't try anything stupid. I'll shoot if I have to. I've got the law on my side, when it comes to trespassers and thieves. You wouldn't be the first one I've shot. Believe me.'

She didn't need to try too hard to convince me. I believed her. I had a terrible vision of Dad rushing to the scene, only to discover his only son – Shit-The-Pants-Tommy – splattered everywhere like spaghetti and ketchup.

As we entered through the back of the house and into the kitchen, I felt like a condemned man, with a pocket of small expectations that would eventually come to nothing. The kitchen stank of stale paint, decaying potatoes and some other terrible smell, alien to my senses. Despite the afternoon's heat, a glow from an old kerosene heater painted pale jaundice on the wooden walls. Unwashed pots formed a metallic pyramid in the sink. A block of butter, touched by afternoon heat, had turned to mush. The room was shelved with the battlefield of decapitated taxidermy: Hares. Foxes. Badgers. A deer's head adorned one of the walls. It regarded me with sad, soulful eyes, as if to say, 'You too?' Below the deer, a bow – its quiver stuffed with arrows – was nailed to the door, alongside a collection of medieval-looking machetes and serrated hunting knives.

'Sit. Over there,' she said, pointing the shotgun at a corner of the room.

I quickly complied, and even though I was terrified to look directly at Miss Jessica's face, I couldn't resist its magnetic pull. Her blonde hair was pulled back tightly, revealing numerous bald patches speckled through the thin, greasy strands. I could see a scant line of discoloration, where some of the hair had recently been removed. Penetrating blue eyes had a life of their own. But it was her striking face that dominated. It was a carbon copy of Devlin's – or at least what Devlin would look like in later years. There was no longer any doubt in my head: this was Devlin's mother.

Miss Jessica slowly sat down opposite me. Not speaking, she chose instead to simply stare at my face, as if knowing the power of a perfect measure of silence. I felt like a bird being watched by a hungry cat.

Minutes ticked by, measured by an old wall clock directly above my head. *Tick. Tick. Tick.* Its wooden sound throbbed in my temples. Fear began playing tricks with my eyes; the raw fear only isolation can produce.

Almost imperceptibly, the silence in the room was slowly diluted. It was only now that I began to hear weird noises, coming from somewhere near. Soft squeals. Little soft squeals of fear.

What seemed an eternity of tense near-silence was broken by the woman's movements. She placed the shotgun at her feet, before reaching into a large metal container, revealing the source of those horrible tiny sounds.

'Hares,' she said, dangling one of the squealing creatures in midair by the ears. 'Don't you just love when they make that sound, their complete hopelessness?'

The creature made the sound a hungry baby makes searching for a nipple; a haunting sound so ominous it reached to the ghetto of my soul, tattooing it forever.

Leaning closer, she held the struggling hare inches from my face, and with sleight-of-hand, produced a pearl-handled knife. In a horrible and bloody instant, she slit the unfortunate creature's throat, releasing a river of blood that covered her fingernails like rose petals. The hare jerked violently. Instinctively, my hand moved to *my* throat. I felt myself grimacing. I tried to unknot the terrified look on my face, but she had seen it, and smiled slyly. The stench of newly hot blood made me retch. I desperately fought the urge to throw up.

'You gonna soil your pants *again*?'

'God, the smell …' I mumbled.

Like lightning, she slapped me across the face with the bloody hare. The slap knocked me off the seat, and I landed squarely on my shitty ass. In an instant, I wanted to do two things: cry, and then rub the sting of humiliation off my face. Instead, I remained motionless. This woman was going to kill me. She would probably mince me up with rabbits' meat, and sell me as pies.

She glared at me, then snapped off a line from a gangster movie: 'I ought to pick that gun up and shoot a hole in your chest, teach you not to take the Lord's name in vain, boy.'

'I'm ... I'm sorry. I didn't mean to –'

'Where'd you learn to blaspheme the Lord? Your filthy ma and pa teach you that?'

'No, ma'am. They ... they'd be very angry with me if they knew I spoke like that – especially ma.'

'Are they good Christian people? Do they attend church and read their Bible?'

Neither of my parents attended church, but that didn't make them bad people.

'Both my parents are good. Dad picks the Bible up every day.' That much was true anyway, though he'd disembowelled his copy of the good book.

'Then you should be ashamed of yourself shaming them, talking such.'

'I *am* ashamed. Truly I am. If Mom heard me, she'd skin the hide off me with her whip,' I said, hoping these were the kind of words she liked to hear. 'I wouldn't be able to sit down for a year, ma'am.'

'"My father scourged you with whips; I will scourge you with scorpions." *That's* the Bible, boy. With scorpions. Think yourself lucky your ma does not use the everlasting sting. Don't *ever* blaspheme the Lord's holy name. His wrath is unmerciful, and His damnation everlasting. Do you want

Him to come after you, with all His power of damnation?'

'I … I'm truly sorry, ma'am. I … I promise never to do it again.'

'Make sure you *do* keep that promise. Dark happenings have a strange and peculiar way of revealing themselves upon us, when least we expect them. Now stop lying there like a pathetic fool, and sit down.'

For the next two hours, I sat there uncomfortably in my own shit. It was hardening like cement, and I wondered if I would ever be able to stand again without walking like John Wayne?

In all that time of torturous waiting, my own torment paled in comparison to the hares'. Twenty of them met a similar fate to their first selected cousin. Their mercuric bluish entrails slipped through her fingers and were deposited into a bucket scabbed with blood and rust. After all the hares had been sent to Hare Heaven, kindly Miss Jessica skinned them, pulling each one inside-out with a single, deft movement, before festooning their pelts upon homemade, bloodstained hooks dangling from the ceiling. Ghoulishly, the pelts retained the hares' tiny faces, each adorned gloriously with a grotesque, posthumous grin.

'Don't pay them no heed,' Miss Jessica said, watching my eyes skim over the dead.

'I … can't help feeling sorry for them, ma'am.'

'Sorry? You're not in a position to feel sorry for anything, boy.

Besides, they're only animals; nothing but simple animals put on this earth for us to eat.' She wiped sweat from her face, leaving a trail of skidded blood across her mouth. The blood glazed her lips, making them fat and obscene.

Eventually, she came to the last of the kill, and cut almost ear-to-ear, before dangling the carcass in front of my face.

'Stick your finger in its throat,' she said calmly.

'I … I can't.'

'*Do it!*' She leaned in so close I could smell all her smells. A faint but malevolent odour, like a residue of hospital, of medicines and disinfectant and illness – all things terrible – was oozing from an opening in her shirt. 'Now!'

Gingerly, I obeyed, poking a shaking finger into the bloody gap where the creature's throat had once been.

'What does it feel like, boy?'

'Sticky … warm …' I willed my stomach to stop heaving.

'Warm? Sticky? Is that how my daughter feels like, you little whoremaster?'

'What …? I … I don't know what you're talking about.' I could feel my face doing a strange little twitching dance, if as someone had shot a million volts of electricity into my nervous system.

'You think I don't *know* why you're here, sneaking about, sniffing the air like a bloodhound? Think you're the first mongrel dog to come here with your little cock high in the air?' She wiped the bloodstained knife very slowly on her gore-covered skirt, as if it were an artist's palette. I wondered if she was planning to plunge the knife right into my throat?

Tiny needles of pain began burning my skull as she reached for the shotgun. She placed the cold barrel tight against my jawbone, and I knew there and then that I was about to die. The side of my face twitched madly, like a freshly strangled chicken.

Miss Jessica reached up slowly and cocked the weapon. The sickening sound ran up the rail of my spineless spine. For a terrifying few seconds, my upper muscles went limp and unresponsive, like stretched rubber bands that could neither expand nor contract. All I could do was hold my breath and wait for my face to be blown to kingdom come.

'I've taken care of my daughter since she was womb-wet. If you *ever* come back here looking for her – you'll be the hare. Do I make myself clear, *boy?*'

I blinked my eyes in acknowledgement of her chilling words.

'I'm gonna give you some advice for free. Be warned of where you crap, boy, because you'll eventually walk in it. If I ever see your ugly face again, I *will* use this gun. Now get the hell off my property!'

Like a drunk let loose, I staggered backwards from the room, into the evening air, then turned and ran as fast as my feet could move. The sky above was more dark than light. God had gone, and the Devil was taking over.

I eventually reached home, bravely ignoring Mom's questioning as I made a dash for my room. Slamming the door shut, I looked in the mirror on the wall. Two perfect circles of red made by the shotgun were branded on my face, giving it a papier-mâché look. I shuddered. I never wanted to see that dreadful woman again.

Quickly changing, I balled the shitty underwear and jeans into a Wegman's plastic bag, and sneaked outside to the garden.

I buried the bag of humiliation deep into the softness of the garden, thankful for last night's rain. I could hear Mom calling my name, but I didn't care. I kept digging and digging, burning with shame and anger.

CHAPTER THIRTEEN

The Hulk and the Thing Pulped to a Pulp

There is always some madness in love. But there is also some reason in madness.

Friedrich Nietzsche

A couple of days after the terrifying encounter with Miss Jessica, I finally acknowledged that in all probability, I would never see Devlin again. So, rather than spending the remainder of the summer alone, or cleaning dirty patrol cars for Dad, I reluctantly decided to swallow my pride and make the first move to reunite with Brent.

'Oh, hi, Tommy,' said a smiling Mrs Fleming, answering the door to my timid knock. Drying her hair with a towel, she was barefoot and evidently bra-less, under a white T-shirt with the words 'Life Is Liberated As Long As I'm Medicated!'

stencilled boldly across it. A tiny pair of cut-off denims cut into her perfect legs. 'I haven't seen you for some time. Everything okay with you and Brent?'

'Yes, Mrs Fleming. Everything's fine. I've just been very busy. Dad had me doing loads of unfinished chores around the house.'

'Sally. Remember?' Her smile lengthened, and I wanted to fall right into it. 'What a great young man you are. That's what *I* need, a man about the place. I wish I could get Brent to do something around here, instead of just lazing about in his room all day long. You know, one day you're going to make some very lucky girl a great husband.'

My face turned as red as the tomatoes in Jack Harding's fruit store. I wondered, would I ever be lucky enough to find a girl as beautiful as Mrs Fleming or Devlin, when I got older?

'*Is* Brent about, Mrs Fleming?'

'Oh, sorry. Yes, he's upstairs in his room. Go on up. I'll bring some cold lemonade.'

Shit! The mere mention of the L word made me sweat. I tried squeezing by Mrs Fleming, but she made little or no effort to move. I could smell soap and shampoo floating from her freshly opened pores. The scent made me feel dizzy in a nice way.

I took the stairs two at a time, before swinging a quick left into Brent's room. He was resting on his bed, reading a comic.

The Fantastic Four. Number twenty-five, the classic Jack Kirby battle between the Hulk and the Thing. The room was filled with comic books and crime magazines. A pungent oniony smell of dirty socks ghosting from beneath his bed caught my nostrils. I decided to ignore it. The smell in my room was probably just as bad.

'How're things?' I said.

Brent didn't even look up. I don't know if he was too engrossed in the fearsome battle taking place within the pages of the comic, or if he just didn't want to see me. I decided it was the latter, and turned to go, sexy lemonade or no sexy lemonade.

'Who d'you think's the strongest?' he said, looking up from the comic just as I turned to leave.

'Huh?'

'The Hulk or the Thing? Who's the strongest?'

I shrugged my shoulders. I hadn't given the question much thought.

'The Hulk, probably,' I said.

'Yeah, that's what I thought. But then, why the hell can't he defeat the Thing outright?'

I shrugged again. 'The problem is, the other three members of the Fantastic Four help the Thing to battle the Hulk. There's strength in numbers.'

Brent considered my words of bullshit wisdom for a few seconds, and then nodded. 'Yeah ... and there were three of us.

We were supposed to be blood-brothers. That was our strength, wasn't it?'

'We still *are* blood-brothers.'

'You're sure of that?'

'Look, if you're talking about the incident at you-know-where, it's over. It was just stupid talk coming from all of us. Luckily, nothing came of it – lucky for all three of us. Between you and me? I'm glad it didn't happen. We could be sitting in the county jail, right now, terrified of taking a shower.'

'You think so?'

'Think so? Are the Hulk's balls green?'

'As green as the Thing's are orange.'

'Damn right!'

We both laughed.

Just then, Mrs Fleming made a welcome appearance. She now had the towel wrapped around her head like a turban. It made her look even sexier, which I hadn't thought possible.

'Here you go, boys. Nice and cold,' said a hot Mrs Fleming, resting the pitcher and glasses on Brent's table. She turned and gave me a smile, and then left the room. I wanted to peep at her denim butt, but resisted the urge for fear that Brent would spot me.

'Why don't we get Horseshoe, and then head over to Jackson's Lake?' I said, reaching for a glass and filling it up with lemonade. I held the filled glass to Brent. A peace offering of sorts. 'It's hot as hell outside. The water'll be great to cool down in.'

He stared at the lemonade for a few seconds. A reconciled smile crawled around the bottom half of his face, making him look like a witness to an execution.

'Are Hulk's balls green? Where the hell do you come up with that shit, Tommy?'

'Who knows? Just shit that's in my head instead of my ass. Take Sue Richards, for instance.'

'Invisible Girl?'

'How the hell does old Reed, Mister Fantastic, manage to see her boobs if they're invisible?'

Brent grinned. 'I never thought of that.'

'And don't get me started about the Human Torch taking a piss!'

He was laughing now. 'Okay, let's get the hell out of here, and pick up Horseshoe,' he said, before gulping the lemonade down in one go.

I followed suit.

As though everything that had happened could be conveniently forgotten, we headed out the front door together, just like the Hulk and the Thing going to meet Mister Fantastic …

We called for Horseshoe, picked up some Cokes at Gino's, and then proceeded onwards to the lake. We were back again – the Magnificent Three. The Three Musketeers. Blood-Brothers

United. Our eyes promised, no more mention of that disastrous night. We all looked relieved, and especially Brent.

'This is the life!' a butt-naked Horseshoe shouted, springing off an old plank we used as a diving board at the lake. Brent and I quickly followed behind him.

Almost an hour went by before we finally dragged ourselves out of the water, allowing the sun to dry our naked bodies on the prickly grass.

'What d'you think of that new X-Men artist, Neal Adams?' Horseshoe said to Brent, reaching for a Coke. 'Isn't he amazing?'

Brent nodded in agreement. 'He is so fucking cool. I love his style, the way he makes the X-Men look so real and angry. He's a god.'

I always felt left out of their comic books conversations, because they only ever discussed Marvel, never DC. Yet today, I was content just to listen to their voices, glad we were here together. I wouldn't tell them that I looked upon my one-time hero, Neal Adams, as a turncoat and a traitor, as he had drawn Green Lantern for DC before jumping ship to Marvel.

'They're advertising real shrunken heads in the back of this month's *Spider-Man*,' Horseshoe said. 'I'm thinking of getting one.'

Brent started laughing. 'Horseshoe, you're such a sucker for all that crap. The shrunken heads are probably just the heads off old Barbie dolls. Someone's trying to make a fast buck from ...' Brent's voice trailed off.

'I want to talk to you – *now*,' Devlin said, appearing out of nowhere and glaring into my face.

I was taken completely by surprise, and no doubt my face registered that. But whatever the look on my face, I knew it was nothing compared to the looks on the faces of Horseshoe and Brent.

'A girl's just seen my dick!' Horseshoe screamed, jumping up quickly and running for his clothes, with Brent right behind him. I never in all my life saw the pair run so fast.

Bold as brass, I stood up, naked. 'Devlin … what … what're you doing here?'

'I told you *never* to go to my house, unless I brought you. Why did you disobey me?' She jammed her finger angrily into my chest. It felt like a hot needle.

'I wanted to see you, that's why. Was that so wrong?'

She leaned her face right into mine. I had never seen anybody so angry. There was spittle on her lips. It made her look vulgar. 'Wrong? It's *wrong* when you don't do as *I* tell *you*. I should've known not to trust you. You're just like all the rest.'

'The rest? Who're you talking about?'

'Hey!' Brent shouted. Now having squeezed into his jeans, he was probably feeling manly again. 'Don't get into my friend's face. Otherwise, I'll –'

Devlin pushed me out of the way, and made a beeline for Brent. Hands on hips, he was grinning with confidence.

'Otherwise?' Devlin said, nose-to-nose with Brent. 'Otherwise what, needle prick?'

I could see Brent's face tightening.

'You better be careful how you talk to me,' he said. 'Just because you're a girl, don't think I won't hurt you.'

I saw it coming a mile away, even if Brent didn't. Devlin's left knee crunched into his balls with such force, he yelped like a wounded dog, before buckling over.

Devlin bent over him, and whispered in his ear. 'Otherwise what, needle prick?'

'Devlin,' I said, quickly approaching. 'He didn't mean anything by it.'

'What about you, sardine face?' Devlin said, turning her flint-like attention to an awestruck Horseshoe. 'Want some *otherwise?*'

'Me?' Horseshoe quickly zipped his jeans closed with one hand, while guarding his crotch with the other. 'No … no, thank you. I've had my fill of otherwise for today.'

I grabbed Devlin by the arm, fearful she was about to beat the crap out of Horseshoe. Her face changed at my touch, and not in a good way.

'*Take your filthy hands off me,*' she hissed menacingly through clenched teeth.

I waited for the knee in the balls, but instead saw Brent rushing her. I tried pulling her out of the way, but Brent was too fast, ploughing straight into her like an out-of-control juggernaut. The two of them went spiralling into the lake.

'Brent! Leave her alone!' I shouted, running towards them. Despite her nastiness towards me, the thought of Brent – *or anyone* – even thinking of hurting Devlin sent blood straight to my eyes.

When I reached them, Devlin was on Brent's back, pushing his head under the water. There was a chilling smile on her face, animal-like in its fierceness.

'Devlin! Let him up!' I pleaded. 'You're drowning him.'

She ignored my plea, and continued holding Brent's head under the water. Little air bubbles began ballooning to the surface from Brent's nostrils. There was little doubt in my mind she wanted to kill him.

Wrapping my arms around her, I tried to pull her away. She screamed at me, reaching to gouge my eyes out with her fingernails. Finally, I managed to pull her off.

We both stood, winded, our bodies heaving up and down with exertion.

Behind me, I could hear Brent gagging and spluttering. Horseshoe stood statue-like, looking up at the sky, not saying a word, not moving, as if fearing the she-tiger would turn her attention and claws on him.

To my surprise, Devlin walked over and kissed me. Then sank her teeth into my bottom lip, biting down so hard I thought the lip had come off. A shaft of pain ran straight through me, bringing tears to my eyes.

She pushed away from me, her mouth covered in my blood. She looked like a vampire, feasting, eyes filled with an insatiable frenzy. I didn't want to, but I couldn't help screaming in agony. My screams immediately stopped when she kicked me in the balls, so hard I feared they would come flying out my ears.

'I don't want to see your face, ever again. If I do, I won't be so tolerant. You'll do more than just crap your pants,' she said, before walking away, back in the direction of the forest, giving Brent's ribs and face a nice kick on the way for good measure.

The scene was a battlefield. Blood everywhere. The pain from my bleeding lip was unbearable. I held my hands against my lip, fearing it would fall off. Horseshoe looked on the brink of vomiting when he saw the bloody state of my mouth. A battered Brent staggered about like a drunk let loose in a liquor store. The Hulk and the Thing had just had their asses kicked, big time, by Catwoman.

'What the hell was all that about, Tommy?' Horseshoe asked. 'You know that crazy girl?'

'I've … got to … get home,' I mumbled through a bloody mouth.

It was left to Horseshoe to quickly bring me straight down to earth.

'You better put your clothes on, first, Tommy. I don't think half the town wants to see you walking about in your bare pelt …'

❀ ❀ ❀

An hour later, I was in the hospital, rushed there by Dad in his screaming squad car. My lip needed eight stitches, but my pride was damaged beyond repair.

When I got home from the hospital, Mom still looked as pale as when she had first set eyes on the lip, despite all her usual tough-as-nails bluster. She had looked on the verge of fainting when I staggered in earlier, covered in blood, practically screaming my head off for Dad. It was the first time I ever saw so much emotion from Mom.

'Well?' she said, looking directly at Dad as he came in behind me, after the hospital treatment.

'He got a tetanus shot, and stitches,' Dad said nonchalantly. 'He'll end up with a bit of a scar.'

'Oh my god … a scar.' Mom looked as if she were about to faint again. 'Not a scar.'

'Don't worry about it, Helen. It's no big deal. Boys love that sort of thing. Isn't that right, Tommy?'

I nodded. I didn't feel like talking. The painkillers were finally showing their strength. Now there was only a dull, relentless throb.

Mom turned to me. 'Despite your denials, I know that Fleming boy had something to do with this,' she said. 'I've a good mind to go over there and see what his mother has to say.'

'Brent had *nothing* to do with this. He wasn't even there. Just Horseshoe and me,' I finally managed to say. My mouth was feeling rubbery with the combination of stitches and painkillers.

I sounded like a ventriloquist's dummy, its wooden mouth needing re-hinged.

'This was a criminal act, Tommy,' Dad said, standing beside Mom. 'Don't you understand? The person or persons who did this should be called to account.'

'It … was a gang, Dad.' This was the story we had concocted between us, knowing the inevitable questioning we would face. There was no way we were going to admit that a single girl had beaten the shit out of us, leaving us with swollen balls and devastated faces. 'They … the gang … took us by surprise.'

'Gang? What gang? Where from?' Dad said, looking even more concerned. 'Did you know any of them? Can you describe any of them?'

'No. It … it all happened so quickly. It was all over in a few minutes. They ambushed the two of us when we were swimming.'

Mom's eyes widened. 'Swimming? You never said anything about swimming.' Her voice was starting to rise noticeably. 'Swimming where?'

'Jackson's Lake …'

I knew that was coming next.

'*Whatttt*!' shouted Mom, making me jump. 'Jackson's Lake! Didn't you listen to your father telling you not to go near that dreadful place, after young Joey Maxwell's tragic accident? How could you?'

'There's nowhere else to go in this town, that's why!'

'Don't dare raise your voice to me, Mister. Go to your room – *now*.' Mom was no longer sympathetic to my suffering.

I did as ordered, glad to be left alone at last. Closing my bedroom door, I went straight to the mirror on the wall.

Shit! What a mess! The ends of the stitches hung ghoulishly from my lip. I looked like one of Doctor Frankenstein's afterthoughts. Yet I was secretly thrilled with them. They were actually fairly cool, and made me look tough, like a movie actor. In a perverse way, the tiny indents beneath the stitching belonged to Devlin. I smiled, causing fresh stabs of pain to shoot across my face.

Someone tapped on the door.

'Yes?' I said, quickly sitting down at my table, grabbing a *Green Lantern* comic.

'Can I come in, Son?' Dad said, easing the door open.

'Sure.'

He gave me a crooked smile.

'You okay?' he said, sitting down beside me.

'Yes.'

'Is there anything I should know, now that we're out of Mom's earshot?'

I thought about repeating the lie, but couldn't.

'It … it wasn't a gang, Dad. I made that up.'

He nodded, looking very serious. 'I suspected as much. You don't lie too convincingly. *Did* Brent Fleming do it?'

'No, that part was true.'

'If not him, then who?'

'I can't say.'

'Are you protecting someone, or is it fear?'

I thought about that for a few seconds, before saying, 'Protecting someone. I know she –' I began stuttering. 'I ... I ... I mean *he*. He didn't mean it.'

'I see.' Dad gave me one of his penetrating looks, as if trying to read my mind. 'You're sure this is never going to repeat itself?'

'Yes ... I mean, no, it won't. It's finished – forever.'

He looked at me for a few more seconds. 'Okay, I'm going to let it go, just this once, but if it ever happens again, I'll not rest until I bring the person before a judge, no matter their gender. Do I make myself clear?'

I hadn't a clue what 'gender' meant, but thought it best to quickly agree to Dad's generous terms.

'Yes, very clear. Thanks ... thanks, Dad.'

He ruffled my hair, his way of showing affection and understanding. He stood to leave, but not before advising me to get some rest.

Before I knew it, mental and physical exhaustion began kicking in alongside the painkillers. I slowly eased on to the bed, and closed my eyes. This was turning out to be the worst summer of my life, and I was only halfway through it.

CHAPTER FOURTEEN

Blood Brothers Spill Blood

Cruel he looks, but calm and strong
Like one who does, not suffers wrong.

Shelley, **Prometheus Unbound**

Two days had gone by since the Battle of the Lake – as Horseshoe had grinningly named it. The fact that he was the only one to come out of it unscathed only added to his delight. The three of us were gathered outside Gino's, drinking Coke, and the fight was still the main topic. Brent was talking about revenge, about how no sucker-punching bitch was going to stain his reputation. I let him know in no uncertain terms that I wouldn't advise any harm towards Devlin, and told him not to be calling her a bitch.

'Why're you defending her?' Brent said, glaring at me. 'Just because she pulled your dick a couple of times, you think she's some sort of beauty queen?'

'Take that back,' I said.

'Fuck you. I'm not taking anything back. She's a sucker-punching bitch.'

'Devlin's got more balls than you, any day of the week. At least she never pissed her pants like a little kid.' *Or crapped them, like me.*

Brent's face turned crimson and distorted. I had gone too far. He took an angry swing at me, missing my nose by a nose.

My aim was better. I cracked him so hard on the chin he was knocked cold, landing sprawled on his back on the path. Pain shot through my hand, but adrenaline eased most of it.

Horseshoe's mouth gaped open. He looked at my fist, and then at Brent on the ground, before saying, 'Shit, Tommy, what're you gonna do when he gets up?'

'We'll see,' I said, not too sure what the hell I was going to see. I wasn't relishing a fight with Brent; he possessed a psycho meanness when dishing out punishment. This was the second time I had landed him on his butt. He would now have to do something to save face.

When he finally did come to, I stood my ground, waiting for the inevitable attack. Inexplicably, it never came. Brent eased himself up off the ground, rubbing his chin a couple of times and glaring at me with daggers of pure hatred. Then he simply turned and left, like a wounded but very dangerous dog. He never said a single word.

'I think that's the end of blood-brothers, Tommy,' said a perplexed-looking Horseshoe. 'Brent looked like he wanted to kill someone.'

CHAPTER FIFTEEN

Death in the Early Hours

Death devours all lovely things.
Edna St Vincent Millay

I would never forget that morning, almost two weeks after my bust-up with Brent. I woke to the sound of Dad's voice filtering up from downstairs. I knew it was early, because of the particular quietness in the house. He was talking with Mom, but secretively, in hushed tones. Something in their voices filled me with dread.

Sneaking out of my room, I hid on the landing, listening.

'Shocking ...' Mom kept repeating. 'And you've no idea who the young girl is?'

'Nothing yet. I've seen some terrible killings, Helen, but this was one of the most violent. Brutal. She'd been raped also, according to the initial coroner's report.'

'Dear God ...' From the stairway, I could see Mom's face cringe. Despite hearing the horrors of Dad's job every day, she had never managed to immunise her feelings. 'To think someone in this town could do such an evil deed.'

'Evil doesn't restrict itself to big cities, Helen. It's everywhere.'

'I hope you find him soon, Frank, before he strikes again. People will be expecting you to catch him – and quickly.'

'I've never rushed an investigation, just to calm people's fears,' Dad said, looking annoyed. 'That's how mistakes are made. I won't be changing my ways just because of pressure.'

'Of course not. I never meant it that way.'

'I haven't got the full autopsy report yet either,' Dad continued. Then, as if reading Mom's mind, he looked straight at her. 'I'm going to take Norman Armstrong in for more questioning.'

'You think that beast has something to do with it?'

Dad's voice went low. 'I think he's got something to do with something, and I sure as hell intend to find out, once and for all, just what exactly that something is.'

Straining to hear, I moved on to the next stair, cursing under my breath as the stair's telltale squeak exposed me. Mom and Dad looked immediately up in my direction.

'Tommy? What on earth are you doing?' Dad said. He looked startled. 'Were you listening in to our private conversation?'

'The girl, Dad? What ... what did she look like?' I walked slowly down the stairs towards them.

Mom glared at me. 'I've warned you before, about listening to –'

'Tell me what she looked like!'

'Don't you dare shout in this house, Mister!'

Dad reached and touched Mom's hand. 'It's okay, Helen. Sometimes it's good to shout.' He was looking at me entirely differently to the way Mom was. The cop in him was quickly kicking in. 'Sit down and we'll have breakfast first, Son.'

'I don't want breakfast. What ... what did the girl look like?'

Dad glanced at Mom again, before returning his gaze to me. 'She had blonde hair, cropped page-boy style. Blue eyes. Her face was covered in –'

'Freckles ...'

Dad's face tightened. It paled slightly. 'You think you know this young girl, Son?'

'It's Devlin.'

'Devlin? The artist girl, the one on the swing? What makes you think it's her?'

'Something ... I don't know, something's telling me it's her ...'

'You said a while back that she lived on a farm outside of town. Do you think you could show me, if we go in the car?'

'No! I never want to see that horrible place again!'

'Okay ...' Dad said, his voice calm and soothing. 'You don't have to go. I'll figure something out from the description you gave me. Is there anything else you can tell me about her?'

'The farm ...'

'Yes? What about the farm?'

'It's ...' I looked at Mom, and then back to Dad. 'It's over in Dust Hill ...'

Mom looked to be on the point of saying something, probably about how she had always warned me about the people of Dust Hill, but Dad gave her a fierce look.

'Anything else, Son?'

'Her ... mother's name is Jessica. That's all I know ...'

My voice was quivering, threatening to quit altogether. Tears began running down my face and into my mouth. I would never forget their saltiness. Ever. Everything was spinning.

Dad quickly stood and came over beside me. 'It's okay, Son. It's okay.'

Of course, it would never be okay. Not now. Not ever.

Just as I made a move to go back upstairs, I collapsed, and darkness swallowed me.

When I finally came to, I was in bed. Doctor Henderson, our family doctor, was sitting beside me, with an anxious-looking Mom standing behind him. Strangely, Dad wasn't there.

Doctor Henderson was checking something scribbled on a pad while his fingers negotiated a pen. The pen rolled with a life of its own, back and forth between his fingers, magically, like water over pebbles in a stream.

'Mom? Where's Dad?'

'He's gone out, on a call. He hopes to be back soon.'

'Devlin's? He's gone over to the farm, hasn't he?'

'Yes, Tommy. Deputy Hillman says he knows the area well, and the people …'

Doctor Henderson coughed. 'Okay, enough talking, Tommy. You need to get as much rest as possible. This should help.'

He handed me a tiny glass, containing an evil-looking green liquid.

'What … is it?'

'It'll help you sleep. Drink it in one go. That's a good man.'

I sniffed it. It stank like fried grease.

'It's not for sniffing,' he said in a scolding voice. 'Down the hatch.'

Reluctantly, I sent it down my throat, just like I'd seen John Wayne do a million times with a glass of whiskey. The foul-tasting liquid punched its way to my stomach. I retched. Wanted to vomit.

'Horrible, isn't it?' Doctor Henderson said.

'Disgusting.' I made a face.

'Good. The more horrible the taste, the better the medicine's strength.'

And with that, he bid me a good day and peaceful sleep.

Mom accompanied him downstairs, and within minutes of their leaving, I could feel my eyes becoming sore with tiredness. Eyelids became heavier, and heavier …

Outside the window, the soft drone of distant traffic could be heard, and kids playing without a care in the world. The way it should be. They were shouting to each other, laughing. One of them kept saying my name, over and over again.

Tommy! Tommy!

It was Devlin, running in the direction of the forest.

I quickly eased out of bed, and sneaked out the window, heading for the forest. I was running in slow motion towards her voice, cursing the swampy sluggishness of my feet. *I'm coming, I'm coming,* I yelled. *Hold on, Devlin! Hold on!*

The forest was covered in a crimson haze, as if the devil himself had come visiting.

Where are you, Devlin!

Here! Over here! Hurry, Tommy! Hurry!

I ran on, finally finding her leaning against an old tree. I thanked God she was okay. She wasn't dead, after all. It had only been a bad dream.

Devlin, I said, smiling with relief. *I thought you were …*

She stepped away from the tree, and what I saw paralysed me with horror. Her collarbone jutted at a strange angle. Swelling and bruising distorted her one-time beautiful face almost beyond recognition. It was a scrambled mess. Eyes swollen shut. Lips split and caked with black blood. Underneath all the red and black and blue, her skin was white as a ghost. From her waist down, she was covered in blood, flesh torn from the bone.

You said you'd save me, Tommy. Why did you lie? Why did you let him do all these terrible things to me? She reached out and touched my face with her bloody hand. I could taste her blood's metallic tang in my mouth.

Don't die, Devlin! Please don't die. Don't leave me … please don't … I can't live without you.

He's coming for you, Tommy. He's coming for you.

Who, Devlin? Who's coming for me?

'Tommy? Tommy?'

'Huh?'

Someone was shaking me.

'You were having a bad dream, shouting in your sleep. You okay?' Dad said, sitting down on the side of my bed. He looked concerned.

'Did you find Devlin's farm?'

Dad nodded. 'Yes, I found it. Deputy Hillman was brought up around there as a kid. He knows the area well. More importantly, I spoke to Mrs Mantle.'

'Mrs Mantle …?'

'Devlin's mother.'

'Devlin Mantle. I never even knew her name. How stupid is that?'

'I didn't know your Mom's surname for about three weeks, when I first stared dating her.' Dad smiled. 'Things like that aren't important to teenagers. Believe it or not, I was one once.'

'Did … did Devlin's mother say anything?' I said, wondering if Mrs Mantle had put two and two together and come up with me being the snooping trespasser? 'About Devlin?'

'No, not yet. She seemed to be in a state of shock. I couldn't get her to talk to me, but I'll go back tomorrow and see how she's doing. I need to find out as much information as possible about her daughter.'

'Did … did Devlin suffer badly, Dad?'

For the longest time, Dad didn't say anything. There was a world of pain and terror in that silence.

'Devlin is in a better place now, Tommy. That's all I can tell you.'

My stomach tightened. I felt like vomiting. The green liquid bubbled in my stomach. I wondered what hell she went through before being murdered.

'You'll get him, Dad, won't you? Bring him to justice?'

'We'll talk about it later, Tommy. Right now, you need to rest.'

'It was Armstrong, wasn't it?'

'I honestly don't have an answer to that. Not yet, anyway. Time will tell. But you must promise me *never* to discuss what you heard between Mom and me this morning. Not to anyone. It could jeopardise any possible charges against the perpetrator. Now, promise me you won't repeat what you heard this morning.'

'Only if you promise to get Armstrong.'

'Mom would be very angry with you if she heard you trying to negotiate conditions for keeping a promise. She'd be even angrier with me if she heard me agreeing to those conditions. Okay, I promise to do everything in my power to get justice for Devlin. Now, your promise.'

'I promise not to discuss what I heard this morning.'

'When you're feeling better, I'll need you to tell me everything you know about Devlin – her friends, how you met. Had she any enemies, people who would hurt her? Any small details you can think of. Leave nothing out. Any little thing could be important. Now, I want you to get some sleep.' He kissed my forehead, something I was unaccustomed to. 'I need you to be strong for the days ahead.'

CHAPTER SIXTEEN

The Monster Caged

Truth from his lips prevailed with double sway
And fools, who came to scoff, remained to pray.
Oliver Goldsmith, **'The Deserted Village'**

Devlin's funeral was a private affair. No mourners permitted, by order of her mother. Worse, Devlin's body was cremated. Dust. As if she had never existed.

I sneaked as near to the crematorium as I could, fearful of being caught by Jessica Mantle. I watched her leave, with a tiny urn tucked under her arm. I couldn't take my eyes from it. I fantasised about stealing the urn, getting my Devlin back.

Over the following days, depression swallowed me. Everything became claustrophobic. I went back to not eating, but this time neither Mom nor Dad said anything, as if they understood what torment I was going through. Of course, they never saw me crying at night, alone in my room, but they showed mercy during the day, and didn't attempt to pry into my grief.

As the days rolled on, details of Devlin's horrific murder, and her equally horrific life, began to emerge: a father abandoning her at birth, leaving her in the care of a seemingly oblivious mother, hooked on drugs and alcohol. Back then, Jessica Mantle earned money for the drugs through prostitution, before finally 'finding religion'. It soon became known that Devlin had been abused by some of her mother's clients, and that concerns raised by neighbours at the time were mostly ignored by incompetent or indifferent social workers. One of those clients had been Norman Armstrong.

The local newspapers soon made Devlin's murder a cause célèbre, putting relentless pressure on Dad to bring the perpetrator to justice – and quickly. Despite this pressure, it took three long weeks before Dad was able to accumulate enough evidence to finally arrest Armstrong for the murder of Devlin, forensics having matched Armstrong's teeth with marks on her body.

I shuddered when I overheard this piece of vile information from Dad, remembering the horrible bruises, shaped like miniature horseshoes, on Devlin's buttocks.

'Thank God that vile creature is in jail, Frank,' Mom said as Dad sat down for breakfast, the day after Armstrong's arrest. I was sitting near the window, gazing aimlessly out at a hazy nothingness. 'The town will sleep a lot more soundly, I can tell you. They owe you big-time for catching him.'

'The town pays my wages, Helen. They owe me nothing,'

Dad said in a slightly annoyed voice. He looked exhausted, the last few days of cat-and-mouse with Armstrong taking their toll.

'Well, *they* appreciate it, even if you don't. At my bridge game last night, people were falling over themselves to tell me what a great job you'd done, arresting Armstrong.'

'That's all nice and fine, but let's not get ahead of ourselves. Justice is a long and very rocky journey. It's almost impossible to predict how it'll finish.' Then Dad dropped a bombshell. 'Armstrong's got Taylor Bradford representing him.'

Taylor Bradford was a living legend in New York State, nick-named The Jugular due to his penchant for going for that particular part of the throat in courtroom battles. He was flashy, arrogant and sly – labels which could also describe some of his past clientele of mafia bosses, movie stars and politicians. He rarely lost a case, having a better batting average than Babe Ruth. Dad had come up against him several times, and the battle always took its toll.

'How can a bum like Armstrong afford such a slick piece of oil as Bradford?' Mom said.

'This one's *pro bono*. Bradford had little choice. Under the American Bar Association's ethical rules, he's obligated to do so many hours of *pro bono* service per year. He hadn't filled his quota this year, apparently. Armstrong got lucky.'

'What does *pro bono* mean, Dad?' I asked.

'It means "for the public good", Tommy. It's Latin.'

'I don't care what language it's in,' Mom said angrily. 'It still stinks to high heaven. Lawyers like Bradford have a lot to answer for in regards to the filth they represent. Public good! That's a joke.'

'Helen, if Bradford hadn't taken the case, he would have been held in contempt of court, or even debarred from practising law. It's his job.'

'Well, if you ask me, it's a damn dirty job, hiding behind a million excuses to try to look clean. I hope he doesn't play his usual games, trying to bewilder the jury.'

'Oh, he'll do whatever he can to get Armstrong off, make no mistake about that. Bradford's reputation is on the line each time he steps into a courtroom. All we can do is put our faith in the system. When the time comes, twelve good men and women will have the evidence placed before them. They'll decide Armstrong's fate, and hopefully see through any smoke and mirrors conjured up by Bradford.'

The doorbell rang, and all conversation ended.

'Who on earth can that be, at this time of morning?' Mom said.

'Tommy?' said Dad, looking at me. 'Go see, please.'

'Okay,' I said, moving slowly to open the front door.

'Is your father in, Tommy?'

It was Mr Maxwell, his rottweiler stare as intimidating as ever.

I nodded. 'Yes, sir. I'll go get him.'

Dad looked questioningly at me as I re-entered the kitchen.
'It's Mr Maxwell, Dad. He wants to see you.'

Mom rose quickly from her seat. 'Well, I'll tell him he'll just have to come back some other time, when you're less busy.'

'No, it's okay, Helen,' Dad said, easing away from the table. 'I'll see what he wants.'

Once Dad had left the kitchen, Mom shook her head.

'People think your father's a robot, on call twenty-four hours a day. The cheek of him, calling at this time of morning.'

I said nothing, quietly slipping into the hallway. I could hear Jeremiah Maxwell's assertive voice clearly from here. It was firm, but there was an emotional shakiness in its tone.

'I warned you that sexual predator would strike again, Sheriff, but you wouldn't listen.'

'I'm afraid you're wasting your time, Mr Maxwell. Discussing the case would contaminate any chance of a conviction. You'll just have to wait until the trial and due process of the law.'

'"Wait" seems to be your favourite word, Sheriff. Wait. Wait. Wait.' Jeremiah Maxwell said the last three words very slowly and deliberate. 'Waiting killed that young girl, and no amount of waiting or fancy legal terms will exonerate you, trial or no trial.'

'I work with what the law gives me.'

'The hell you do! The law? Don't lecture me about the damn law. Armstrong sexually abused Joey, forced him to commit suicide. Where was the law then, when Joey needed it? Oh, that's right, I have to *wait* for that. You knew from the beginning what type of sadistic animal Armstrong was, when you had him in your office, interrogating him. But you did nothing.'

'I did everything in my power to apprehend him.'

'That's bullshit, and you know it. Just remember this, *Sheriff*: that young girl would be alive today, if you had done your job. Her blood is on your hands, and no amount of legal washing will erase it – ever.'

Jeremiah Maxwell turned and walked out, leaving Dad standing at the doorway, looking terribly alone.

CHAPTER SEVENTEEN

Blood Gone Bad

How haughtily he lifts his nose,
To tell what every schoolboy knows.

Swift, **The Journal**

Summer ended, and school started. I never thought I would say it, but I was glad to be back, if just to get into some sort of mundane routine. Horseshoe and I still hung out together, but Brent avoided us now. I didn't know if it was just paranoia taking over, but I felt that everyone was watching me. Everybody was discussing Devlin and Joey, and wondering about my part in their deaths.

At break time, Horseshoe brought up the Battle of the Lake, how he had never seen anything like it in all his life.

'Devlin was incredible, Tommy, wasn't she?' Horseshoe said, still in awe of the happenings that day.

I nodded, not really wanting to speak of Devlin in front of Horseshoe, the lump in my throat threatening to make me cry. In my head, I sometimes tried desperately to conjure some kind of sequence, some chronology of events that explained her disappearance.

'I hope Armstrong fries, Tommy. I read in one of your crime magazines about this real bad villain given the electric chair. The guards hated him so much, the executioner lowered the power in the electricity, so that it would take longer for the villain to die. His eyes popped out and rolled onto the floor. That's what they should do to Armstrong. Make him suffer. Perhaps your Dad could have a word with the executioner when Armstrong goes to the chair, Tommy?'

I didn't know if I should laugh or cry at Horseshoe's habitual naïveté.

'I don't think it works like that, Horseshoe.'

'I keep thinking about that night, at Armstrong's trailer,' Horseshoe said, lowering his voice.

'Stop thinking about it. It never happened. The less people know the better, otherwise we'll really be in the shit.'

'The only thing Brent shot off that night was his big mouth. I keep thinking about it – if Brent had done what he said he was going to do, perhaps Devlin would still be alive.

'You can't think like that, Horseshoe.'

'Do *you* ever think about it like that?'

Of course. I thought about it all the time, the *what if* question. I tortured myself about it constantly, the alternative outcome if we had killed that bastard on that fateful night. If we had, Devlin would still be here, with me, instead of dust and memories. And what about Dad? Was Jeremiah Maxwell right – would Devlin still be alive if Dad had done something as well, instead of just talking? Everyone had deserted her in her most wanting hour.

'Let's change the subject, Horseshoe, before someone over-hears us. How're the Bills gonna do this season?'

Horseshoe shrugged. 'They'll probably reach the Super Bowl and then get beaten.'

'Perhaps they'll take it. They look good enough on paper.'

'Yeah, on toilet paper.'

'Miracles can happen.'

'Look over there. Speak of the devil. It's Brent.' Horseshoe indicated with a nod of his head towards the basketball court.

Brent stood alone at the wire fence. He glanced over at us, before quickly looking away.

'I don't think he's forgiven you, Tommy.'

'I don't give a shit. Let him sulk all he wants. I don't miss him.'

The truth was I did give a shit, and missed hanging out with him. I wanted us all to be a gang again, just like old times. Brent's problem was that no one really liked him at school. They either feared him or detested him. I had Horseshoe and a bunch of other friends to always fall back on. Despite the fight, I couldn't help but feel sorry for Brent. He was his own worst enemy. Little did I know then, but soon he would become my worst enemy also.

CHAPTER EIGHTEEN

Trial and Revelation

A nice man is a man of nasty ideas.

Swift, *Thoughts on Various Subjects*

Horseshoe was right about the Bills losing that season, but the town had more on its mind than football. The trial of Armstrong had started, despite numerous objections from Bradford that his client would not get a fair trial in the town. Bradford's many requests for a change of venue fell on deaf ears. Judge Louisa Pickford made it quite clear that she had full faith in the honesty and integrity of the good citizens of Black's Creek – Armstrong's peers would assure that he received a fair trial. Bradford then complained about the limited pool of people his client could select potential jurors from. Judge Pickford said she would give some consideration to Bradford's concern. Eventually, she permitted people from the nearby town of Webster to be included in the jury selection.

It was impossible to escape the trial. Local media fed a hungry and eager public with every grisly detail. Facts – with little pieces of fiction – were added to the recipe to give spice whenever the media detected the public tiring of the tasteless banquet. And I kept my ear pressed against the wall of the hub, to get even more of the inside track.

When arrested, I learned, Armstrong had at first denied even knowing Devlin, but finally admitted having what he called paid, 'consensual' sex. The bite marks were part of the sexual act, he claimed; an act both he and Devlin enjoyed. She was sixteen, and there was no law against having sex with a consenting adult. Dad suspected the abuse of Devlin by Armstrong had started many years ago, when she was very young, but suspecting and proving were two different animals entirely.

I hated the pervert even more now, when I had overheard Dad discussing with Mom what Armstrong had said. Armstrong was a liar. A filthy rotten liar. Devlin wasn't like her mother, a prostitute. She wouldn't have had sex willingly with an old and ugly pervert, I kept telling myself, over and over again, fighting the snickering voice in the back of my head to the contrary.

According to Dad, not a seat could be had in the courtroom. It was the biggest thing to hit our town in decades. I was under strict orders from him not to show my face at the court. No doubt he feared I would hear further graphic and disturbing details about Devlin's rape and murder.

'I don't think I like the fact that Judge Pickford brought people in from Webster,' Mom said to Dad one evening. 'It's almost as if we can't be trusted to do the right thing. We're not all rednecks, you know.'

'Don't take it personally, Helen. She's a very shrewd but fair judge. She's making sure Bradford has little scope in asking for a retrial, if Armstrong is convicted.'

'*If?* Surely you mean *when*, Frank,' Mom said, giving voice to the question in my head.

'There's no guarantee of anything. Bradford is no fool. He was very careful about the jury members he managed to select. They say he keeps a profile on each potential juror, on their personalities, beliefs and opinions. All it takes is one juror to plant doubt in the minds of the others.'

I could detect doubt in Dad's voice. He always seemed a bit that way, and chose his words very carefully, whenever he was involved directly in a trial, and had to give evidence. This time, however, the doubt seemed more marked.

'What would happen to Armstrong, if he wasn't found guilty, Dad?' I asked.

'Happen?' Dad seemed to be mulling over my question. 'Well, nothing would happen. He'd be freed, Tommy. That's the law.'

'To come back here, to kill again?' I was horrified at the thought of Armstrong roaming the streets at night, looking for other victims. Looking for me, perhaps.

'Let's not think negatively,' said Dad, looking directly at Mom.

I stood, and pushed away from the table. 'I need to use the bathroom.'

'You okay?' said Dad.

I didn't reply.

I stood in front of the cool porcelain of the sink, feeling like I was going to throw up. I had taken it for granted that Armstrong would simply be found guilty, and either be executed or forced to spend the rest of his sordid life in prison.

'Just how bad is it, Frank?' I heard Mom ask.

'Could be better. I spoke to Flynn, the prosecutor, this afternoon. He now gives it a fifty-fifty chance of conviction. Said the evidence I gathered may not be enough to convince or convict.'

'What? How can that be? Any fool can see Armstrong's guilty as sin.'

'Unfortunately, we don't have any fools on the jury, Helen. Bradford knew exactly what type of people to select. All professionals. People who think with their minds – not with their hearts. We don't have any witnesses placing Armstrong at the murder scene. Most of the evidence is circumstantial.'

'But he has no alibi for the night in question. And what about all those filthy movies in that run-down trailer of his?'

'You'd be surprised how many people wouldn't have an alibi for that night, if asked. And as for the movies? There's no crime against them, per se. Truth be told, probably quite a few well-respected homes in town have had them through the door, at one time or another.'

'But the teeth marks on the young girl? Surely no intelligent human being could believe the disgusting explanation given by Armstrong about his teeth marks on her body?'

'Armstrong claims it was all consensual. But there's worse to come.'

'Worse?'

'The autopsy revealed Devlin had had an abortion.'

'An abortion? Dear God ...'

I didn't know what an abortion was, but by the sound of Mom's voice, it must be something frightening.

'Bradford's trying to get it brought into evidence. I'm not sure how he'll convince the judge that it's relevant, but he'll try. He wants the jury to believe Devlin was promiscuous, and not the innocent little girl the media is portraying her as.'

'That young girl is dead, brutally murdered, Frank,' Mom said, anger in her voice. 'It would be a travesty if this ... this animal escapes justice.'

'Armstrong is sitting there, sombre, clean-shaved, nice suit, playing to the jury. He looks like a model citizen. What we need is a living, breathing witness. Someone able to testify against Armstrong's past; someone able to show a pattern of *his* deviant behaviour, rather than –'

Dad stopped abruptly when I came out of the bathroom.

'Sure you're okay, Tommy?'

I nodded. 'I'm going to my room. I've homework to finish.'

In my room, I gazed out the window at the falling snow, thinking about the strange and unnerving words Dad and Mom had used: *Abortion. Promiscuous. Travesty of justice.* Could all the people in charge – the police, the judge, the lawyers, the jury – really let it all go so horribly wrong? Dad had said they needed a living, breathing witness. It was then, as I watched the tiny snowflakes amassing into something much greater, that some of the pieces of the puzzle began falling into place.

'Shit …'

CHAPTER NINETEEN

Sharp as a Knife

The truth is rarely pure, and never simple.
Oscar Wilde, **The Importance of Being Earnest**

School was cancelled the next day, because of snow. I took this as an omen to advance the plan germinating in my head from the night before.

'I'm going over to Horseshoe's,' I said to Mom. I hated having to lie, but I knew it was necessary.

'It's freezing out there. Wouldn't you rather stay indoors?'

'I'm well wrapped up,' I said, making my way towards the front door.

'Make sure you are. Don't stay out too long. There's a possibility of a whiteout later on.'

The snow was ankle-deep, and made a crisp, crackly sound under my boots. Every house and building was covered in a blanket of purest white. Postcard perfect. A few kids were out, throwing snowballs at each other, or making ridiculous-looking snowmen. I smiled to myself. It wasn't too long since my gang would have been doing the same.

Brent's house was eerily quiet as I approached. I stopped a small distance away, trying to figure out the best way to approach him. That was when I heard a window being opened.

'What the hell're you doing here?' shouted Brent, sticking his head out of the bedroom window.

'I need to talk to you,' I said, loudly, but not too loud, in case Mrs Fleming heard.

'We've nothing to talk about. Now scram.'

'It's about Armstrong.'

'I don't care who the hell it's about, just get off our property – now!'

'It's about the teeth marks.'

Brent's face immediately changed. I swore it turned as pale as the snow along the edge of his windowsill. He stared back at me for a few seconds before disappearing out of sight.

I waited for what seemed an eternity, wondering if he would come down. When he finally did, he came towards me like a rhino in pre-charge, his face knotted with anger.

'I told you to get off our property.'

'We need to talk first. Then I'll go.'

'There's nothing to talk about – ever.'

'There's plenty. Let's start with the teeth marks.'

'What fucking teeth marks?'

'You know what I'm talking about, Brent. The marks that were on your … butt.'

I'd accidentally noticed marks on Brent's butt, almost identical to those on Devlin's, as we skinny-dipped at the lake two years ago. When he caught me looking, he became angry, calling me a 'homo' and a 'butt watcher'. We didn't speak to each other for almost a week, until he eventually calmed down, and we were able to laugh about it.

Brent grunted. 'You mean the time I caught you looking at my ass, like the little faggot you are? Those weren't teeth marks. I told you what they were. Bruises.'

'How did you get them?'

'That's got fuck all to do with you.'

'You can't remember what you told me, can you?'

'I … I … slipped in my room … the carpet was sticking out … I tripped over it.'

No, that wasn't even close. He had told me a story about a raid on Mister Johnson's apple trees, and a weak branch.

Lucky I landed on my ass rather than my head, he had laughed, by way of explanation.

At the time, I thought Brent's explanation sounded pretty reasonable. Not now.

'You told me you got them falling from a tree in old man Johnson's yard.'

He blinked, as if he'd just been slapped. 'Oh, yeah … right. Now I remember. So? Big deal.'

'We both know they weren't bruises caused by a fall,' I said. 'The were the exact same teeth marks that were on Devlin's body. They were Armstrong's teeth marks. The first time I saw them on her, I knew I had seen similar marks, but I just couldn't remember where. Last night, I finally remembered.'

Brent looked as if he had been kicked in the balls. His mouth opened, but no words came out.

I reckoned Brent had been lured to Armstrong's trailer with the incentive of money – something Brent was always in need of. That must have been how he knew about Armstrong's comings and goings at the trailer, so inch-perfectly; how he knew about the liquid in the cupboard, which I suspected was some sort of knockout drug. That's why Brent insisted Horseshoe say he was thirsty, knowing Armstrong would go to the cupboard at the end of the trailer, where Brent waited in the darkness with his gun. I shuddered at the thought of what must have happened to Brent; now I fully understood why he wanted to kill Armstrong, rather than simply blow his nuts off. It all made sense. Brent. Joey. Devlin. But how many other victims had there been, all nameless and as yet unknown? How many more would there be if Armstrong escaped justice now? I couldn't allow that to happen.

'Brent, you've got to tell my dad everything you know about Armstrong, what he did to you. Otherwise, the murdering pervert could walk free and commit another –'

Without warning, he lunged, pinning my body to the snowy ground.

'Nothing happened, faggot! Nothing!' he said, trying to wrap his hands around my throat.

'You want Armstrong to escape justice, and continue to do to others what he did to Devlin and Joey? What he did to you!'

'Armstrong did nothing to me! You can't prove a fucking thing.'

'You've got to testify, otherwise he could get off. Dad needs more evidence. You have it.'

I tried to roll him off, but his anger increased his strength. His features were changing, right before my eyes. It was scary. He was Bruce Banner becoming the Hulk, a sick smirk appearing on his face.

'Twice you got away with making me look like a dick in front of Horseshoe,' Brent hissed. His spittle showered my face. 'I'll not let that happen again – ever.'

I didn't see the penknife until it was too late. He plunged it towards my left eye. In slow motion, I saw dried speckles of our blood on the blade. *Blood-brothers forever.*

I managed to move my head slightly, but not enough. The knife sliced into my forehead, just above the eyebrow. Hot blood crawled down the side of my face. I should have screamed with pain, but a combination of cold and adrenaline probably prevented the injury registering in my brain.

He tried plunging the knife again, but I managed to grab him by the balls, and squeezed for all I was worth. He groaned terribly before slipping off me. Quickly jumping on top of him, I grabbed the knife and held it tight to his throat.

'What're you gonna do, faggot? You gonna kill me?' He glared defiantly at me. 'Go on. I'd rather be dead, anyway.'

'It was never about Joey, that night at Armstrong's trailer. It was about you getting revenge for yourself, wasn't it? You didn't give a damn about Joey. Not then, not now. You're a coward.'

'If you think I'm gonna tell anyone what Armstrong did to me, you've another thing coming. You're right. I don't give a fuck about Joey, and I don't give a fuck about your little whore girl.'

'Don't talk about Devlin like that.' Despite the cold, I felt my face flush.

'She was a whore, faggot. Nothing but a little whore. Did you know I fucked her, behind your back? The whole town fucked her, and you couldn't see it because you were *in love*. Know something? I'm glad she's dead. I wish I'd killed her.'

He began laughing. It was an evil, sandpapery laugh, grinding my skull.

Mad thoughts began flooding my brain. Something was happening to me; something uncontrollable. I pushed the knife tighter against his neck. A small line of blood appeared under the blade.

'*Take back what you said about Devlin, or I'll kill you,*' I hissed.

'Fuck you! Kill me.' Tears began pooling in his eyes. 'I don't give a shit. I've nothing to live for anyway. I'd rather be dead.'

I believed he really did want me to kill him, now that I knew his terrible secret. He was probably thinking that I'd tell everyone at school about what Armstrong did to him, but that I'd change the story to say Brent loved every second of it; that he was a regular at the rundown trailer, giving and receiving blowjobs. How could he ever show his face again?

'You can't do it, can you?' he mocked. 'Who's the coward now, faggot?'

'Tommy!' shouted a voice behind me. 'What on earth are you doing with that knife? Get off Brent!'

Mrs Fleming grabbed me from behind, pulling me off Brent. She had the strength of a mother bear protecting her cub, and held me vice-like in a hold.

'Let me go!' I shouted.

'Not until you drop that knife and tell me what's going on here. Why were you trying to stab Brent?' She tightened the grip, her breathing laboured. 'Tell me right now, otherwise I'll call your father.'

For the longest time, Brent and I stared at each other with sheer hatred.

'He said things he shouldn't have,' I said, nodding in the direction of Brent.

'Liar!' Brent shouted. 'You just don't like hearing the truth.'

'I know you're lying about Devlin!'

'Ha! You're the one lying to yourself. She was dirt. The whole town knows she was dirt.'

I tried breaking free from Mrs Fleming, but to no avail. I wanted to rip his stinking, ugly face in half, but I was drained of all strength.

'Brent? Get inside – *now*!'

Brent mumbled something under his breath about Devlin, before slowly walking away towards the house. He looked back at me before entering, a greasy smirk on his face.

Mrs Fleming flung me around. She was no longer beautiful, but ugly with anger and hatred.

'I don't know what's going on with you two, but I never want to see you near my home again. Do you understand?'

'Yes …'

'Thank yourself lucky I don't have you charged with trying to kill my son. Now leave. Get away from here before I get really angry and do something to you.'

I walked slowly away.

'And to think, I thought you were a nice kid …' Mrs Fleming said, before I was out of earshot.

CHAPTER TWENTY

In Stitches and Needled

The court is obliged to submit the case fairly, but let the jury do the deciding.

Chekhov

The cut above my eye needed six stitches, but, as Dad pointed out on the way home from the hospital, it could have been a lot worse.

'You're lucky you didn't lose your eye, Tommy. Damn lucky. Collecting stitches seems to have become a hobby with you.'

'It was an accident.'

Snow was beginning to fall. The windscreen wipers made hypnotic whooshing sounds, making me drowsy. I could feel my eyelids becoming heavier. I wanted to sleep, badly.

'I'm not going to question your explanation about slipping on ice, but that doesn't mean I believe you. Your mother also suspects something's going on with you and your friends –

chiefly Brent Fleming. She's talking about sending you down to New Jersey, to stay with Aunt Katherine, if just to get you away from here for a few months.'

'What?' I was shocked at this revelation, and quickly became alert. 'Dad, you can't let that happen. Aunt Katherine drives me nuts. She never tires of saying that New Jersey is home to more scientists and engineers *per square mile* than anywhere else in the world.'

Dad tried to hide his smile.

'That's not a good enough excuse. Jerseyites have little to boast about, but when they do, they sure do boast.'

'I hate her house. It smells of cat pee, and she always tries to make me go to bed early. *And* she drinks like a sailor, singing for all the neighbours to hear. It's embarrassing.'

'Don't ever let me hear you talk about Aunt Katherine like that.' Dad's tone became serious. 'She's a good person. She has gone through hell in her life, and has her reasons for drinking so heavily. Clear?'

I nodded. 'Okay, but I'm not going there. Mom can't make me.'

'Really? You know if your mother says you're going, you're going. She doesn't believe in negotiating. Anyhow, she may be right. Perhaps getting away from here would be good for you.'

'Please, Dad. I won't be any more trouble. I promise. I really need to be here, to see Armstrong finally get what's coming to him.'

Dad stopped to think about this. It was a few seconds before he responded.

'Don't take it for granted that Armstrong'll be found guilty. We've all got to prepare ourselves for a worst-case scenario, just in case.'

I didn't like the sound of that. 'What does worst-case scenario mean?'

'Worst-case being he'll get off, or a mistrial is declared. Even a hung jury.'

'A hung jury? The judge will hang the jury if they don't get it right?'

Dad laughed out loud at that. It was good to hear his old laughter back. He hadn't been himself since the trial began. Everything depended on his evidence, and it was clearly weighing on him.

'No, they don't hang the jury, Tommy – though God knows, sometimes with the decisions they make, they could do with a good hanging. No, "hung jury" is a legal term, meaning that the jury can't come up with a unanimous decision.'

Dad slowly brought the car to a halt at an intersection. I gazed out the window at the leaden sky. The snow was becoming heavier, the winter wind more fierce. I wanted desperately to tell Dad about Brent, about my suspicions – *beliefs* – but couldn't. What good would it do anyway? It would be Brent's word against mine. He'd simply deny it, no matter the strength and skill of Dad's interrogation.

Realistically, there was nothing I could do.

The moment we walked through the door, Mom shouted to Dad that he needed to get over to the courthouse, straight away. Prosecutor Flynn had been calling for him. The jury had finally reached its verdict. Everyone was waiting for Judge Pickford to arrive. The judge had been delayed by the snow, but would be in her chamber within the hour.

Dad rushed out to his car. I watched him speeding away, wishing I could be there, if only to see Armstrong's face.

Mom looked at the new stitches adorning my face. She looked angry rather than sympathetic. Shook her head.

'When are you going to grow up? We're tiring of your nonsense. I'm shipping you out of here, the first chance I get.'

No, you're not, I wanted to say, but didn't have the balls.

'Get out of my sight,' she said. 'I don't want to see you the rest of the day.'

Her words didn't bother me, because it was all coming to an end. The nightmare would be over soon. Armstrong's fate was now firmly in the hands of twelve men and women.

Little did I know then, but my fate was also in their hands.

CHAPTER TWENTY-ONE

Scapegoats Aplenty

A false witness shall not be unpunished,
and he that speaketh lies shall not escape.
Proverbs 19:5

Armstrong's shock acquittal reverberated through the town and beyond. I sat in the living room, watching the aftermath unfold on live television. Prosecutor Flynn was standing on the snow-covered steps of the courthouse, looking uncertain and drained, giving hesitant responses to the media's bullet-like questions.

'Prosecutor Flynn, what on earth happened?' a local hack asked, notepad in hand. 'You kept telling everyone this was an open-and-shut case. Looks more open now than it did at the beginning. What went wrong?'

Despite the freezing temperature and falling snow, Flynn's face was greasy with sweat. 'I wouldn't characterise it as anything gone wrong. It's the nature of the system.'

'Would you not agree that perhaps someone with more experience with murder trials should have been in charge of this one?'

'I have plenty of experience with murder trials.' Flynn's face constricted. 'I felt there was sufficient evidence to get this case before a jury. That's my duty. Don't forget, Mr Armstrong may have been acquitted, but the jury didn't say he was innocent, or that –'

As Flynn tried to finish his sentence, behind him a beaming Bradford could be seen, exiting the courthouse. The media swarmed towards him as one, leaving a relieved-looking Flynn to hurriedly disappear down the snowy courthouse steps and out of sight.

'Mr Bradford! Mr Bradford! How does your client feel, now that he's a free man?'

Bradford gave his best Hollywood smile before answering.

'Mr Armstrong feels as good as any innocent man feels after being vindicated and released from a nightmare. His good name has been restored to him by the clear-thinking men and women of the jury. All he asks now is to be left alone to try and pick up the pieces of his life, a life possibly irrevocably damaged by vindictive law enforcement officials and their despicable gung-ho attitude. Arresting someone simply because they live alone and do not follow the norms of society, cannot go unchallenged.'

'There's talk your client will be suing the county for wrongful imprisonment. Is that true?'

Bradford's smile disappeared. 'The travesty of imprisoning the innocent should never be permitted. Nor should we passively accept what the system tries to impose upon us when the system is clearly wrong. More than likely, the killer of young Devlin Mantle was a drifter. Rather than pick on Norman Armstrong, the police should have been out looking for the real killer. They wasted time. They wasted taxpayers' money. Worse, they allowed the real killer to slip through the net and escape justice and –'

Mom appeared out of nowhere and clicked the television off.

'That's enough of that windbag spewing out his nonsense,' she said angrily. 'Didn't I tell you I didn't want to see you the rest of the day?'

'I wanted to see if Dad was going to be on television.'

'Well, he's not. Now, go to your room and clear up all those comic books scattered about the floor. I'm tired looking at them.'

She was upset, and I should have simply done what she wanted. But I had to go and open my big mouth instead, by saying, 'Armstrong got off. How could Dad let that happen?'

For a second, Mom looked at me as if I were a slithering worm she had almost stepped on. Then she turned on me like a hungry tiger, her eyes tightening like Clint Eastwood in a spaghetti western.

'I *ever* hear you say anything like that again about your father, I guarantee you won't sit down for a week.' She pushed her face up against mine. Our noses touched. 'Your bare butt isn't too old to escape my handprint all over it, Mister. Now, get out of my sight and into your room – *pronto!*'

'They're saying I arrested Armstrong too soon, Helen,' Dad said, holding up the newspaper later that evening. 'God the night! When can it be too soon to arrest a monster like Armstrong? After he kills again?'

'Stop crucifying yourself, Frank. There's enough Judases in this town with hammers in their dirty hands. You did the best you could with what little you had.'

'Well, according to the newspapers, my best wasn't good enough.' Dad began reading from the evening newspaper he had brought back with him.

Justice is only as good as the case that can be made. Unfortunately, in the case of the Armstrong trial, the case wasn't very good. Prosecutors claim they did their best with what they had, but it wasn't enough. Many important questions remain about the murder of young Devlin Mantle, not least of which are the identity and whereabouts of her killer. Sheriff Henderson plans to continue pursuing answers. That's commendable but not very reassuring, if this farce of a trail was anything to go by. Unless there is new and substantially stronger evidence, the killer, whoever he is, might just get away with murder.

Dad flung the newspaper at the far wall.

'If Flynn or the media think I'm going to allow you to be made into a scapegoat, they better get their heads in gear and out of their asses,' said Mom defiantly.

I was shocked. The word 'asses' sounded so foreign coming from her mouth. It carried a whole new level of crudeness.

'Helen Henderson! What on earth's gotten into you, talking like that?' Dad said, smiling.

'When it comes to this family, I'll be doing more than swearing if someone thinks they're going to hurt us.'

Dad reached over and kissed Mom.

'Dad?' I said, looking directly at him.

'Yes? What is it, Tommy?'

'I'm … I'm sorry for blaming you for Armstrong getting off. I was angry.'

'I didn't know you blamed me, but that's okay. I know how you feel about Devlin. I'm just sorry I couldn't bring her killer to justice … this time.'

This time? The way he said that and looked directly into my eyes, made my heart tighten. Was Dad sending me a cryptic message of his determination to see justice done? Those two words gave me hope. He hadn't given up.

'They should have hung the jury, Dad.'

Dad laughed, and nodded. 'I can't argue with the truth, Tommy.'

'Can I be excused, Mom? I'm tired. I think I'll have an early night.'

Mom nodded and gave me a reluctant half smile. I think she was pleased at my apology to Dad. She didn't even insist I eat the broccoli languishing at the side of my plate like some alien creature from outer space.

From the stairs, I could hear Dad going over the case with Mom, examining where it all went wrong.

'It was Bradford's endless innuendo about the mother's lifestyle that muddied the water. That swayed the jury more than any other factor. Bradford didn't say it, but he more or less hinted that mother and daughter were cut from the same cloth, and that the killer could have been any of the mother's many clients. It was sickening to listen to, but it worked.'

'Bradford's a despicable creature, Frank. How on earth he sleeps at night is beyond me.'

Hate and anger burned in me as I listened. It was hard to decide whether I hated Bradford more than I hated Armstrong. One thing I did know: I wanted to kill both of them. I thought of Brent, also. Would his testimony have sent Armstrong to prison for life? I believed it would, and quickly put Brent down on my list of hate.

Bone-tired, I began undressing in my room, watching the snow fall outside on the front lawn. It was covering everything with its cleansing beauty, but I knew it was just an illusion that couldn't be sustained. Eventually the snow would fade, and all the filth and dirt would emerge again, triumphantly.

I crawled into the refuge of my bed. An arrowhead of moonlight entrenched itself upon the wooden beam directly above my head, as if someone had taken a potshot at me with a crossbow. Quickly pulling the blankets up over my head, I achieved shelter and warmth simultaneously. Before I knew it, sleep touched me on the shoulder, and took me to the land of Nod.

Just how long I had been permitted to visit the world of sleep, I couldn't tell. I awoke in the middle of the night with a feeling of trepidation. Probably a bad dream, I reasoned, as I peeped over the roof of the blankets to glance about my room. I thought I'd heard a sound. Something? Nothing. Imagination? Probably.

Then, just as I closed my eyes, I heard it again. The sound grew and fell and then grew again. It was coming from outside the house. I listened. It was like an enticing hum, like someone blowing on an empty bottle, and the unnatural progression of my thoughts led repeatedly back to it until I could no longer tolerate its torturous whisper.

The swing ...? It sounded like the swing groaning under the pressure of too much weight.

I got out of bed to investigate, tiptoeing to the window. Pressing my face against its coldness, my breath quickly fogged the glass. I wiped it, and stared out across the snow-covered garden. To my amazement, the swing *was* moving, but almost imperceptibility, as if being pushed by invisible hands. *The wind ...?*

I thought of Devlin, laughing on the swing, being pushed by me on a beautiful summer's afternoon.

Oh, Devlin ...

I continued looking out the window, scrutinising the snowy scene. In the play of light and shadow, the moon's luminous glow was pale, yet bright enough to hurt.

'What the ...?'

Something had moved. Something was out there, in the winter wonderland. I quickly wiped the fogged window again. Nothing. Just snow playing tricks with my tired eyes. Then I saw him. Armstrong. He was staring up at the window. Partially camouflaged by the falling snow, and totally naked, his luminous and hairless body looked diseased, like a withered funeral candle. In his right hand he held a large knife. The knife's blade was as long as his massive hand was wide. His whole being radiated something terrifyingly arrogant.

I quickly ducked beneath the window, hoping beyond hope he hadn't seen me.

Easy ... steady your nerves. It can't be him. He wouldn't have the balls to come here ...

I eased up to the window's edge, and sneaked a peek. To my horror, he was walking towards the house. I wanted to shout, but the electric shock of fear stunned my mouth. I tried to run, to get Dad, but my feet seemed glued to the carpet. A dark sickness began rising up in me. Armstrong had used his evil powers to make me immobile, and he was coming here, into our home, to kill me, just like he'd killed Devlin, just like he'd promised in the Strand's toilet.

I tried to control my breathing while listening to the sounds from within the house: the soft hum of electricity ticking from the basement; the fridge moaning and shuddering; the wind sneaking through cracks and holes.

A door sounded from downstairs. *He's in.* The bastard was in the house. Sneaky footsteps began registering on the stairs.

Finally freed from Armstrong's spell, I moved in slow motion for the door. Just as I neared it, the door began slowly to open. I threw my entire weight against it. The door slammed shut.

'Bastard! Get out, you murdering bastard!' I screamed. 'Dad! Dad! *Heeeeeeeeeeeeeeeeeelp!*'

I pushed against the door with all my strength. I could still feel force coming from the other side.

'Tommy? What on earth's going on? What's all the shouting about?' Dad was banging on the door.

'Dad? Dad! Armstrong's in the house!' I shouted, opening the door quickly. Dad was in uniform. 'He was outside, now he's in.'

'Armstrong? Get back inside.'

'But –'

'*Now!*' he hissed, pushing me back and slamming the door, just as Mom's voice said from their bedroom, 'Frank? What on earth's going on?'

'Helen!' shouted Dad. 'Get back in and lock the door.'

It all went quiet. After a few moments, I opened the door inch-wide, peering through its spine. Dad was cautiously going down the stairs in the darkness, gun in hand, halting on each step for a second before proceeding. He kept pointing the gun in different directions, just like I'd seen on TV.

Careful, Dad …

Minutes crawled by painfully. Not a sound. Then the lights came on in the house, followed by Dad's distant voice. 'Come on down. I've got him!'

'Frank, what's going on?' said Mom, rushing down the stairs in her nightgown. 'Got who? And why is the back door open, all that snow coming in?'

'Tommy's intruder, Helen. Out in the back,' Dad said, pointing the gun towards the back garden.

'An intruder?'

'You got him, Dad?' I said, rushing down the stairs, almost breaking my neck in the process.

'I've got him covered, Son. Don't worry. I've told him to freeze, and take that silly grin off his face.'

Gingerly, I walked to the door, and looked out.

'That's your intruder, Tommy.' Dad was pointing at the Klein's snowman, languishing smugly in their garden.

'Can someone please tell me what's going on?' Mom said, her voice becoming increasingly prickly.

'It's okay, Helen. False alarm. Tommy thought he saw an intruder.' Dad started laughing. 'Mister Snowman.'

'I know what I saw!' I said angrily. 'It was Armstrong. I heard him coming into the house.'

'That was me you heard, Tommy. I got called out in an emergency, a couple of hours ago.'

'No, it wasn't you. I know what I saw. It was Armstrong. He was naked, and –'

'That's enough, talking about naked men again!' said Mom. 'Frank, close those doors before we become the laughing stock of the neighborhood. Tommy? Get to bed.'

'But I'm telling you –'

'Mister, you're telling me nothing other than *yes Mom, good-night Mom, three bags full Mom.*'

Dad ruffled my hair.

'Go on, Son. Get some sleep. You're overtired. We're all going straight to bed.'

'I know what I saw …' I mumbled, heading back up the stairs. 'It *was* Armstrong.'

CHAPTER TWENTY-TWO

Beneath the Icy World

For believe me: the secret for harvesting from exist-
ence the greatest fruitfulness and greatest enjoyment
is – to live dangerously.

Friedrich Nietzsche

As days turned to weeks, Devlin's murder slowly faded to the back of the town's consciousness. The economy was in turmoil, and people had more pressing things to think about, such as jobs and livelihoods. Only those who cared about Devlin kept her memory alive. I couldn't stop thinking of her.

It was Saturday afternoon. The snow had fallen persistently for three days, and was causing major power failures. Many homes – including ours – had no electricity. No electricity meant zero television, my main source of entertainment on Saturday afternoons. I was going stir crazy. I was driving Mom crazy also, so she did what she was good at: stirring.

'That driveway could do with some shovelling,' she suggested, meaning get off your lazy ass and get the snow cleared, pronto.

'What's the point? A whiteout's been forecast for later in the day. It'll only cover it up again. Can't I just read some comics in my room?'

'When you're finished shovelling the snow away, I've a couple of other chores in mind,' Mom said, ignoring my feeble attempt at negotiation. As usual, there was no reasoning with her. It was either her way or the driveway – and make sure you have a snow shovel in hand.

'Some Saturday this has turned out to be! I'd rather be at school,' I said, angrily grabbing my hooded coat and gloves, and heading out the door.

The second the shovel touched the ground, the falling snow became serious, laughing at my futile attempt to keep the driveway clear. Thick flakes parachuted from the sky with a vengeance, like an invading army. I endured the humiliating shovelling for about twenty more minutes, before finally deciding I'd had enough of the pointless task. I speared the shovel into a mound of snow, but instead of going back indoors to face Mom's wrath, I headed in the direction of Black's Wood.

Despite the snow adding to the difficulty, I believed I could conjure up a mental map of the exact spot where Devlin's body had been found. Perhaps she would speak to me, help me unearth a clue missed by Dad and the rest of the investigators? Maybe tell me something not yet known about Armstrong? I knew it sounded mad, but stranger things had happened. I was desperate, and more than willing to take desperate action. I had let her down in life, but now I'd rectify that by helping to bring Armstrong to justice, one way or another.

When I finally arrived at Black's Wood, it resembled a frozen lunar landscape left behind from a million years ago. Eerily quiet and beautiful to behold, it took my breath away, literally. My icy breath streamed out each time I opened my mouth, and then paddled right back, as if seeking shelter where it had just been evicted from.

It had taken me over an hour to reach the woods, but it took less than five minutes to realise I would never realistically locate the spot where Devlin's body had been discovered. Despite this, I trudged aimlessly in different directions.

Hours filtered away before I finally admitted I was lost. Everything was too blindingly white. There was texture, but no shape. Tree branches besieged with ice created a picture of an elevated Edgar Allan Poe boneyard to my over-stimulated imagination. Every once in a while, I could hear a tree branch groaning under the strain of so much snow, and the soft hollow thud of snow falling to the ground from up high in the trees.

Ominously, a stark moon had slowly replaced the weak sun. Nerves began setting in. I stopped for a few seconds, and began surveying the snow-enveloped landscape, desperately trying to figure out my best way of getting home.

The forest was becoming darker. I wished the dirty-grey sky was clear, so that I could see the stars – the stars that had stopped Mom with a sharp intake of breath on a frosty night not so long ago, leaving her motionless, speechless and utterly still. I remembered how she stood in the back garden, her mouth agape with awe and wonder, as if she had seen a UFO.

What is it, Mom? I asked her.

God, she replied solemnly. *When you think things have become too dark in your life, always remember, that only when it's dark enough, do we get to see the brilliance of the stars.*

Just as I was about to make a move, I heard a sound, like a rough whisper.

'Who … who's there?' I listened intently. The whisper was gone, replaced by the stretching tremor of wind skimming over the hardened surface of iced snow.

'I said, who's there?' Despite the sound of my voice granting me a little bit of assurance, I was freaked out. A crafty little breeze began turning the resting snow into quivering white sails, like invisible mice running over the ground.

I decided to head in the direction of Ferguson's Bend, at the eastern end of the woods. It took me almost twenty minutes to complete what normally would have taken five, emerging just where the lake began. The lake had completely frozen over and looked like a plate of solid steel. I stopped momentarily, gazing in awe at the strength of Nature to silence and tame the restless water. It was a clean freeze. No ripple lines scarring the surface. A mist danced across the icy surface.

As my eyes lingered on the lake, I spotted something stuck in its centre. From the safety of the lake's lip I strained my eyes to see. The moon reflected blindingly across the hardened surface, conspiring with the mist to make visibility difficult.

'Looks like a wounded bird ...' I spoke out loud to give myself company.

Easing closer to a group of trees, I now wished I had Dad's binoculars for a clearer view, though in all honesty they would afford me little help at this time of night. The mist was less heavy out from under the trees, so I could see just a little bit clearer.

'A seagull or a swan. Got to be some sort of bird, trapped in the ice. What else can it be?' I needled my eyes along the surface, trying to gauge the ice's thickness. 'Might still be alive. Shit, I can't just leave it like that, in pain.'

Cautiously placing my right boot on the ice, I began springing my knee slightly, testing the ice's integrity. It seemed okay. Pretty solid. Delicately standing with one half of my body-weight resting atop the icy surface, I brought the rest of my body on board, breathing a sigh of relief when I didn't go crashing through.

I waited a few seconds before bringing my right boot forward, followed slowly by the left. I tested the ice again, slightly forcing my weight upon it. If I fell through at this stage, it wouldn't be too bad. The water would barely reach my waist.

'Easy … easy …' I moved gradually along the frozen surface, gaining confidence and momentum with each step. Something was tickling my stomach. Adrenaline coupled with nerves. Creeping closer, I now realised it wasn't a trapped bird. Wrong shape. Wrong everything.

My eyes were playing tricks, making the middle of the lake wobble and warp. Cramps were beginning to plant themselves in the calves of my legs, but I willed myself on, knowing I would be within touching distance of the object in a moment.

'Oh, shit …' I almost fell backwards, slipping on my ass. Looking up at me from beneath the ice was the face of a girl. Pitiful. Young. Her skin had a purplish hue, but it was the penetrating eyes I was forced to focus on. Dark blue. They looked like bluebottle flies, fat and greasy, feasting on her face. Her hand stuck up out of the ice, as though trying to grab hold of the air and pull herself free.

I stood still, hardly daring to breathe. I wanted to be away from this hellish place, but fear immobilised all movement. The girl's face was bobbing slightly against the ice beneath me, her lips in a perpetual 'o' as if caught by surprise. Or terror.

Without warning, the ice started making a whispery sound. Beneath me, tiny cracks began emerging, slowly webbing out in competing directions. A sickening feeling was rapidly entering my gut. The tension in my neck began trafficking all the way down to my spine, forcing muscles to stiffen like dry clay.

'Oh … no …'

I quickly stepped back, but not before reaching instinctively for the arm, pulling on it forcefully in the hope of keeping my balance. No such luck. Instead, I skidded, slip-sliding backwards before crashing downwards onto the icy surface, force opening a new, gaping wound – a wound large enough to pull me in and under. In an instant, I was inverted beneath the ice, totally disorientated. Freezing water rushed into every cavity in my body. I began pushing frantically at the iced ceiling. I groped in the darkness for the entrance wound I had caused, but found nothing but iced resistance.

Don't panic. There has to be a way out …

Without warning, the dead girl's arm attached itself my clothes. Then her face rubbed up against mine. The face looked spongy, the eyes full of pain. She had died horribly, but all I could think about was pushing her away from me, with all the force I could muster.

I kept struggling to unite a small gathering of positive if somewhat patchy thoughts on how to escape. My burning lungs, though, were not taking part in the positive thinking, and they began inflating, ready to implode.

Think!

A dull drum of death was sounding. Echoing in my brain, it began counting down from five, mocking me.

Five ...

Think!

Four ... You're finished ... you're going to die for allowing Joey to die ...

Shut up!

Three ... It's over ... No point in struggling ... Open your mouth and let the water take you ... You're dead ... You, Joey, Devlin ...

I could feel my body being jolted slightly by the water's undulation as I groped blindly along the ceiling. I was quickly becoming mentally and physically exhausted.

The escape hole where I fell through has to be here. Find it ...

Two ... Goodbye, fool ...

Bizarrely, an old horror movie entered my head. It was about a man who had been buried alive. Frantically, when he realised his fate, he began using his fingernails to scrape at the coffin's lid in a futile effort to escape the death he had always dreaded.

Now I was the one scraping frantically with my nails on the icy ceiling, no longer able to feel my fingers because of the cold. My head started ballooning. Any second now it would explode. The pain was becoming unbearable. Then, just as quickly as the pain had started, it subsided, leaving a beautiful calm throughout my entire being. I had endured the storm before the calm, and this was my reward: the serenity of the dead. Blissful death. Everything became still. I was an ice sculpture, ready to depart from this world.

Directly above the iced ceiling, my fading eyesight caught an eerie figure. It was bright, like a lamp shining through the ice.

A face? An angel?

Without warning, the figure raised one of its arms.

Kartachhhhhhhhhhhh!

A knife came rocketing through the thick ice, narrowly missing my face. The iced ceiling disintegrated into particles. Two seconds later, a hand hooked itself onto the hood of my coat, and winched me violently to the surface.

With a tormented howl, I emerged, my mouth sucking the beautiful icy air, *suck suck sucking*, drinking the freezing air too quickly, making my burning throat gag and choke.

'Hold still!' screamed the figure. 'Don't breathe so hard, otherwise the cold'll suffocate you.'

My eyes were curtained with ice. Blinded, I strained to look at the figure towering over me.

'Devlin …?' I mumbled, before finally blacking out.

CHAPTER TWENTY-THREE

Mad Momma's Murky Mystery

… with every secret thing, whether it be good,
or whether it be evil.

Ecclesiastes

I kept floating in and out of consciousness. I was in a poorly lit bedroom of sorts. The room was filled with a jarring darkness, offering no clues to my whereabouts other than a nocturnal sense of dread.

Slowly, the surrounding space began morphing into colours and shapes. Smells of incense and melting candles quickened the air. I felt hot. I felt cold. A flotilla of blood-red balloons floated above me, each depicting Devlin's face in different moods. Every now and then, one of the faces got near to mine, planting a kiss on my lips, followed by a heart-rending smile.

'I'm sorry, Devlin, for letting you down,' I mumbled. 'Sorry for –'

Pop! Pop! Pop! The balloons began popping loudly, making me jump.

'Devlin? Where are you? Come back!'

A grinning Joey Maxwell appeared out of nowhere. In his hand he held a large, lethal-looking hatpin, dipped in blood. He brought the pin's apex to my left eye, and rested it on the pupil. I waited for him to plunge the pin in, but all he did was throw his head back in laughter, mouthing the words, *pop, pop, pop.*

'You're a foolish boy.' The voice startled me, breaking my nightmare. 'Could have gotten yourself killed out there.'

A face came into view. I strained to focus. Not Devlin. Her mother, Jessica. She was sitting beside me, rubbing some sort of liquid into my skin. The pungent stench of alcohol riveted my nostrils, making them burn.

'Where … where am I?' I tried easing myself up, but had little strength. I felt lethargic, as if all my bones had been removed by some mysterious and sadistic surgeon.

'Short memory, boy? Don't recognise the place you trespassed, not so long ago?'

She continued rubbing and kneading my doughy skin.

To my embarrassment, I realised I was naked, with only a coarse blanket covering me. 'Where're … where are my clothes?'

'Getting washed and dried. The woollen blanket covering you is more than capable of keeping you warm. You don't want to be putting too much covering on this moonshine.' She rubbed harder. 'It needs to breathe. Moonshine can peel skin if it doesn't get to breathe.'

'What am I doing here?' Then it all came back in a flash. 'You ... it was you who pulled me from the water. You put yourself in danger over me.'

'Don't over-value your body's worth, boy. I was ice fishing. You were nothing more than an interruption of my cash flow.'

'You saved my life.'

'Saved your life?' There was a pane of frozen silence. Jessica Mantle kept studying me, like a cat within reach of a bird. 'I thought you were a large fish, but you turned out to be a minnow I should have thrown back.'

'How long've I been here?'

'Two days, come evening.'

'Two days!'

'You've had a fever, and done a lot of mumbling in your sleep.'

'But ... but my mom and dad, they'll be looking for me. Have you contacted them?' I tried pushing myself up from the bed, but I'd become rubberised.

'Phone lines are down. According to the radio, they're not expected to be up again until tomorrow at the earliest. Main roads are impassable, otherwise I'd have taken you to the hospital in the pick-up. Anyway, I don't know your ma and pa, so I couldn't contact them.'

'You know my dad. He's the sheriff.'

'The sheriff …?' She paused to consider this as she stared at my face. 'Yes … I can see the likeness now; not then, not when he came to inform me my daughter'd been murdered. What's your name? I can't keep calling you *boy*.'

'Tommy.'

'Tommy.' She said my name strangely, as if it meant something to her.

'He's smart, my dad. He'll find Devlin's killer, bring him to justice.'

'Will he? He's already let the killer escape justice, or don't you follow what your pa does?'

'That wasn't Dad's fault. He did everything he could.'

'But did he do everything he could? If my daughter'd belonged to a rich family, her killer would be in jail now, for life. My daughter was on trial because of me.'

'Dad said Armstrong's lawyer did that. Filled the jury's heads with shit – sorry for swearing. Said he got them to believe things they shouldn't have.'

'They believed what they *wanted* to believe. They didn't care what happened to my daughter.'

'Dad will get Armstrong in the end. You'll see.'

'Will he?' She looked at me as if I had just tried to sell her a box of lies. She wanted proof, not empty rhetoric.

'The girl!' I exclaimed, remembering. 'What happened to the girl?'

'Girl?' Jessica Mantle's forehead crinkled. 'What girl?'

'The girl, in the water, underneath the ice. You must've seen her. She was near me.'

'There wasn't anyone else in the water. You've been hallucinating since you got here.'

'I wasn't hallucinating! There *was* a girl. Young, dark eyes, sad smile … I think … I think she was dead …'

'Dead?' Jessica Mantle looked at me with something I never thought possible: pity. 'Guilt can do strange things to a soul. Can torment it to breaking point. You're filled with it, and it's crushing you. I know.'

'What?' I felt my face twitch. 'Why would I have guilt? I've nothing to be guilty about.'

'We're all guilty of something, at one time or another. Your guilt rests with Devlin. You've been talking a lot in your sleep. I've been listening. It was hard not to. The day I caught you trespassing, you were here looking for her. Weren't you? You can no longer deny that.'

I tried to think of a good lie, but couldn't. 'I just needed to see her.'

'You blame yourself for her death. Why?'

'I don't blame …' I was about to argue a lie, but didn't. 'I don't know. I should have protected her, or something.'

'That's how guilt operates. It sits in a corner like a spider, weaving silently in the dark. There was no protecting Devlin. There was nothing you could have done – nothing any of us could have done. The wheels of evil were in motion that day, and there was no bringing them to a halt until they reached their destination.'

'Devlin told me never to come here alone. Said it was dangerous.'

'She meant me.'

'You?'

'She hated me.'

'Hated? How can you say that when she took care of you?'

'She told you that, did she? Oh, she took care of me, all right.' A smile as thin as a knife blade appeared on Jessica Mantle's lips. 'In more ways than one. She was good that way. Making people dependent on her, only to snatch what she had given away when they needed it most.'

'She wasn't like that …' *Or was she? Hadn't she done the same to me?*

'No? She always gave me my medicine on time – except when she couldn't find it. Usually that happened right after I had annoyed her, or said the wrong thing. Sometimes she couldn't find my medicine for days, until I was near Death's door. Want to know how I got all these bald patches on my head, the ones you keep staring at?'

'I … I wasn't staring.'

'From bottles being smashed against it. The numerous dead wounds have left tracts where my hair will never grow again. Pretty, aren't they? Know who caused them? Devlin. Oh, she apologised, later. Even helped clean up the blood and the broken glass. But I can still see the gleam in her eyes when she saw the damage. She was glad she'd done it.'

'Don't say that.' I was getting angry. Not with Jessica Mantle, but with myself for believing her words. 'I ... I don't believe you.'

'Yes, you do. Remember when I caught you trespassing in the barn?'

'Having a shotgun stuck into my face is hard to forget.'

'I said at the time your eyes did a strange twitching when you're lying. Well, they're doing the same twitching right now. Eyes don't lie. God gave us eyes, but the Devil created tongues, the meat of deception. Devlin was a great user of people's emotion. She could make you do anything – *anything she wanted* – when she turned on the charm. As long as she was in control of the tap, and could turn it on and off when *she* decided, then everything was fine in her world.'

'I want you to stop saying bad things about Devlin.' I tried making my face look mean, but it probably looked sickly and pathetic.

'You need to hear the truth, bad or good, about her. That's the only way to break the hold she still has over you, even in death. Just over a year ago, she went into one of her blood rages, screaming at me, accusing me of being a witch, able to cast spells on her. She came at me with an axe, but I was able to run and lock myself in the bathroom. While I'm in there, it all goes quiet, and I'm trying desperately to hear where she is, what she's up to. I'm expecting her to axe the door down. Instead, there is only the soft sound of liquid sliding under the door. I thought, perhaps she's peeing outside the door, just to anger me. But just as I smell and understand what that liquid is, her chilling voice breaks the silence. "I've just poured gasoline under the door. If you don't come out, you'll burn in Hell, where you belong with all the rest of the witches." She rattled a box of matches close to the door, and sniggered. The sound was terrifying ...'

I tried to picture Devlin standing outside that door, creating a puddle of gasoline, match in hand. I shuddered, as the picture came easily to mind. I didn't want to believe it.

'Did ... did Devlin set fire to the gasoline?' I asked, not really wanting an answer.

'I could hear her fumbling with the matches, then I heard the striking of a match against the sandpapery side of the box; smelt the stench of sulphur in the air ...' Jessica Mantle seemed to recoil slightly at the memory. 'I knew that if I stayed in there, I would be burned to death. So I rushed out the door, physically tackled her down, and I knocked her out accidentally. Soon after that, they came and took her away. Six months of shock treatment she needed, before they deemed that she was no longer a threat to herself or others. No longer a threat ...'

'Was ... was she okay, then, after ... what they did to her?'

Jessica Mantle looked beyond me for a few seconds before finally answering. 'I think it made her worse, more paranoid, more mean …'

Silence crept into the room. I no longer wanted to hear bad things about Devlin.

'The lake,' I said. 'What were you doing there, at that time of night?'

'What I was doing there, was minding my business, until someone came along and interfered with that business; someone who shouldn't have been walking on thin ice.'

'I need to know. It's important to me.'

'If you really need to know, I was out hunting. That's how we … that's how *I* normally eat in this place, what the land gives. Strange, I usually avoid the lake area, as there is little game to be had, but …'

'What?'

'Something … I don't know. Something ushered me in that direction, the wind, strong, pushing me …' Her voice fell silent.

'Do you believe in ghosts?'

'Ghosts?'

'Or walking souls? Someone who protects, even if they are no longer with us?'

'No. When you're dead, you're dead.'

'I think … I think Devlin directed you to the lake, to help save me.'

'If that's what you believe, believe.'

'If she hated you, she wouldn't have brought you to the lake, to save me. Don't you see?'

Jessica Mantle walked to the door without answering.

'Mrs Mantle?'

She turned. 'Yes?'

'I'm sorry.'

'For what?'

'For thinking … for thinking you were some sort of … monster.'

My words seemed to catch her off-guard.

She pulled a tight smile across her mouth. 'Oh, but I *am* a monster. Devlin would have testified to that, had she not been murdered.'

'You shouldn't say things like that.'

'The abortion? You heard about it during the trial?'

I nodded slowly. 'I overheard my parents talking about it, when I shouldn't have. I didn't know what an abortion was, so I went to the library, over at Kansas Avenue. I searched book after book until I found what I needed. I almost threw up. The pictures inside were frightening.'

'Life is frightening. No fairy-tale ending. You better get used to that.'

'But … a baby? How could Devlin do such a horrible thing?'

'She had no say in the matter. No say whatsoever. I sent her to a … friend. Devlin thought she was going to have that baby.

What she didn't know was that I'd already decided not to allow that — couldn't allow it. The person I sent her to was an abortionist, not a doctor. Now you know the truth about why she wanted to kill me. Now you know I really am a monster.'

I stared at the door, long after Jessica Mantle had left.

CHAPTER TWENTY-FOUR

Guilt. Love. Motherly Smells.

What profit is there in my blood,
when I go down to the pit?
Psalm 30:9

'The phone lines are finally up,' Jessica Mantle said, placing a humongous breakfast in front of me, just as I sat down at the kitchen table. Her voice was matter-of-fact, as if last night's terrible revelations had never revealed themselves. 'I just got off the phone to your pa.'

'Dad? How'd he sound?' I asked, dreading the answer.

'Very concerned, as can be expected, but relieved that you're safe and well. He said he'd get here as soon as possible, but with the snow still falling, it might take some time.'

I had asked Jessica Mantle not to call Mom, who was probably waiting to flay the skin off my ass for not doing the driveway, on top of all the trouble I'd caused falling into the lake.

So inconsiderate of me, destroying all my clothes in that icy water. I doubted very much that she'd have any sympathy in her pockets with my name on it. I could picture her now, arms folded defiantly, waiting for me with her scary war-face.

'Thank you, for everything, Mrs Mantle,' I said, tucking into the enormous stack of pancakes and syrup.

'Eat,' was all she replied, before exiting the room.

It was almost two hours later, watching through the window, that I spotted the pickup approaching from the snowy nothingness. The large, bulbous vehicle with its plough attachments resembled a metal pig feeding nervously at a trough, as it gingerly worked its way through the snow. As it got closer, I recognised it as belonging to Jim Johnson, one of Dad's buddies.

The pickup stopped directly at the door and Dad stepped out from the driver's side, glancing about. I couldn't help but notice that he didn't have his happy face with him. He looked tired. I waved from the window, but he didn't acknowledge it. Perhaps he hadn't seen me? I hoped that was all it was.

Jessica Mantle met him at the door. Dad said something to her, and then reached out his hand. After a few seconds of hesitation, she took it, and they shook hands. They talked some more, and then she showed him inside.

'Here he is,' she said, opening the kitchen door.

Dad entered, stared at me, and said, 'I've had the entire force out looking for you, Tommy, along with neighbours and friends. Everyone's been sick with worry.'

'I'm sorry.'

'Sorry doesn't cut the mustard with your mother. I hope you understand that?'

'Am I in for it, with Mom?'

He ignored my question, matching it with one of his own. 'Did you thank Mrs Mantle, for all she did?'

Mrs Mantle cut in. 'He's thanked me a hundred times, Sheriff. No need for any more.'

'Okay, then, Tommy. Ready to go?'

I nodded. 'Yes …'

'Go on out to the pickup,' Dad said. 'I'll be along shortly.'

It was twenty long minutes before Dad emerged from the house. I don't know what was said between him and Jessica Mantle, but he looked anxious, an emotion he rarely exposed in public.

The moment he got back inside the pickup, I told him of the young girl in the lake. He said nothing. He probably thought I was trying to avoid the inevitable justice that awaited me from Mom, by inventing an outrageous story. Then I waited for a lecture about my conduct. Troublingly, only silence prevailed, and I was forced to listen to the drone of the engine all the way home.

The forty-minute journey seemed to last for hours, until we finally drove up our driveway. The snow shovel was still there, sticking out of the mound like a salient cross on a grave – mine.

Dad turned off the annoying engine, and then looked at me. 'I guess it's time to pay the piper.'

I wasn't too sure what he meant, but it didn't sound good.

'Pay the piper? Who's the piper?'

'Remember the Pied Piper of Hamelin?'

'The guy that chased all the rats?'

'Remember the townspeople didn't pay him, after agreeing the deal?'

'Yes, they went back on their word.'

'The consequence was losing their children to the lure of his pipes. That's why you must always pay your debts, Tommy. Always. No ifs, ands or buts. Clear?'

'I … I think so.'

'Good. Well, you're about to pay the piper in the form of your mother. You've put her through Hell on earth, this last couple of days, and I don't think she's in a debt-forgiving mood.'

I knew I still had Mom to contend with, but strangely, I was more concerned with Dad believing me about the girl in the lake. 'You don't believe me, about the young girl in the lake, do you?'

He sighed. 'Right now, Tommy, I've other things on my mind. Come on. Let's go.'

I followed him to the door, feeling like a condemned prisoner going to the electric chair.

Dad opened the door, and there stood Mom in the hallway, her face knotted.

'I'm taking the pickup back over to Jim's. See you both later,' he said, leaving me alone with my executioner.

'Well, Mister? What've you got to say for yourself?' Mom said, looking as if she were about to give me a karate chop in the neck.

I shrugged my shoulders. 'I'm sorry ...'

'Sorry? *Sorry*?'

The way Mom said the second 'sorry' made me jump. The word sizzled with venom, like fat burning on a hot pan.

'I ... I just wasn't thinking,' I finally mumbled.

'Thinking? Ha! That's your problem, you *never* think about anything other than what *you* want. Do you know what we've gone through, this last couple of days? No word from you. Nothing. We thought the worst had happened. That you'd been ...'

Her words trailed off, but I was certain 'abducted' would have come next.

'The phone lines were down, Mom, so there was no way I could call.'

'An answer for everything, as usual. What on earth were you doing, walking on the frozen lake? I suppose you have an answer for that too?'

'I ... I thought I saw something, someone, in the middle of the lake. I *did* see someone. I just ... well ...'

Mom made a movement towards me. I held my breath, steeling myself for the parental punishment, hoping it would be swift and not too painful. But instead of a whack to the head, she grabbed me, and pulled me into her warm and lovely-smelling body.

I could feel her warmth oozing through the sweater Dad had bought her last Christmas. She smelled of soap and that special smell all moms have. It made me feel safe, tenting in her clothing, feeling all lost parts rushing together; parts I had never experienced before. Everything was going to be okay. My only wish was to stay in this embrace for as long as possible, because I knew she would probably never embrace me again. It wasn't in her nature.

'Don't *ever* do anything like this again. Do you understand?' she said, tightening her grip, as if fearful I would flee back to the woods.

'Yes,' I feebly replied.

'Good. Now, go and have a hot shower,' she said, ushering me away, not allowing me to see the tears staining her eyes. 'You stink.'

CHAPTER TWENTY-FIVE

Guardian Angel

Nothing contributes so much to tranquillise the mind as a steady purpose.

Mary Shelley, **Frankenstein**

'I just got off the phone to Mrs Mantle,' Mom said, sitting down at the table for dinner later that same day. 'What do you say to a woman who has just saved your son's life?'

Mom seemed to be directing the question at herself, but Dad answered her. He looked uncomfortable. His tone was edgy.

'There's nothing you can say, except "thank you". That's the answer in a nutshell.'

Mom stared at Dad for a few seconds. She obviously didn't like his tone of voice. I thought she was going to say something in response. She didn't.

'Do you realise just how lucky you were that Mrs Mantle was in the area when you fell through the ice?' Mom said, directing this next question to me. 'Your guardian angel must've been watching over you.'

'I suppose so ...' I mumbled through a mouthful of spaghetti. What I really wanted to say was that Mom was right on the money about the guardian angel. A guardian angel named Devlin.

'You still haven't explained to us why you were out on the lake in the first place.'

I swallowed what was in my mouth before answering. 'A ... girl. I saw a girl.'

'Girl? What girl?' Mom looked confused. 'No one told me about a girl.'

It sounded like an accusation, the way she said it.

'That's the reason I was on the ice. I thought it was a wounded bird, but it was a girl.'

'You saw a girl on the ice? What on earth was she doing out there, at that time of night?'

'She wasn't *on* the ice, Mom, she was *underneath.*'

'Underneath ...?' Mom's face went into total puzzlement.

'I saw her when I fell through ... she was dead.'

A brick of silence fell into the room, landing directly on the table. A horrified Mom looked across at Dad, who in turn looked at me. It was hard to read his face, but he looked very uncomfortable.

'There really was a girl, Dad. I saw her.'

Dad put his fork down, and looked at Mom, then me.

'Tommy, you were in a state of shock. You almost died out there. People see things in terrible situations. Unexplainable things.'

'I wasn't seeing things.' Anger was beginning to rise up in me.

'You said that about the snowman, don't forget.'

'I *know* what I saw.'

'We can discuss this later, Tommy. Right now, I want to enjoy this meal.'

'Shouldn't you check it out, Frank?' Mom said, looking terribly concerned. 'Just to make sure?'

'There's been no report of any girl missing, either here or in surrounding counties. I checked, as soon as I got home. Anyway, I don't have the resources, Helen. It's not realistic to just go and dredge the lake, looking for a supposedly dead girl. Do you know how many men and hours it would take, in these conditions?'

'I suppose an awful lot. I'm sure Mrs Mantle didn't wonder about resources, when she risked her own life to save your son.'

Dad looked as if he had just been kicked in the balls by an angry mule. 'That's unfair, Helen.'

Mom stood. She had hardly touched her meal. 'There's hot apple pie in the kitchen. Help yourselves. I'm going to bed.'

Unlike the pie, Mom's voice was cold. I couldn't look at Dad. The last thing I wanted was to cause an argument between him and Mom, but I knew what I had seen out there beneath the frozen grey ice, and it wasn't a figment of my imagination.

Dad stood up, looked at me for a moment, and then left the room. A few seconds later, I heard the hub door slam, hard. The prodigal son had screwed things up, big time. As usual.

CHAPTER TWENTY-SIX

The Dummy Exposed

Don't let us make imaginary evils, when you know we have so many real ones to encounter.

Oliver Goldsmith, **The Good-Natured Man**

Fourteen men were involved in combing the lake, beginning at first light the next day. They were mostly volunteers – part-time firemen, ex-deputies and a couple of lumberjacks. Most owed Dad something for some favour or other he had done them, over the years. Now he was calling in those favours.

I could tell his pride wasn't too happy about asking all these men for help, as he stood beside me on the embankment, walkie-talkie in hand. He had tried to keep the search secret, restricted to those taking part, but a couple of local reporters had somehow gotten wind of it. They were taking photos of the search team, and doing their utmost to find out what the hell was going on.

The search was organised into three teams, armed with an assortment of misfit contraptions, ranging from lethal-looking chainsaws to downright ugly and rusted augers. From the embankment, they looked like a medieval hunting pack.

For two grueling hours, they tormented the ice, taking turns to chip and erase, all the while inching three small rowing boats agonisingly slowly towards the aperture of my departure into Hell. The original hole was practically refrozen, with barely visible telltale scars on the surface. But it didn't fool me for one second.

'That's it! That's where I fell through the ice!' I said, as one of the boats touched the frozen, jagged scar.

'You're sure, Tommy?' said Dad.

'I'll never forget it.'

Dad quickly spoke into the walkie-talkie. 'Okay, Jack. Let's take it from there. Tommy reckons that's where he crashed through the ice.'

'Okay, Frank,' came the metallic reply on the walkie-talkie. 'Bob and Red are suited up. They're gonna take the first dive.'

'Tell them to be careful. Not to take any chances. The freezing temperature won't be long resealing any holes we make.'

'You got it.'

Bob Hays and Sean 'Red' McRae were both part-time deputies, the other part of their time – the major part – being taken up with hunting, fishing and all means of outdoor activity. They had both rescued people from the lake in the past, and both knew the deep waters like the backs of their gnarled but skillful hands.

The rest of the men frantically hacked at the ice, creating enough space for Bob and Red to work in. Then, about twenty minutes later, the two divers slipped into the hole. They looked like James Bond in *Thunderball*, slick and cool. But just watching them disappear into the freezing water made me shiver.

'Dad?'

'Yes?'

'You're not mad at me, are you, for all this?'

Dad looked at me, and then removed his pipe from his pocket. He lit the pipe up and exhaled smoky curlicues above his head. The smell of burning tobacco made me think of home, warmth and comfort. I wanted to be back there, right now, reading *Green Lantern* or *The Flash*.

He didn't answer my question, preferring to ask me one instead. 'Do you know what a paradox is, Tommy?'

'No,' I said, shrugging my shoulders. I could hardly pronounce the word without slaughtering it, let alone know its meaning.

'I hope you're right about this, Tommy. But I'm also hoping you're wrong. That's a paradox.'

I was still confused, but didn't ask him to explain further. Instead, I just took in the aroma of his pipe, and sealed the scene into memory. Years from now, I would remember it with fondness, rather than with the trepidation gnawing my stomach at that moment.

Twenty minutes went by. Nothing. Then Bob and Red reappeared. I could barely see the tops of their heads, but they resembled sea lions. They seemed to be talking to one of the other men in the boat. Then they slipped back into the water.

'Frank?' said the metallic voice of Jack on the walkie-talkie. 'Bob and Red think they've spotted something. Not too sure what, but they're going back down to investigate further.'

'Jack, I don't want them down there too long, in case of hypothermia,' Dad said, bringing the walkie-talkie close to his mouth. 'The next time they come up, they stay up.'

'Okay, Frank, but you know what they're like, once they get the scent of something. Two damn bloodhounds.'

For the longest time, Bob and Red stayed submerged. Dad was looking increasingly worried. He was just about to speak into the walkie-talkie when Bob and Red surfaced. A commotion ensued as the other members of the team pulled them onto the boat. A few seconds later, a third person was pulled on board.

'I told you!' I said triumphantly. 'I told you she was there. Now you believe me?'

'Jack?' Dad said, frantically talking into the walkie-talkie, ignoring me. 'Jack, what's happening? Did they find her?'

The walkie-talkie crackled. Dad held it to his ear.

'Frank …? We've got her, but …'

'But what? What the hell's going on?'

'Frank … we're coming back. Don't want to say anything on the air, in case someone's eavesdropping. Be there shortly.'

There was a terrible stone of silence. Dad looked at the walkie-talkie as if it were an unexploded hand grenade.

'What is it?' I asked. 'What's happening?'

Dad didn't answer. Instead, he watched the boats slowly edging towards us, returning to the embankment.

Jack quickly jumped out and came straight to Dad.

'What the hell happened, Jack?'

'It … it was a mannequin, Frank. Lifelike, yes, but a damn mannequin, all the same.'

'No way!' I shouted. 'I know what I saw.'

'*Quiet*,' said Dad, in his don't-have-me-say-that-twice voice.

We stood in silence, as the team carried the naked and mud-covered mannequin over, dropping it onto the snow beside me.

'Give her a kiss, Tommy,' Red grinned, still in his diving suit.

'A mannequin …' Dad just shook his head. His face had an expression on it, but I couldn't tell if it was shock or anger.

I stared at the mannequin, the large eyes and sad smile, and for the first time, doubt took over. It hadn't been a girl, after all. Just a life-like piece of moulded plastic, no better than one of Horseshoe's *Aurora* monster kits. Jessica Mantle had been right.

Guilt confuses the mind. Guilt had made me see things that were never there in the first place.

'Sorry about this, Red,' Dad said.

'Think nothing of it, Frank. Better safe than sorry, says my book. What do you want me to do with that?' Red said, pointing at the mannequin.

'I'll take it home and dispose of it. Damn clothing stores, dumping their crap in the lake …'

Over the next hour, the men slowly packed up. Dad thanked each of them as they left. He looked terribly embarrassed. A couple of them looked at me, grins on their faces.

'Put that mannequin in the trunk,' Dad said gruffly, not looking at me as he headed for the vehicle.

I grabbed the mannequin by the feet and dragged it to the car, before opening the trunk and dumping it inside.

I walked to the passenger side and slid in as silently as possible, trying to pretend I wasn't there. Dad was glancing out at the lake, the scene of his humiliation. I'm sure he wanted to kill me at that particular moment. He seemed lost. It was the same look he had when speaking to Jessica Mantle the day he came to collect me.

'There *was* a girl in there, Dad,' I said, finally breaking the tormenting silence. 'I know what I saw.'

Dad turned, and glared at me. 'Just like you saw Norman Armstrong standing naked outside our house, freezing his ass off?'

'Armstrong *was* there.' I felt frustrated anger bubbling up in me.

'You made a mistake. That's all. A person who makes no mistakes makes nothing. Making mistakes is nothing to be ashamed of. We all do it. I've made quite a few of them lately.'

'I know what I saw.'

Dad sighed. 'Look, Tommy, I understand you're going through a lot right now. It hasn't been easy for you, but now it's time to move on. I don't want to hear another word about any girl in the lake – ever. Clear?'

Reluctantly, I nodded. 'Yes …'

Little did we know, we were *both* going to hear plenty more words about it. *Lots* of words, in fact. The fan was just about to get hit with an awful lot of proverbial shit.

CHAPTER TWENTY-SEVEN

Who's the Real Dummy Now?

No life that breathes with human breath
Has ever truly longed for death.

Tennyson, **The Two Voices**

'Dummy Discovers Dummy,' shouted the headline on page six of the evening newspaper, two days later. The story claimed Dad had lost the plot, and that he was looking for a mysterious girl, only to find a wax dummy: 'The bigger mystery is why on earth is Sheriff Henderson wasting our hard-earned tax dollars and resources on a wild goose chase? Is he deliberately trying to make the town look like it's full of chawbacon fools? Shouldn't he be out looking for the murderer of Devlin Mantle?'

It made little difference that all the people involved in the search had volunteered their time and equipment, and that the town wasn't out one red cent for the search operation.

No, that particular salient fact of the story wouldn't sell newspapers, so better to disregard it. Better something with a bit more *oomph*.

'Who do they think they are, writing that garbage?' Mom seethed, barely controlling her anger.

'Don't let it upset you, Helen. It's just a story to sell newspapers,' Dad said, cleaning out his pipe, ignoring the newspaper glaring up at him from the table. He looked blasé, but I could see it was an act. He was obviously upset about the whole stinking episode – big time. 'It'll be forgotten by tomorrow.'

'I've a good mind to go down to their office and punch him right on the nose, that Mister – what's his name?' She grabbed the newspaper, and glanced at the hack's name. 'Mister Jonathan Pistorious ...' Her face flushed. 'Well ... an appropriate name, if I should say so myself.'

Dad burst out laughing. I grinned, even though I didn't really get the joke at first.

For a second, Mom looked uncomfortable at Dad laughing. Then *she* started, laughing like a schoolgirl on a first date. I had never heard her laugh like that. So strange. Then Dad was at it, laughing louder than Mom, like it was a laugh-out-loud competition. I just sat quietly, embarrassed and slightly unnerved by their weird behaviour. Was something deeper happening here? Something my adolescence and spongy brain couldn't absorb?

Mom reached over and touched Dad's hand, tenderly. They looked into each other's eyes, as if meeting for the first time in their lives. My neck became hot.

I was totally invisible to them, so I slipped secretly out, heading for my room. Just as I reached the first stair, the phone rang.

'Answer that, Tommy!' Dad shouted.

I did. It was Deputy Hillman.

'Your father there, Tommy?' he said, in an excited voice.

'Yes. Hold on, I'll get him.'

'Who is it, Tommy?' Dad said, coming to the phone.

'Deputy Hillman. Sounds urgent.'

Dad took the phone. He had a short conversation with Deputy Hillman, before hanging the phone up. He went very quiet. Looked at me gravely.

'What? What'd I do now?' I said.

'Two locals, ice fishing, have just discovered a body, not too far from where Red and Bob originally dived. It's a young girl.'

CHAPTER TWENTY-EIGHT

The Monster Again

Deep into that darkness peering,
long I stood there wondering, fearing ...
*Edgar Allan Poe, **The Raven***

The unknown girl in the lake quickly became a household name in town. The media began filling pages and airwaves with detail after detail on her tragic life.

Jordan Taylor was only thirteen when a monster decided to torture her young body, sexually and sadistically, and then savagely murder her. Jordan had been placed in an orphanage at age six, before being bounced from foster home to foster home, eventually boomeranging full-circle back to the orphanage at age ten. Three weeks ago, she had 'simply disappeared', never to be seen alive again. The orphanage, Saint Peter's on the Rock, issued a terse and somewhat impassive statement to the press. Jordan had a habit of absconding from the orphanage, it said, and the 'excellent and dedicated' staff had done all in their power to prevent her from leaving.

Prevent her from leaving ... a more telling statement than they had intended, I suspected.

From the pictures in the newspapers, Saint Peter's on the Rock looked more like the other infamous Rock, Alcatraz, than a caring institute for orphans. The intimidating gates of the building were cloud-touching in height, crowned with spikes shaped as spearheads. Lethal-looking razorwire snaked over the filthy grey walls, like some prehistoric reptile searching for victims. The creepy place gave me the burning shits, just looking at it. Edgar Allen Poe would have loved to roam its corridors.

Almost a week had now slipped by since the recovery of Jordan's body, but the media were still carrying stories about her – albeit now relegated to the pages of lesser importance. She'd long been moved from the front pages, replaced by some political scandal in Washington.

On Saturday at breakfast, I spotted the photo of Jordan in the morning newspaper. The grainy image, taken the previous year, could have been from fifty years ago. She looked like an old lady. Unsmiling. Haggard. Tormented eyes. I wondered what hell she'd gone through in that terrible place?

Alongside Jordan's photo was one of me. It was the same photo used by the newspapers when I had tried to rescue Joey. There was an accompanying article by Jonathan Pistorious – the same creep who had done the hatchet job on Dad. Pistorious had tried to give the article an air of mystery, obviously hoping to hook as many readers as possible.

'*What is the strange – and as yet, unexplained – connection between Sheriff Henderson's son, Tommy, and the three young people whose lives have all ended violently in and around Jackson's Lake? Sources have informed me that Tommy Henderson and Devlin Mantle were actually young lovers, and that –*'

'I don't want you reading any more about that young girl, and especially anything written by that disgusting man,' Mom said, snapping the newspaper from my fingers, before sitting down for her breakfast. 'Your father should have brought this rag with him to work, instead of leaving it here.'

Oddly, Dad had left the house just before I came down, even though it was his day off.

'But I want to know about Jordan, what sort of life she had.'

'You won't get her real life from newspapers, I can assure you; just the parts they can sell for profit. Now, eat your breakfast. I don't want to hear any more discussion about Jordan Taylor. Her death has cast a dark cloud over this house, and made everyone miserable. Even your father has become quieter than usual since her body was recovered.'

Mom was right about the dark cloud, but wrong about Dad. His mood had changed dramatically, all right, but that change dated from the time he went to pick me up at Jessica Mantle's house, and had that long and whispery discussion with her. Something was gnawing at him, but knowing Dad, he would never discuss it. Now, most evenings after work, he would go and sit in the hub, in complete silence, not even listening to his music. Mom said to just leave him be, that he'd soon be his old self again, given a bit of time.

As far as I could see, the more time he was given, the darker his mood became. I knew he was drinking in the hub – something he very rarely did. I also knew Mom had had words with him about the drinking, the thin walls of our house being a great conduit for all things private. I had never known why Mom disapproved of alcohol so much, until a few nights ago, when she was having one of her 'silent' arguments with Dad in their bedroom.

'Why are you doing this to yourself, and to me, Frank?'

'I'm only having a drink, Helen. Stop making such a big deal out of nothing.'

'Big deal out of nothing? How can you say that, Frank Henderson? You know my father died an alcoholic. You know I've always detested it and –'

'*I'm* not a damn alcoholic – though God alone knows how I've never become one, listening to your persistent nagging. And what about your sister? She's a walking – when she *can* walk – advertisement for Jack Daniel's.'

There was a terrible silence after that last statement, then a loud banging of a door. I could hear Mom making her way downstairs, into the kitchen. It was the first time I had ever heard them argue like that. I hoped it was the last.

Over the next couple of days, frostiness quickly developed between them – and it had nothing to do with the sub-zero temperature outside.

'Stop daydreaming and finish your breakfast,' Mom said, getting up from the table.

'Where's Dad? Thought he was off today?'

'After you've finished, go outside and play,' she said, deliberately ignoring my question.

'But it's freezing out there.'

'Do something useful then. Get your room sorted out. It's a mess. I'm going to stay with Aunt Katherine for a few days, and I want you to behave yourself while I'm gone. Don't be getting up to any tricks.'

'Aunt Katherine's? Why?' I said, as if I didn't know about the arguing.

'She …' Mom looked flustered. 'She isn't well. I'm going to look after her for a while. That's all. If you didn't have a few more days left in school before the Christmas break, I'd have brought you with me. I know how much you love visiting her.'

'That's okay,' I said, trying to sound disappointed, all the while hoping she wouldn't see the joy in my eyes. 'You'll be back before Christmas, though, won't you?'

Christmas? That was a joke. The Christmas tree languishing in the corner, unlit and unloved, was a depressing-looking specimen. The decorations, thrown haphazardly at it, had anger written all over them. This was the festive season? A wake would have had more festivity.

'Of course I'll be back for Christmas. What a silly question. I'm only going for a few days. Now, there's lots of food in the fridge. I've frozen plenty of pasta for you and your father, and there's meatloaf for tonight. Now, while I'm away, I don't want you leaving the television on all day. Do you understand?'

'Yes.'

'Make sure you clean your teeth and wash your face.'

'Mom, I'm not a kid. I know what important things have to be done.' And cleaning my teeth and washing my face wasn't on the list.

'Right then, I'm going to clear up here, but before I do I want you to go and tidy your room. I'll be in to have a look.'

'Okay,' I mumbled, pushing my chair out from the table and heading in the direction of my room. I'd tidy the room up a bit, just enough to keep Mom out of my hair, and then finish off my latest *Green Lantern* comic.

I spent at least an hour arranging and tidying my room. Sort of. After that, I counted my towers of comic books for the umpteenth time, like a miser with a hidden cache of gold. I thought about going over to Horseshoe's, to watch 'Valley of The Dinosaurs' and see if the Butler family could finally get back home with the help of their caveman friend Gorak. It wasn't the kind of thing I boasted about, watching kids' TV shows, but I enjoyed cartoons. Horseshoe, on the other hand, couldn't care less what anyone thought about his viewing habits.

'Tommy?' Mom called from the bottom of the stairs. 'I'm going now.'

'Okay,' I shouted back.

'Don't you have a message for Aunt Katherine?'

Yes, but I doubted she'd like to hear it. 'Tell her I hope to see her soon.' *When I'm about sixty.*

'Get to bed early. I'll be checking. And don't forget to clean your teeth at night and in the morning.'

Before I could lie, the front door slammed. Then silence. I listened as the car started up, and slowly eased down the snowy driveway.

I thought again about heading over to Horseshoe's, but instead made my way downstairs. I peeped out the window, just to make sure Mom *was* gone, and not up to some trick, trying to catch me doing something I wasn't supposed to be doing. Like what I was about to do any second now.

I left the window and went directly back upstairs and into the hub. Inside, I glanced about. The place looked unusually cluttered. Dad wasn't a neat freak, but he was tidy. Some of his *National Geographic* magazines had fallen on the floor, and had been left untouched. Worryingly, the Jim Beam bottle was empty, and two others had joined it, each having met the same fate.

Newspaper clippings lay scattered on the desk. I sat down

on his chair and picked a couple up. They were all about killings and deaths: Joey's, Devlin's and now Jordan's, all intermingled in a grisly trilogy. A couple of the clippings showed Armstrong leaving court, trying to hide his smirking face from the cameras. From the grey paper, his penetrating eyes peered up at mine. I shuddered, and looked quickly behind, as if expecting him to be standing there.

Go over to Horseshoe's, said a voice in my head. *You don't need to be reading these clippings.* But instead of listening, I went to the Bible, retrieved Dad's diary from its stomach, and began flipping through the pages until I found the entry I wanted. It was dated two days after he had picked me up at Mrs Mantle's.

Went to pick Tommy up at Jessica Mantle's home. What a relief when we received that phone call from her, saying Tommy was safe. Helen and I had gone through Hell the past couple of days, thinking the worst had happened to Tommy. How could any parent survive mentally after burying a child? I simply can't comprehend. I know I would die of a broken heart if anything ever happened to Tommy. My talk with Jessica Mantle brought it all home to me. Modestly, she brushed away all talk of being a hero for saving Tommy. I'm indebted to her. Always ...

Perhaps if I had listened to Theodore Maxwell the night he appeared at my home, Devlin would be alive? Perhaps if I hadn't been so stringent with the law, I could at least have put Armstrong on notice that I was watching his every move, even if it violated his 'rights'? Perhaps my eyes on Armstrong's back would have unnerved him? Too late now. Far too late for the dead.

I stood for what seemed an eternity, staring at Dad's words, before turning to leaf through the rest of the pages. I stopped at the very last entry, made three nights ago, obviously in reference to Jordan.

Another innocent life brutally taken. Where is the justice, people ask me? Where is the justice, I ask myself? I'm beginning to have doubts about justice, about my job, and about myself.

The end of this last entry chilled me:

Payment of some sort has to be made. Ultimately, we all have to pay the piper, sooner or later, if we are to prevent any more of our young people from being abused and murdered.

I sat staring at the page, as if it were a dead thing in my hand. There was little doubt in my mind that Dad was planning to do something to Armstrong. It was only a question of when. He wouldn't get away with it, of course. Dad was a great cop, but a lousy detective. He'd leave telltale clues everywhere, because he wasn't thinking clearly. The alcohol would see to that. He simply didn't have the imagination for what needed to be done – more importantly, to get away with what needed to be done. I pictured him being arrested and hauled off to Sing Sing, where all his enemies waited for him, nursing ancient grudges, shanks in their filthy hands.

An hour went by before I finally decided to go over to Horseshoe's. I decided he would be a good distraction, to help clear my head.

I arrived too late for 'Valley of The Dinosaurs', but Horseshoe enthusiastically filled me in on all the details, even mimicking the characters' voices in a creepy low droll. Later, Mrs Cooper made pizza, and we all sat around a blazing fire, listening to Horseshoe's dad playing a harmonica and acoustic guitar, just like Bob Dylan – though not as good.

The entire house was one giant aromatic smell of Christmas: cinnamon, cut oranges, cloves, apples, gingerbread cookies, mint candy canes and fallen pine needles from the flawlessly decorated Christmas tree.

I looked at Horseshoe, and then at his parents, thinking how perfect a family they were. For one sad moment, the beautiful scene made me feel terribly alone. I thought of Dad, hiding in a whiskey bottle, and of Mom gone to her sister's, for God knew how long. I thought of our miserable Christmas tree, and a house filled with silence and animosity. I thought of the bastard responsible for it all. Armstrong.

'Are you okay, Tommy?' a concerned-looking Mrs Cooper said.

'Huh?'

'Is everything okay? You ... you seem a bit sad.'

'Sad? No! I'm fine, Mrs Cooper. Really ...'

'Why don't you stay tonight, do a sleepover?' Mrs Cooper looked unconvinced by my answer, as if she knew something sure as hell was wrong. 'If you like, I'll give your mom a call, get her permission.'

'Yeah, Tommy, that'd be great!' Horseshoe enthused. 'You can even have the top bunk.'

'I ... thanks, Mrs Cooper, but ... I've a lot of homework to get through,' I lied, not wanting Mrs Cooper to know about Mom and Dad fighting. 'Perhaps some other time ...'

'Any time you want, Tommy.'

Horseshoe looked as if I had just rammed my fingers into his eyes. As soon as his mom left the room, he said, 'What the hell, Tommy? What was all that bullshit about doing homework?'

'It's not bullshit, Horseshoe. I'm behind in my schoolwork.'

'So? That never stopped you before. You always catch up eventually.'

'Yeah, I know, but Dad's really clamping down. Don't you think I'd rather stay here and have some fun with you, than have my nose stuck in homework books?'

Horseshoe sighed. 'Yeah, I guess you're right. I was just thinking we could have done a Monster Night, with you telling one of your horror stories with the lights out. You're a great storyteller, Tommy.'

'We'll definitely do one, Horseshoe. Don't worry. I've more scary stories than you can imagine ...'

It was late evening when I left Horseshoe's, heading for home. Snow was coming down with a vengeance. A whiteout. The first warning sign to hit me in the face was Dad's car, parked outside the house. The driver-side door was wide open, and exposed to the elements.

I ran to the car, and looked inside. Dad wasn't there. My stomach tightened. Something was wrong. I slammed the door shut and quickly headed for the house. The front door was open also, the whipping snow gathering inside in increasing mounds. I quickly closed it, shouting, 'Dad! Dad, where are you?'

A light from upstairs caught my attention. The door to the hub was ajar. I knew I had closed it behind me – I always carefully covered my tracks. I ran upstairs, fearful of what was waiting there.

'Dad? You in there?'

Inside was Dad's body, sprawled out on the carpet, motionless. Suspecting the worst, I threw myself down beside him. But instead of blood, it was the overpowering stench of booze that attacked my nostrils.

I wrapped a floppy arm around my neck and attempted to heave him up from the floor, but his dead weight was far too much for me.

'Dad? You've got to get up. C'mon!' There was annoyance in my voice now. I tried again to shift him, and once again failed. Defeated, I stood over him. 'If Mom could see you now. Look at the state you're in.'

A groggy, hesitant response came from his mouth. 'What … is it? … What do … want? Who … who you?'

Dad was never a drinker, per se. Yes, he would have a beer watching baseball on the TV while cheering on the New York Mets, but other that that, he was little-league, especially if you compared him to Aunt Katherine down in Jersey, with her .300 batting average of slugging down Jack Daniel's Old No.7. I had never seen Dad drunk. Ever. After tonight, I wouldn't be able to say that again.

'C'mon, Dad. Let's get you to bed.' I pulled at his arm. 'It's me, Tommy.'

'Tommy …? Oh! Tommy! Good old Tommy … let's have a drink to good old Tommy.' His voice was slurred. It scared me to hear its ragged rhythm. Slowly, he moved, pushing himself up, guided by my pull. The skin of his face was crisscrossed with carpet creases and angry red blotches. Beside him lay the diary, open.

'C'mon, Dad. I'll help you into bed.'

Dad swooned slightly before steadying himself. Bloodshot veins collected at the corners of his tired eyes. He patted me on the cheek.

'You're a good son … a damn good son …'

'I know. The best in the world. Now, let's be having you. You'll feel a lot better in the morning.' That was when I noticed the dried stains on his face, like a snail trail on garden stones. He had obviously been crying. I was shocked. Dad always said, crying never solved a single thing. Crying was for the *dying* – not the living, not even the dead.

'A bourbon. I need a shot of bourbon, Tommy. Get me the bottle of Jim Beam from the bottom drawer in my desk, will you? Just to dampen my thirst. Know what I mean?' Dad winked.

'You've had enough to drink, Dad. Let's get you to bed. Mom'll be home shortly. You don't want her to see you like this.'

'Mom? Ha! Didn't you hear?' Dad laughed sarcastically. 'She isn't coming back. It's just you and me, Son. Your mother's had enough of a failure like me for a husband and sheriff.'

'Don't talk like that,' I replied, trying to sound calm. The alcohol was confusing him. He had his facts all wrong. Mom *would* be back. I was certain of it. Almost. 'You're the best sheriff the town has ever had. Everyone knows that. You're not a failure.'

'Not a failure? God help us if that's true. All those kids dead because I let a monster outwit me ... useless ...' He pulled at his badge, ripping the cotton from his shirt as if it were paper. He flung the badge angrily across the room. 'I'm not worthy to have that, pinned like a peacock to my chest.'

It took me almost half an hour to coerce and cajole him into bed. By the time I was finished, I was exhausted mentally and physically. I wished now that I'd stayed at Horseshoe's, instead of witnessing Dad's drunken humiliation.

I went back to the hub to get Dad's badge, and just as I spotted it in the corner, something else caught my peripheral. An object, black and lumpy. I knew what it was, even before I picked it up: Dad's service revolver.

Something wasn't right. Dad was strict when it came to guns. Drunk or sober, he would empty the gun's chambers and lock it away in the gun cabinet.

Cautiously but expertly, holding the weapon away from my face, I checked it. I was shocked. It was loaded. Even more worryingly, the safety catch was off. A big no-no in Dad's bible: *Never* ever *take the safety off. Once you take that off, you only have the safety net of quick thinking to prevent your happy little trigger finger determining the outcome …*

'What were you going to do, Dad?' I picked the diary up from the floor. I read the open page in a whisper. *'Payment of some sort has to be made. Ultimately, we all have to pay the piper, sooner or later …'*

That was when I finally decided to kill Armstrong. For Joey and Devlin, for Jordan Taylor and all the other nameless victims whose lives he had shattered. I wouldn't allow Armstrong to torment Dad any more, or to destroy our family. I wouldn't allow Dad to go to jail.

It was time to face the monster. To slay it. On my own.

CHAPTER TWENTY-NINE

Preparing to Hunt the Monster

*Facing it – always facing it – that's the way
to get through. Face it!*
Joseph Conrad

The next morning at breakfast, Dad was hurting – in more ways than one. He hadn't shaved, and looked old and dishevelled. His bloodshot eyes squinted across the table at my own lack-of-sleep bloodshot eyes. I couldn't read his mind, but I could guess he was more than embarrassed about last night.

I placed a plate of burnt toast and watery eggs down in front of him, alongside a cup of coffee. Dregs, larger than nail heads, haplessly rearranged themselves in iffy oily patterns on the surface of the coffee. Dad looked at the liquid suspiciously, before turning his attention on me.

'Did you go to bed late, Tommy? Your eyes look kinda red.'

'No later than usual.' *Oh, I was up all night, planning the perfect murder.*

'What … what time did I come home at?'

I shrugged my shoulders, and tried to sound casual. 'Don't know. I was at Horseshoe's. Oh, I'll be staying over there tonight, if that's okay?'

'Is it okay with the Coopers?'

'Yes.'

'Then it's okay with me.'

'We're doing a Monster Night special.'

'Monster Night? Shouldn't you keep that stuff for Halloween?'

'Any dark night's good for Monster Night.'

'Well, just make sure you behave yourself.'

'Mrs Cooper doesn't take any crap.'

'No, she doesn't. That's why Horseshoe is such a good kid. Got good parents.'

'You haven't touched your breakfast. It's not too bad, if I say so myself.' I forced some nearly-cooked egg down my throat, even though my stomach was knotted. I almost retched.

'I don't feel like eating right now. I'll have something later.' He pushed the plate away, before sipping bravely on the coffee. 'Great coffee, though. Hitting the spot.'

'Good to the last drop,' I sang.

Dad forced a smile, and then became serious. 'Listen, Tommy. I've a load of work to do, over at the jail. I'll probably be out most of the day. You're going to have to fend for yourself until I get back. Is that okay?'

'Sure.' Since sitting down, neither of us had dared to mention Mom.

'There's plenty of food in the fridge. Any problems, you've got my number.'

'I'll probably be in Horseshoe's anyway, so I'll probably not see you until tomorrow.'

'I'll do the washing up,' Dad said, pushing away from the table, coffee in hand. 'Then I'll get going.'

An hour later, he was dressed and shaven and looking almost like his old self. He was preparing to leave when I stopped him at the door.

'You must have dropped this, Dad,' I said, reaching out my hand, revealing his badge. 'I buffed it up a little, to make sure it shines.'

Dad stared at the badge, and then sheepishly at me.

'Thanks, Son,' was all he said, before disappearing out the door, badge in a closed fist.

The moment I heard the car leaving, I quickly ran upstairs to the hub. I grabbed Dad's flashlight, before heading into my room to get dressed in heavy winter clothing. Suitably attired, I made my way to the back of the house and grabbed a shovel. There was only one thing on my mind, and I needed to act fast.

On the journey to Black's Cemetery, I hoped for two things:

firstly, not to run into Horseshoe or Brent; and secondly, that what I had come to look for was still there.

The snow-covered cemetery gave me the shits even more than usual when I finally arrived. It was deathly quiet – as Horseshoe liked to wisecrack – but there was something additionally ominous about today's deathly quietness. I kept looking over my shoulder, expecting to be ambushed at any moment by some sort of graveyard ghoul; worse, Armstrong, leaping from behind one of the tombstones, grabbing me.

It took me almost twenty minutes to locate the old uprooted tree, and as I began shoveling away the snow surrounding it, I hoped beyond hope that it still concealed the Luger. I wasn't certain the gun was still here. There was a strong possibility that Brent would have moved it to another spot, after the botched 'hit' on Armstrong. But one thing I *was* certain of – he wouldn't have got rid of it totally. Too tempting. Too powerful a tool in his inventory of bad-guy muscle.

When the shovel finally hit something metallic, my heart skipped a beat. Suddenly, I was torn. It was one of Dad's paradoxes – I wanted the gun to be there, knowing what had to be done; but a big part of me wanted the gun gone, fearful of the consequences that would most certainly follow if my plan went belly-up.

I kneeled down, and pulled away the remaining dirt with my hands. The Luger had been rewrapped in its protective covering of polythene. I quickly picked it up. It felt heavier than before. I glanced nervously over my shoulder, before shoving the gun inside my winter jacket.

As I left the cemetery, the gun inside my jacket seemed to be coming to life, almost breathing. As if it had found its rightful owner. Finally.

CHAPTER THIRTY

Bloody Revenge

As you value your life or your reason
keep away from the moor.
Arthur Conan Doyle, **The Hound of the Baskervilles**

Mrs Cooper went all-out in making me feel wel-come, with a meal that would have choked a giraffe: fried chicken, corn on the cob, mashed potatoes, homemade apple pie, all washed down with buckets of fresh orange juice. It was more a banquet than a meal. I think Mrs Cooper still sensed something was wrong back at home, and was trying to 'food comfort' me. Perhaps all moms had this uncanny gift of knowing things just weren't right, without being told?

'More chicken, Tommy?'

'Phew! No thank you, Mrs Cooper. That was great. I'm stuffed.'

'Don't offer Tommy any more, Mom,' Horseshoe grinned. 'He'll be stinking tonight with his farts.'

I felt my face go on fire, as Horseshoe and Mr Cooper burst out laughing. Thankfully, Mrs Cooper came to my rescue.

'Don't speak so crudely, Charles Cooper, and especially in front of guests. I never find it funny.'

She gave Horseshoe the same kind of look Mom gave me whenever I became a bad page in her book.

About an hour later, we went up to Horseshoe's room to get everything prepared for Monster Night.

Horseshoe's room was a shrine to superheroes and monsters. He had every Aurora monster kit on the market, ranged on shelves lining the walls of his room. Frankenstein, Dracula, Wolf Man, The Mummy, et al., all meticulously constructed, each intricate and tiny piece lovingly attached, shaping and granting life to them.

The one that always gave me the creeps was 'The Forgotten Prisoner of Castel-Maré', with its raggedly-dressed skeleton chained to the dungeon wall. It always made me shudder to think of being left to starve to death in a dungeon, alone, with no family or friends to remember you. A horrible way to die. *No family or friends to remember you ... just like Jordan.*

'How do you sleep in here at night, Horseshoe?' I said, trying to get Jordan's face out of my head. 'Wouldn't you rather have Green Lantern or Spider-Man up on the shelves, watching over you, instead of all these monsters?'

'Where's the fun in that? Night and darkness belongs to monsters. It doesn't belong to superheroes.'

For a moment, I thought about what he had just said. It was profound in a way, and made me think about what I planned to do. *Night belongs to monsters. Was I a monster or a superhero?*

'C'mon, Tommy. Let's close the curtains, and get some sheets to make the tent. I can't wait.'

'Do you ever feel guilty, not inviting Brent to your house?' I said, as we pulled the curtains across.

Horseshoe made a face. 'Yeah, course I do, but my parents don't even know he's my friend. They'd freak out. They say his parents are criminals.'

'That's not fair, calling Mrs Fleming a criminal,' I said, a bit too forcefully. 'She's got nothing to do with all that crap about drugs in Florida.'

'Why're you snapping at me? It's not my fault what my parents think. Anyway, you've never invited him to your house either, so don't talk. Bet your parents don't like him.'

Even though he was right, I didn't like the tone in his voice. I was about to let him know what I thought of it when I realised I would be blowing everything for the sake of an argument. I decided to change the subject.

'You better have extra underwear for tonight,' I said, an evil grin forming on my lips. 'When I'm finished with my special horror story, you're gonna be shitting tons.'

'Yeah? We'll see, Vincent Price. I don't scare easy …'

Monster Night was 'a howling success', Horseshoe wise-cracked afterwards, as we sat on the floor, finishing off the last of our Swiss Miss hot chocolate and marshmallows.

'Shit, Tommy, that was your best one yet. Bet you're gonna be a bestselling author one day.'

'Dream on.'

'Seriously, I almost jumped out of my skin when you grabbed me in the dark by the neck, just as the zombie was about to strangle the old lady in the kitchen.'

'I told you you'd need extra underwear.'

We both laughed, Brent long forgotten.

'I don't know about you, but I'm beat.' Horseshoe yawned loudly.

'Yeah, me too.' I forced a false yawn. The night was getting heavier outside, and I needed to be out there in its hidden blackness.

'We had a great time, didn't we?' Horseshoe said, crawling into the bottom bunk.

'We sure as hell did. Thanks for letting me stay over, Horseshoe. I really enjoyed it.'

'It's great having you stay. I only hope I don't have any nightmares from your stories.' I could detect Horseshoe's voice tiring, as he fought the wave of sleep about to engulf him.

'If you don't have nightmares, then I failed as a storyteller.'

'Wake me if you hear me screaming.'

'Okay.'

'Goodnight, Tommy,' were his last words, half-muffled by his quilt.

'Goodnight, Horseshoe. See you in the morning, pal.'

With the lights dead, Horseshoe's monsters glowed eerily on the shelves, like miniature lighthouses bathed in fog. I wished now I could stay in bed, warm and safe, rather than face what awaited me out in the freezing snow and wind.

Before the dark shifted too far into morning, I checked the luminous face on my Dick Tracey watch. Two hours had almost gone by, touching the dangerous side of three in the morning. I listened to Horseshoe snoring softly from below.

'*Horseshoe?*' I whispered.

No answer.

'Horseshoe?' Much louder.

Nothing. He was dead to the world. Just as I thought of that phrase, I wished I hadn't.

Easing out of the top bunk, I dressed as quickly and as silently as possible. Under his warm covers, Horseshoe tossed and turned, mumbled something about zombies, farted, and then went quiet.

I quickly made a body shape in my bed, just in case the Coopers came snooping, and then went to the window. Outside, snow was falling thickly, and the wind was violently whistling. I steeled myself for the cold, then eased the window open just enough to squeeze through. Edging my way precariously onto the thick branch protruding from the tree, I closed the window behind me, leaving a notch of a gap for my return.

If I returned …

The branch was covered in icy, compacted snow, and I almost slipped off twice. Finally managing to secure myself, I made it into the tree house. Inside, I steadied my nerves for a few seconds, and then began unrolling the rope ladder.

Safe on the ground, I made a dash for the side of the house. The streets were deserted, everyone already where they wanted to be. The darkness had settled, curling cat-ways for the night, and the town was a startlingly quiet wasteland.

In scattered windows, fluorescent lights flickered like candles on forgotten birthday cakes.

Ignoring all last-minute appeals for reason coming from my subconscious, I quickly exited the street, feeling a strange momentum hurrying me along. The wind, strong and gusty, tore up the last layers of thought swimming through my head.

I quickly proceeded in the direction of Armstrong's lair. The twisty road looked eerie. A ghost's entrails. Overhead, telephone wires were iced, trembling like piano strings. They made a creepy sound, like a dirge for the dead.

The take-no-prisoners snowstorm had seriously dulled and diluted visibility. What would normally be a twenty-minute walk took almost an hour. Every now and again, the chalky headlights of a lone car would come my way, and I had to find a shadow to hide in. Strange, despite the temperature being sub-zero, I couldn't feel the cold. Adrenaline was burning throughout my body. I wondered had I left it too late to reach Armstrong's lair before light would start pouring over the hills? I had to get back to Horseshoe's before morning. He would be my iron-clad alibi. Not that I would need one, hopefully. I kept thinking of what Brent had said, during that summer: *We're just three kids. Who'd suspect us?* He was right – who'd suspect a kid of carrying out a murder? The bigger question was, *could* this kid carry out this murder?

At last, the derelict hardware store came into sight. Déjà vu. I entered the building from the side. The interior was heavily dark, funerary, like the lining of a painted jar. I quickly switched on the flashlight. It created a spooky effect, making elongated shadows dance in jittery motion. To make matters worse, a large rat scurried out of nowhere, unhinging my already frayed nerves. I instinctively threw the flashlight at the vile creature. In a moment, the room was plunged into total darkness as the flashlight smashed upon a wall instead of the rat.

'Bastard!'

I groped about in the darkness for what seemed an eternity, but to no avail. Even if I had found the flashlight, it probably would have been useless. Was this the beginning of my luck running out?

I took a couple of deep breaths, steadied myself, and then walked gingerly to the smashed-out window, trying not to trip over any debris in the dark. At the window, I saw my face and weary eyes in the fingers of broken glass. I hesitated. It was like a stranger looking back at me.

Across the snowy wasteland, Armstrong's trailer sat solidly, defiant and arrogant. Just like its owner.

'Bastard,' I said again, but this time my rage was directed at the bigger rat inside the trailer. I hoped he was sleeping, so that he wouldn't hear me when I entered his kingdom to slay him.

I removed the Luger from inside my coat, and cocked it expertly.

'One bullet. That's all it'll take. One to the head.' My grip tightened on the gun, as if I were fearful of it deserting me, along with my courage. I thought of what Mrs Fleming had said, in the kitchen, on that beautiful summer's day: *That's what distinguishes a hero. Doing what others fear to do, even if you are terrified when it's happening.*

I *was* terrified. This was no longer daring thoughts dreamed up in the safety of my imagination, but the tangible and stark reality of *now*. Here. On my own. Showtime or shittime.

Theodore Maxwell's shocking conversation with Dad in the hub kept coming back to me: *The system didn't serve my son. Joey was sexually molested, and so far the perpetrator's not been brought to justice. Joey committed suicide because of the animal that raped him, and took away his innocence.*

'This is for Joey, for Devlin and for Jordan. For all the kids you destroyed, Armstrong, you filthy bastard.' I was immediately comforted by the sound of my own voice, all the names of the victims. I began reciting the names, over and over again, a holy incantation for an unholy act. 'For Joey. For Devlin …'

Outside, the night sat watching, an infinite black sheet of nothing, waiting patiently. It had no place else to go for at least another couple of hours, before the early morning light came to relieve it from its duty.

I took a deep breath and began walking towards the door.

Time to slay the monster …

CHAPTER THIRTY-ONE

The Monster Slain

Down, down to Hell; and say I sent thee thither.

Shakespeare, **Henry VI**

It was four days before Christmas when the town learned the news of Armstrong's body being found at his trailer by old man McGregor. Raccoons had gotten in to the trailer and feasted on the corpse, paying particular attention to the face. People in town said Christmas had come early – especially for the raccoons – and that kids could now go to bed feeling safe. According to reliable sources in the media, Armstrong had 'received three shot wounds to the genital region'. We were further informed that '… in all probability he had lived for hours, before bleeding to death. Most certainly, he'd have been in terrible agony while he lived.'

The media speculated that the number of times he was shot was deliberate, a symbolic punishment for the number of victims known to have suffered at his bloody hands.

I'll always remember the look of relief on Dad's face, when he phoned Mom at Aunt Katherine's to tell her the news.

'Armstrong's gone, Helen. Gone forever …'

Mom returned home early on the day before Christmas Eve, looking relieved to be back. I hoped it was because she had missed me, but more than likely Aunt Katherine had drained her. The news of Armstrong's death probably played the biggest part in her return.

Dad was clearly happy to see Mom home, and vice versa. The boil of tension between Mom and Dad had finally been lanced.

Mom also brought back a couple of Christmas presents from Aunt Katherine, one for Dad and one for me. It was the first time Aunt Katherine had given either of us anything for Christmas. Mine turned out to be a book about New Jersey's history. It smelled faintly of cat piss and the edges of most of its pages had been gnawed by what looked like cat teeth.

'It was the thought that counts,' Mom said, seeing the look of disappointment on my face.

Dad's present was pipe tobacco – though not the brand he smoked. It looked like a bunch of old withered leaves, wrapped up in a dirty polythene bag.

'It was the thought …' Mom said, reflecting the look of amusement on Dad's face.

'Well, you can say that to me after I make dinner.' He kissed Mom on the cheek, and she smiled. Warmly. Everything was good again. A Norman Rockwell painting.

After dinner, we all sat down with popcorn to watch It's a Wonderful Life, Mom's favourite Christmas movie after White Christmas. Near the end of the movie, George Bailey finds a gift from Clarence the guardian angel – a copy of *The Adventures of Tom Sawyer*, with the inscription: *Dear George: Remember no man is a failure who has friends. Thanks for the wings! Love Clarence.*

Dad stopped eating his popcorn, and looked over at me. He seemed embarrassed. Probably thinking about that time he had called himself a failure. I was just about to say something to him, when Mom spoke in a calm but chilling voice.

'Sometimes justice takes time, but when that time comes, it sure as Hell takes. Norman Armstrong was pure evil. He destroyed many families. Murdered and abused children. I hope he's burning right now, and if it's a sin to think like that, then God forgive me. May he burn in Hell for all eternity. Amen.'

'Amen,' Dad and I said in unison.

The three of us went back to eating popcorn and watching the movie.

CHAPTER THIRTY-TWO

An Unusual Suspect

Am I therefore become your enemy,
because I tell you the truth?
Galatians 4:16

T wo days after Christmas, I went over to Horseshoe's. We were in his room, finishing off the last of the chocolate Santas, and drinking Coke. Normally, the post-Christmas conversation would be about comparing gifts, but Horseshoe only had one topic in mind.

'He did it, Tommy,' Horseshoe said, looking terrified as well as excited.

'What? Who did what?'

'Brent. He actually did it!'

'Brent …?'

'He shot perv Armstrong. He really did it.'

I was stunned at Horseshoe's speculation.

'It's … it's very important that you don't talk about it,

Horseshoe. You understand that, don't you? You don't want trouble coming to our doorsteps, do you?'

'Of course not.'

I wasn't convinced by his assurance.

'We're still blood-brothers, Horseshoe, the three of us. You haven't forgotten the oath, and what will happen to the person breaking that oath?'

Horseshoe looked uneasy. He nodded. 'Shovelled in the ass by Old Nick's dick ...'

'Worse than that can happen. A whole lot worse.'

'What could be worse than a flaming ass?'

'Could be a big muscular con in Sing Sing, dinging you in the ding-ding, three times before breakfast. And that's just for warm-ups.'

'What the hell's that suppose to mean? We didn't do anything that would make them put us in jail.'

'Think so? We can be done for conspiracy. Big time. We agreed to go along with Brent's crazy plan, remember? Withholding information on a murder can get you twenty big ones in the big house with all the big cons. Once they've finished with you in that place, your ass'll have more holes in it than a bowl of Cheerios. You wouldn't be able to sit down for the rest of your life.'

Horseshoe grimaced in a painful way. I pictured him pulling in his butt cheeks.

'That isn't funny, Tommy.'

'You can say that again. Think of spending *one day* in a place like that, never mind twenty years.'

He looked petrified. 'Okay, I get the message. I won't be saying a word to anyone. Trust me on that.'

'I trust you, blood-brother.' Now I did. I forced a smile. 'Look, if it makes you feel better, I once heard my dad saying that snowflakes are one of nature's most fragile things, but just look what they can do when they stick together. That's all we've got to do. Stick together.'

'I hope you're right. Will you be telling Brent the same thing, if you see him?'

I had never told Horseshoe about the knife attack. It would have led to other questions being asked; questions I wanted to avoid. At the time, I had quickly fed Horseshoe the same story I had fed Dad. The difference being, Horseshoe believed me.

'I'll not be going near Brent again, Horseshoe. Ever.'

'Oh …' Then, as if hit by a revelation, he said, 'Of course! I get it. Someone might be watching. Right? See you two together, and figure you'd something to do with it?'

'I … right. That's it. Too dangerous to be seen with him – ever. You'd best do the same. I'm not telling you what to do, just giving you some good advice.'

'I probably won't be seeing Brent anyway, even if I wanted to.'
'Oh?'

'I meant to tell you, Tommy, as soon as you got here, but …'
'Tell me what?'

'We're leaving Black's Creek.' Horseshoe looked crestfallen. 'Dad got a promotion. We're moving to New York City.'

Before I met Devlin, Horseshoe's news would have devastated me. But I had changed, seen wider horizons. In a way, it was a relief to hear that Horseshoe would no longer be here. The further away, the better, for all our sakes, lest he let something slip.

'That's great, Horseshoe. You'll be able to walk right into Marvel's office in downtown Manhattan. You might even get to see Spider-Man webbing his way across all those skyscrapers.'

'Yeah, how cool would that be?'

We both laughed. Kids again, if only for a few precious moments.

'If I were you, Horseshoe, I'd go speak to Stan Lee. Show him your art. It's good enough.'

'Stan Lee?' To Horseshoe, Stan Lee – the co-creator of a million superheroes and villains – was a member of the God Club. 'You really think so?'

'Big time. He'll see what a great artist you are,' I smiled, but there was sadness in it. 'I'm gonna miss you doing all those sketches of Spider-Man.'

'Hopefully, I'll be able to come back, every now and again. It's only a train journey away.'

He was lying, probably, about coming back. Not maliciously. Just not wanting to hurt my feelings. I'm sure he was glad to be getting out of here, away from Brent's uncontrollable rage and madness, away from this town of monsters, bogeymen and strange happenings.

'I'm gonna miss you, Tommy,' he said.

I believed that part.

'I'm gonna miss you, too, Horseshoe. This town is gonna be one lonely place without you.'

I returned home that evening, having said my farewells to Horseshoe and his parents. Just as I got a foot in the door, Dad popped his head out of the hub.

'Tommy? I need to see you. Up here, please.'

I tried to read the expression on his face. It was a blank page. Paradoxically, Dad's blank page usually had trouble written all over it.

'Close the door, Tommy,' he said as I entered.

'What is it, Dad?' I tried to sound casual.

He went behind his desk, sat down, picked up his pipe and a box of matches. He struck one of the matches along the top of his desk, leaving a thin, ice-skate mark embedded into the wax. The match's strike was as crisp and bright as the flame.

'Sit down, please,' he said, lighting the pipe.

The aroma of burning tobacco filled the room, as the smoke formed a thin cloud on the ceiling. Normally, it had a calming influence on me. Not this time. I suspected Dad was merely using it as a prop, hoping to catch me off-guard. I sat down on the leather chair, but not before unbuttoning my heavy winter jacket.

He looked straight into my eyes.

'Is there anything you would like to say to me, before I continue, Tommy?'

'Say? What … what about?'

'Have you been in here, when I'm at work?' he asked, stretching his legs out onto the edge of the desk.

I shrugged my shoulders. 'Sometimes.'

'Good. Not good you disobeyed me by coming in here, but good you're being honest. I respect and admire that. It takes courage to tell the truth, Tommy.'

I nodded, not knowing what to say. I left it to Dad, hoping he'd do all the talking.

'When you come in here, Tommy, what is it you do?'

I shrugged again. I was getting good at that. 'Nothing … I just look about. Sometimes, I look in your crime mags. Sometimes I just sit in your chair.'

'I see,' he said, bringing the pipe to his mouth and taking a long steady draw. He had yet to take his eyes from mine.

'Can I take my coat off?' I said, trying to deflect the stare.

'Of course. Hot in here, isn't it?'

I suspected he used that line when interrogating suspects. I quickly removed my coat. It did little to ease the rising temperature in the room.

'I have a little book, Tommy. A very private little book. Some people call them diaries. Some might call them journals. I just call it my book. Ever see it?'

'No,' I said, too quickly.

He reached into the drawer, and produced the accursed diary.

'This is it. Nothing fancy. Normally, I keep it hidden in an old hollowed-out bible.' He held the diary in his hands, and flipped the pages with his thumb. Then he held it out to me. 'Here. Take a look inside.'

I edged away from it.

'I don't want to look inside.'

'No? Why?'

'Because …'

'Because isn't an answer.'

'I … because … because it belongs to you.'

'You mean it's private, and should not be read by anyone without permission?'

I nodded. 'Yes …'

'Do you know what killed the cat?'

Was this a trick question? Had a cat been killed, and he suspected me?

'No,' I said.

'Curiosity. Prying. Inquisitiveness. Take your pick, only never – *ever* – steal people's private thoughts by reading their private things. No one likes a snoop. Clear?'

Chastised, I surrendered without a fight. 'Yes ...'

I stood to leave, glad the verbal reprimand was over.

'Sit down. I have something else I need to discuss with you.'

I slowly fell back in the electric chair.

'I never got to ask you how Monster Night went, over at the Coopers' house.'

'Monster Night ...? Oh, it went great. Just great. Mrs Cooper filled us with so much food, I was nearly bursting.'

Dad smiled. 'Great people, the Coopers. I spoke on the phone to Mrs Cooper about an hour ago. Told me they're leaving town in a day or two. Off to live in the Big Apple. A pity. This town needs good people.'

I nodded. 'I'll miss Horseshoe. He's my best friend.'

'I think you were upstairs with Horseshoe when I called, to thank Mrs Cooper for having you over. She said you and Horseshoe had a great time on Monster Night. She said you and he went to bed almost immediately after the show.'

'That's right. We were both kinda tired.'

'That's exactly what Mrs Cooper said. She even checked in on the two of you, a few times during the night.'

Shit! My stomach became a bucket of rats. 'She did?'

'Well, you know, with all that's been going on, parents are nervous. I suspect *all* parents in Black's Creek were checking their kids at night, just to make sure they were safe.'

'Oh ...' This train of conversation was speeding down the wrong track, and I needed to get off quickly before Mister

Conductor asked for a ticket I didn't have. 'That ... that was real nice of her, checking to make sure we were safe.'

'It sure was. She said each time she looked into the room, you were both sleeping like babies.' Dad grinned at that.

'Babies? Is that what she said? Sleeping like babies?'

Dad nodded. 'Her exact words.'

'That's embarrassing.' And comforting. Thankfully for me, Mrs Cooper's powers of observation did not match the power of her motherly instinct. Thank you, Mrs Cooper!

'Tommy, have you ever been to Johnson's Timber Store?'

I shook my head. I'd never heard of the place. 'No.'

'You're sure?'

'I've never even heard of it, never mind been to it.'

'It's no longer a timber store now, of course. Just a dilapidated old building, directly across from Norman Armstrong's trailer.'

Numbness began pulsing down from my neck, spreading out in waves to my shoulders. My entire body tightened; ribs crushed against lungs, making breathing difficult.

'Are you okay, Tommy? You look a bit pale.' Dad's legs dropped down from the desk, springing the rest of his body forward towards me.

'I'm ... okay. Just tired.'

'Myself and Deputy Hillman were up all morning at Armstrong's trailer, checking out the scene of the crime, hoping to discover some clues as to the killer's, *or killers'*, identities.' Dad reached beneath his desk, and produced a large plastic bag. 'Deputy Hillman found this. Ever see it before?'

Shit! Inside the bag was a smashed flashlight. It had once been perfect, until I decided to crown a rat with it. With all the shit and nerves at the time, I'd forgotten to bring it back, smashed or not.

'Looks like a flashlight,' I said, trying to keep my voice steady.

'It *is* a flashlight, but not just any old flashlight. If you look carefully at the rim, you'll see my faded initials written on it. Here, take a look; only keep it in the bag. That's evidence now.'

'Evidence?'

'That's right. Probably got fingerprints all over it. Somehow, that flashlight walked all the way from here to Johnson's Timber Store on the night Norman Armstrong was killed, and splattered itself against one of the walls. How do you think it got there?'

'I don't know.' Sweat was trickling down my arms, pooling in the palms of my hands. All Dad had to do was look to see the sweat dripping onto the carpet. 'Maybe you had it the night old man McGregor reported the scuffle outside Armstrong's trailer, and you dropped it.'

'*Hmm.* That sounds feasible. Let me consider that scenario for a moment.' He rubbed his chin, nodded to himself, shook his head, nodded some more, and mumbled a bit. He seemed to be debating with himself, weighing up possibilities. 'I'm afraid that doesn't work.'

'Oh? Why?'

'Daylight. I went to talk to old man McGregor during the day, you see. I wouldn't have brought a flashlight with me. Wouldn't make sense, would it?'

'No … I guess not.'

'Can you think of any other explanation for how it could have got there? Perhaps between the two of us, we can figure this puzzle out. What d'you say?'

'I … I can't think of anything, right at this moment, Dad. Too tired.'

'Too tired?'

'Yes.'

'I want you to look me in the eyes, Tommy.'

I reluctantly did as requested.

Dad joined his fingers in prayer mode, and rested his chin gently upon them. His face had the determined look of rolled-up shirtsleeves.

'I have become utterly mystified at the emergence of this situation, at the dilemma facing us. I need you to tell me if you're in any sort of trouble; trouble that might be heading this way soon. It's always best to be prepared. Can you think of anything coming our way?'

My eyes began watering, I was staring that hard. I thought Dad was trying to hypnotise me. I waited a few seconds before answering. 'I … I can't really think of anything.'

He sighed. 'Norman Armstrong was a monster. You know

that. I know that. The entire town knows that. The person responsible for his death probably had a very good reason for doing what he did. But that doesn't make it right. That's why we have the law, Tommy. If we allowed people to take the law into their own hands, we would have anarchy and lynching. You understand that, don't you?'

I hadn't a clue what anarchy was, but lynching was right up my street. 'Yes ...'

'Okay then. Now, can you think of how that flashlight got there?'

'I've already told you no. Why d'you keep asking me that?'

'Because this puzzle isn't going to go away, that's why. Deputy Hillman is pretty good at solving puzzles. He enjoys doing jigsaw puzzles and crosswords. He has great patience. He sits for hours – days even – until he comes up with a solution. Good plans always start with a piece of paper. You add things together; you subtract things that don't fit, and you arrive at your final answer. His sums usually tally up in the end. The flashlight is Deputy Hillman's piece of paper.'

'If he's so smart, then ask him to solve it,' I said defiantly.

'Don't get mouthy with me. Clear?'

'Yes ...'

'We need to keep examining the situation in front of us, before time runs out. We need to come up with an answer that adds up, before Deputy Hillman does. He asks the type of questions most cops don't. That's what makes him very smart. Once he figures out the motive, he believes the answers will follow like a stagecoach behind horses. Is there anything else you can think of? Something … something he might discover?'

'Discover …?'

'Will you think real hard, just for me?'

'I can't think of anything, right now.'

A little zing of tension entered the room, slipping between us.

'Okay, Tommy, I want you to listen to what I'm going to say. Listen very carefully. That night you went over to the Coopers, to do Monster Night?'

'Yes. What about it?'

'Do you remember all the clothes you were wearing?'

'I think so. Yes …'

'I want you to gather them all up for me, tonight – boots, socks, everything. Understand?'

'Why? What for?'

Dad looked at me as if to say, you know damn well what for. 'It's best you just do as I say. Clear?'

'Yes.'

'Now, this is very important: Is there anything I should know about Horseshoe?'

Horseshoe! I almost burst out laughing.

'What like?'

I could see Dad consciously controlling his breathing,

doing his best to remain calm. I wasn't helping him by playing dumb. 'When the police take in a suspect, they usually offer him some sort of deal, provided he's willing to turn against his accomplices.'

'Dad, I don't know what this is all about.'

'Enough, Tommy! Damn it!' He banged his fist on the desk. I had rarely seen Dad lose his temper. It made me feel very uncomfortable – and guilty. 'I think you had something – *directly or indirectly* – to do with Norman Armstrong's death. To what extent, I don't know. I believe your entire gang was somehow involved. Horseshoe, perhaps, certainly Brent Fleming. I suspect Fleming was probably the instigator and brains behind it, and suckered you and Horseshoe into it. Am I right?'

'No! None of us had anything to do with killing Armstrong. This is all a simple coincidence.'

'A simple coincidence? Perhaps I'm not as smart as some people, but in my tiny world, simple coincidences are neither simple nor coincidental, Tommy. This investigation has led me on a very dark journey, and uncovered unpleasant people doing the most unpleasant of acts. One way or another, I'll find a way to see that justice is done.'

'The way you brought Armstrong to justice?' I blurted out, wondering where the hell I had grown the balls to talk to Dad like that. 'Perhaps if someone had killed Armstrong a long time ago …' My voice trailed off.

'Go on. Finish what you were about to say.'

'I just wish someone had done something to Armstrong after what he did to Joey. Perhaps Devlin would still be alive. Maybe even Jordan. I'm glad he's dead. I hated him.'

Dad looked at me as though I had just plunged a dagger into his heart. I had hurt him, deliberately, by paraphrasing Theodore Maxwell.

'Okay, Son. Some of what you say could be true. You can blame me for Devlin's death, if that's what you're thinking. To be honest, I blame myself also, for not doing enough.'

'Yeah, well, it won't bring her back, will it?' I willed away the tears threatening to form in my eyes. 'Words, always fancy words and sayings from you, Dad. Nothing else.'

Dad could no longer hold my stare.

'We're both tired,' he said. 'Let's call it a night.'

I wanted to say something else, something more hurtful, but thought better of it. Nothing would be gained by drawing this out; nothing but implications and questions without answers.

I left the room with a terrible dryness in my mouth, but with the rest of my body soaked in sweat. It would only be a matter of time before Dad – or more likely, Deputy Hillman – proved my involvement in Armstrong's death.

CHAPTER THIRTY-THREE

The Perfect Killer

*With as little web as this will I ensnare as great a fly
as Cassio.*

Shakespeare, **Othello**

'Either my cooking has turned sour, or you two are keeping something from me,' Mom said, two days after Dad had interrogated me in the hub. 'Which is it?'

Dad was barely eating, no doubt worried sick at the prospect of Deputy Hillman pulling a rabbit from his wide-brimmed hat. I was a carbon copy of Dad, picking at my food.

'There's a stomach bug doing the rounds down in the jail, Helen,' Dad said. 'I probably caught it, and gave it to Tommy as well.'

'Well, I don't abide by good food being wasted. So either get yourselves over to Doctor Henderson's, or mouthwash with Raid to kill the bugs. And Tommy?'

'Yes?'

'I still can't find those jeans I bought you three months ago. Any idea where they are?'

Burnt to ashes, then scattered to the wind, along with socks, shirt, and everything else I was wearing that night. 'No ... I'll search again for them, later.'

'Make sure you do. Your clothes seem to be doing some sort of disappearing act, and frankly, it annoys the hell out of me, your careless attitude. Those jeans cost money, you know.'

Yes, I know, because you keep telling me the price of them. You're still looking for my shitty ones too, buried in the garden. Wait until you find out my new winter boots are missing as well! That should be fun.

Mom headed into the kitchen, leaving Dad and me alone with our thoughts. He looked over at me, as if to speak, but stood instead.

'Helen? See you later,' Dad said, directing his words towards the kitchen. 'I'll probably be late coming home for –'

That was when I heard the sirens blasting in the distance.

'Is that Deputy Hillman making that racket?' Mom said, coming in from the kitchen.

Dad's face paled. He looked over at me, at my pale face.

The sirens got louder. My stomach tightened. Body felt weak. I quickly gripped the sides of my chair for support, trying desperately to will away the threatening blackout.

Ominously, the sirens came to a dying screech right outside. A car door slammed shut, followed by the sound of footsteps on the porch. Someone banged loudly on the front door. Dad jumped slightly. I squirmed on the chair, as if I had just sat on a thumbtack.

'Tommy?' Mom said, glaring at me. 'Don't just sit there like a dummy. See who's at the door.'

I moved off the chair, walking towards the door in slow motion. Dad kept looking at me. Mom looked at both of us. I looked at my hand on the handle on the door. It was slowly turning. The door opened. It was an excited-looking Deputy Hillman. He removed his hat and stepped inside, ignoring me.

'Hello, Mrs Henderson,' he said, before nodding to Dad.

'Someone chasing you, Pete?' Mom said. 'All those sirens. My goodness.'

'An emergency,' Deputy Hillman said, looking slightly embarrassed and out of breath. 'Needed to get here ASAP. Sheriff? Can I talk to you, please? In private?'

A worried-looking Dad nodded. 'Okay.'

They left the house, walking as far as Deputy Hillman's car. Deputy Hillman removed what looked like a piece of paper from the top pocket of his jacket. A warrant! He handed it to Dad.

'Tommy Henderson!' Mom shouted, making me jump. 'Stop gawking out the door, and bring the rest of those dishes into the kitchen. Your nose is going to get you into an awful lot of trouble, one of these days. Keep it attached to your own face, and out of other people's business.'

I quickly stacked up the remainder of the plates, while Mom slammed the front door closed. I knew it was only a matter of time before Dad and Deputy Hillman walked back through that door, to arrest me.

'After you wash those dishes, I want you to –'

Suddenly, Dad walked in, just as I had predicted.

'Did you forget something, Frank?' Mom said.

In his hand was the piece of paper Deputy Hillman had handed him. Dad looked badly shaken.

'It's a letter,' he said.

'A letter?' Mom looked at him, puzzled.

'From Theodore Maxwell. A confession.'

'I don't understand, Frank. What sort of confession?'

'Theodore Maxwell's body was discovered a couple of hours ago. He shot himself.'

My mouth opened, but I couldn't speak.

'Dear God …' Mom brought a hand to her mouth. 'How terrible.'

'He left this letter, confessing to the killing of Norman Armstrong. In it, he explained he was suffering from an inoperable cancer, and that the only thing keeping him alive was the thought of killing Norman Armstrong. He gives details of how he killed Armstrong – details only the killer would have known. He said he acted alone, and wanted to make sure no innocent person was ever charged for what he did. That was why he wrote the confession, apparently …'

For minutes, a tent of silence covered the room. We all stood, not saying a word, until Mom eventually said, 'I don't agree with suicide, but what that poor man went through with his son more than pays the bill. I sincerely hope to God he rests in peace.'

Dad nodded, and then looked over at me.

'You okay, Tommy?'

'Yes … fine …' I lied.

'We'll talk later. Okay?'

'Yes.'

'I've got to go, make a report,' Dad said. 'I'll see you both later tonight.'

I waited until Dad had left, and then went upstairs to my room. I felt slightly dizzy, and lay down on the bed. Closing my eyes, thoughts of Theodore Maxwell came flooding into my head; thoughts of all that had happened the night I went to kill Norman Armstrong …

That night, as I looked out at Armstrong's trailer, I'd been encouraging myself, bolstering my nerves, by reciting the names of the kids destroyed by Armstrong.

'This is for Joey. For Devlin. For Jordan. For Joey. For Devlin …'

The trailer waited in the snowy darkness, taunting me to make a move, get on with it. I made my way towards the door, and just as I was about to step out into the snow, all hell broke loose. I remember hands grabbing me; the terrible streak of fear railing my spine. Blue sparks danced in my brain. Armstrong had outwitted me, waiting like a fox in the darkness. I was so pathetically predictable.

I tried to break free, pulling, pushing and kicking, but it was useless. My feeble struggling only seemed to galvanise him, to make him stronger. His grip tightened on my throat. I couldn't breathe as his filthy murderous hands covered my mouth. I was sinking fast.

That was when I blacked out.

How long I had succumbed to the darkness was anyone's guess. It felt like hours, but was probably no more than a couple of minutes. My neck felt as if it had been placed into a vice and squeezed. I was propped up in a filthy corner of the room, my body shaking. All that lovely adrenaline was long gone. My teeth wouldn't stop making that terrible noise caused by fear and cold.

Somewhere in the heavy darkness, someone was coughing badly.

'Are you okay, Tommy?' said a gravelly voice. 'I hope I didn't hurt you, but I couldn't allow you to scream.'

I tried to focus my eyes, but they seemed fogged.

'Who … who are you? What do you want?'

'I want to save you from doing something you'll regret for the rest of your life, while rotting in prison.'

The voice sounded familiar. The words, despite the continued coughing, were clear and forceful, just like its owner. I could see him now, despite the darkness shrouding that intimidating face. His skin was pale, like bleached bone, his eyes the colour of dead coffee. He looked lost, like a mourner at the wrong funeral.

'Mister Maxwell?' I said.

The coughing started again, and then slowly faded.

'I need you to listen very carefully to what I'm going to say, Tommy. I need you to go home. Forget about vengeance. Leave that to the old and to the dying ... especially the dying.'

'I can't do that.'

'There's no can't about it. You're going to do it, one way or the other. Things happen, sometimes in a complex pattern of events called destiny. And that is what we have in our hands at this very moment. Destiny. Everything in its place, a place for everything.'

'But Armstrong ... what about him, all the kids he murdered and ... done things to? He'll keep doing the terrible things if he's not stopped.'

'You don't need to worry about Norman Armstrong any longer. He's dead.'

'Dead ...?' The word caught me like a meat hook to the throat. 'But when ... how ...?'

'Oh, he doesn't know he's dead, just yet, but he will. Very soon. I've waited the last three nights for him to show up at his trailer. He has to come back to it, eventually, just like a dog to its own vomit.'

'I … I wanted to do this for Joey,' I said. 'For letting him down.'

'You didn't let him down, Tommy,' said Theodore Maxwell in an almost affectionate voice. 'Others let Joey down – myself included – but not you. Always remember that. I'm indebted to you. And I'll never forget what you intended to do, here tonight, for Joey. For the other children, murdered and abused.'

'Can't I at least do something else to help? I can be a look-out. Something. Anything.'

'You can help by leaving, right now. Quickly. I'm sure your mother and father will discover you missing very shortly, if you don't make it home in time. Your father, in all probability, will send out a search party, and they might just come here. They would find me with a loaded and unregistered gun, and no explanation. That would give Armstrong a warning that something was coming his way. You wouldn't want that, would you?'

'No, sir. I wouldn't.'

'Then you'll do as I ask?'

I nodded. 'If … if that's what you want.'

'It's what I want. It's what –' He began coughing violently. Quickly held a handkerchief to his mouth. Spat into the cloth. 'It's what Joey would have wanted.'

'The … the Luger? I need to put it back where I found it.'

'A beautiful weapon for ugly deeds, eh? I have a better idea. I think it best that I dispose of it, someplace where it'll *never be found* – or used. Are you in agreement with that?'

'I suppose …' I wondered what would happen if Brent went looking for it?

'There's doubt in your voice. Doubt is the gate through which slips the most deadly of enemies. Trust me. Better for all concerned that this gun no longer exists after tonight.'

'If … if you think that's best, then it's okay with me.' I stood, wiped the dust and other pieces of crap from my clothes.

'Thank you, Tommy, for everything,' Theodore Maxwell said, extending his hand.

I reached and shook it. His grip was iron, but despite that, something wasn't right with Theodore Maxwell. All that coughing. He looked pale. Gaunt. Seeing him in the stark light, heavy coat buttoned to his neck, eyes expressionless, made me feel nothing but pity for the man, something I once would have thought impossible.

'You haven't told me not … not to tell anyone, of … of what you're gonna do,' I said. 'Aren't you afraid that I might say something to my dad?'

For the first time since I met Theodore Maxwell, I saw a smile on his sad face.

'You won't. Goodbye, Tommy. Get home safe.'

Later, when I was back, warm and secure in Horseshoe's room, I thought of Theodore Maxwell, biding his time in that freezing old building. Waiting there patiently, alone with just his thoughts and demons. Horseshoe's dad had been right: 'Better to fuck with the devil, than with Theodore Maxwell. He neither forgives nor forgets …'

CHAPTER THIRTY-FOUR

Puzzle Solved.
Sort Of.

The more a man knows, the more he forgives.
Catherine the Great

If Theodore Maxwell's life had been measured by the number of people attending his funeral, the measuring tape would have stretched for miles. His death attracted the largest crowd of mourners our town had ever seen. Even Dad attended, accompanied by Deputy Hillman. After the funeral, Dad brought me home in the car. Neither of us said a word. It wasn't until we stopped, outside the house, that Dad eventually spoke.

'Deputy Hillman finally figured out the last piece of the puzzle, concerning how my flashlight was found at Johnson's Timber Store.'

'Oh?'

'The way Deputy Hillman figures, it was the night Theodore Maxwell came to see me in the hub. He was left there alone, before I came up to talk to him. He must have seen the flashlight over in the corner, and decided to take it.'

'Why would he do that?'

Dad looked straight into my eyes.

'I don't know *why* he'd do it, and I no longer care. All I know is that the case is officially closed. Clear?'

I nodded. 'Yes. Very clear.'

'Good. Now get out. I've something I want to show you in the trunk.'

We both got out of the car, and walked to the trunk. Dad opened it, and removed a package wrapped in brown paper.

'Here. Mom has reluctantly agreed to let you keep it, but not up on the wall. Put it away until you get older, or get married and have your own house.'

I quickly tore the brown paper away. My heart did a little flip-flop of excitement. It was Devlin's drawing of me.

'I thought you'd like to have it back. I'm sure Devlin would have wanted you to keep it,' Dad said, smiling.

I was overcome with emotion. I felt like crying, but forced a smile instead. 'Thanks … thanks Dad. This … this means …' I couldn't finish the sentence.

'You don't have to explain, Son. I know what it means to you. Just keep it out of sight from Mom. She's still not one hundred percent convinced that we should have a drawing of a mysterious naked man in the house.' He grinned. Ruffled my hair. 'Come on. Let's go in.'

I watched Dad walking up the porch, a slight swagger to his gait, and suddenly realised for the first time in my life, that I, not Horseshoe, was the lucky one. He would never have a dad like mine.

EPILOGUE

Painting is just another way of keeping a diary.

Pablo Picasso

'Here's some fresh coffee, Tom. That cup you have is cold by now.'

Belinda's caring voice brings me back from the old home movies playing in my head. I hadn't even heard her coming out into the garden. She hands me the fresh cup of coffee, and sits down beside me.

'Thank you.' I sip. The coffee is lovely. I finish reading the last part of the newspaper article.

DNA Evidence Reopens Murder Case

Newly discovered DNA evidence proves that Norman Armstrong was not the killer of a young girl, Devlin Mantle, over twenty years ago, in the town of Black's Creek in upstate New York. Norman Armstrong was the chief suspect in the brutal rape and murder of Devlin Mantle. Armstrong would eventually be gunned down at his home, by prison guard Theodore Maxwell, whose son, Joey, died tragically in Jackson's Lake. Rumours at the time claimed Armstrong had sexually molested the young Maxwell boy.

Police have arrested a sixty-eight-year-old local drifter, Bob McCoy, on suspicion of the Mantle murder, along with that of another child, Jordan Taylor. McCoy worked as a handyman of sorts at the now-discredited and closed Saint Peter's on the Rock orphanage.

The story continues with the confession of McCoy in prison, wanting to clear his conscience of all the murders he was involved in: Devlin, Jordan and three other young people.

Armstrong was not the killer of Devlin or Jordan. I thought about all of the implications of this for a few minutes, and then about Joey. Wasn't Armstrong responsible – even if indirectly – for Joey's horrific death? What about the terrible things he did to Brent and Devlin, and all the other lives he messed up because of his perverted and sick nature? Was Theodore Maxwell wrong in what he did? Was I wrong in what I had intended to do?

Perhaps if I had studied Devlin's paintings more carefully, I would have noticed the clues. As I gazed at the picture in the newspaper, I realised that I knew that man's face, from the painting she had titled 'Guilt of Man'. The boar, that ugly animal, its bestial face transforming into the brutal Bob McCoy.

The paintings were Devlin's diary, right there under my nose, to be read by me or anyone else with claims of loving her. She was trying to tell us things, terrible things, but not one of us listened.

'Tom? Tell me what's wrong. I know you, and I know something's wrong.'

'I'm fine,' I say, knowing now that I'll never be fine, ever again. I sip the coffee, but I no longer feel like drinking it. It tastes strangely bitter.

Other books by Sam Millar

'Mesmerizing and fascinating, *On The Brinks* is one of the most revealing and powerful memoirs you will ever read.'

New York Journal of Books

In 1993, $7.4 million was stolen from the Brink's Armored Car Depot in Rochester, New York, the fifth-largest robbery in US history. Sam Millar was a member of the gang who carried out the robbery. He was caught, found guilty and incarcerated, before being set free by Bill Clinton's government as an essential part of the Northern Ireland Peace Process.

This remarkable book is Sam's story, from his childhood in Belfast, membership of the IRA, time spent in Long Kesh internment camps and the Brinks heist and aftermath. Unputdownable.

Karl Kane

'Crime noir doesn't get much darker or grittier'
Booklist

Karl Kane is a private investigator with a
dark past, his mother murdered when he
was a child. Years later, Karl has a chance
to avenge his mother's murder, but allows
the opportunity to slip through his hands.
When two young girls are sexually molested and then brutally murdered, Karl
holds himself responsible.

Young homeless women and drug addicts
are being abducted before being brutally
mutilated and murdered, and a city is held
in the grip of unspeakable terror. By ab-
ducting Katie, the young daughter of private investigator Karl Kane, the killer has
just made his first mistake, which could
well turn out to be his last.

Private Investigator Karl Kane returns to
the streets of Belfast, investigating the dis-
covery of a severed hand. He's convinced a
serial killer is on the loose, and that he may
be the next victim ...

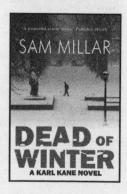

A tense tale of murder, betrayal, sexual abuse and revenge, and the corruption at the heart of the respectable establishment.

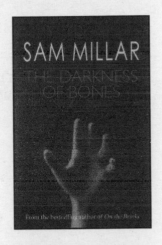

In a wood at night, a young woman witnesses the murder of a whistle-blower by a corrupt businessman, owner of an abattoir. Paul Goodman, a would-be snooker champion who works at the abattoir, has never known his father and believes that he deserted him when young. But he is befriended by the one man who holds the key to the mystery of his disappearance, the man responsible for his death.

Sam Millar is a bestselling crime writer and playwright from Belfast. He has won numerous literary awards and his books have all been critically praised.

AN IMPRINT OF O'BRIEN